THE MATCHMAKING KITTEN

The kitten turned up the steps leading to Emma's front door, where it placidly settled on its haunches and attempted to lick the tip of a tail that refused to be still.

The viscount lunged for it, but it made no attempt to escape his grasp. Straightening, he turned the unprotesting kitten over in his hand and poked at its front paws. Emma, with a startled gasp of outrage, broke into as rapid a run as she could manage, hampered both by her narrow skirts and by her accompanying feline entourage.

Breydon looked up as her footsteps sounded on the paving stones, and his gaze narrowed. A slow, rueful smile tugged at the corners of his mouth. "I should have known," he said, exaggerated resignation in his voice.

She slowed to a stop at the foot of the steps. "What are you doing to Penelope?" she demanded.

"Examining her. She seemed to be in some frightful pain after she jumped into my breakfast parlor."

"Jumped—" Emma reached up to stroke the furry head, her alarm evaporating.

Breydon repositioned Penelope to a more comfortable spot in the crook of his arm. "She scrambled through the open window while I was eating breakfast, then set up the most dreadful screech. While I was trying to catch her, a footman came in to see what was toward, and she took off out the door."

"And you followed." The first stirrings of amusement crept into her voice.

"Well, of course I did. I thought she was hurt. But all she seemed to want to do was lead me a merry chase. Directly to you, as I should have guessed she would . . ."

—"A Shocking Faux Paw" by Janice Bennett

BOOK YOUR PLACE ON OUR WEBSITE AND MAKE THE READING CONNECTION!

We've created a customized website just for our very special readers, where you can get the inside scoop on everything that's going on with Zebra, Pinnacle and Kensington books.

When you come online, you'll have the exciting opportunity to:

- View covers of upcoming books
- Read sample chapters
- Learn about our future publishing schedule (listed by publication month *and author*)
- Find out when your favorite authors will be visiting a city near you
- Search for and order backlist books from our online catalog
- Check out author bios and background information
- Send e-mail to your favorite authors
- Meet the Kensington staff online
- Join us in weekly chats with authors, readers and other guests
- Get writing guidelines
- AND MUCH MORE!

Visit our website at
http://www.zebrabooks.com

SUMMER KITTENS

Janice Bennett
Valerie King
Martha Kirkland

Zebra Books
Kensington Publishing Corp.
http://www.zebrabooks.com

ZEBRA BOOKS are published by

Kensington Publishing Corp.
850 Third Avenue
New York, NY 10022

First Printing: June, 1999
10 9 8 7 6 5 4 3 2 1

Printed in the United States of America

Contents

A SHOCKING
FAUX PAW

by
Janice Bennett

ONE

One star shone brighter than the others, a brilliant, sparkling jewel in the velvet fastness of the sky. Its light glinted off the dark waters of the ocean, shimmering as the wavelets lapped the sandy shore. Only a thin crescent moon, not far past new, vied for supremacy of the night.

Midsummer's Eve. Emma, Lady Stanyon, drew a deep breath, tasting the salty tang of the cooling breeze. Even the warmth trapped in the sand had begun to fade. She was alone, here on the deserted beach. To be alone, in Brighton, in the summer, seemed a miracle.

No, not quite alone. She felt the sensation of pleasure that emanated from a stray cat even before the animal reached her, before its furry body rubbed against her leg and its whiskers tickled her ankle. She was never completely alone. Cats seemed to sense her presence from miles away and came running to surround her.

With the purring feline keeping pace with her, Emma strolled aimlessly along the shore, the gentle roar of the ocean underscoring the longing in her heart. Yet what she wanted, she couldn't say. She had no reason to be depressed. On the contrary. Her life perfectly suited a lady of her practical disposition.

She certainly lacked nothing from a material standpoint. Her jointure far exceeded her needs, enough so she found herself able to rent an elegant establishment on the Marine Parade for the summer. As for the rest of the year, the Dower House on her late husband's estate boasted every amenity, and her stepson, now Lord Stanyon, welcomed her with delight to the town house in Cavendish Square whenever she wished to visit the metropolis.

Loneliness couldn't be the problem, either. Her stepdaughter, Sophie, adored her, and had removed with her to the Dower House the previous year upon the marriage of her brother. With Sophie making her curtsy to Society this past Season, they had embarked upon a round of balls, *soirees, al fresco* nuncheons, boxes at the opera, and visits to modistes and mantua makers. She'd barely had a moment to herself.

Until now. Her steps slowed, allowing a second cat to catch them up. Had Sophie's first Season resurrected memories of her own, abbreviated, debut into Society only a few years before? Its joys had evaporated for her in the face of her father's failing health; they had returned to the estate in early May, only weeks before he succumbed to that final illness, leaving her orphaned. Her straightened financial circumstances had made it impossible to return to London when she at last had emerged from mourning.

She had been saved from poverty by her neighbor, Lord Stanyon, the elderly friend of her late father. A widower desirous of a loving mother for his twelve-year-old daughter Sophie, he had offered a marriage of convenience, which Emma, ever practical, had accepted. She had always been fond of him. He'd treated her as a second daughter, and when he died just over two years ago, she found she missed him every bit as much as she'd missed her own parent.

Then Sophie's brother had married, and she'd rejoiced for him, for he'd brought a sweet, gentle bride into the family, one who would make him happy, and in time would fill her position to perfection. And now it would be Sophie's turn. It was the wish of Emma's heart to see her beloved stepdaughter happily established. That her own life would seem very empty when Sophie wed, she tried to ignore.

She halted on firm sand, dampened by an earlier high tide. The water looked so peaceful, showing no more than ripples in the glimmering light of the myriad stars and tiny moon. And that one star, so very bright in the midnight sky. On impulse she closed her eyes and wished upon it, not in words but with the aching, nameless longing of her heart. When she looked up again, the star seemed to grow brighter until a halo gleamed about it, pulsing and alive. The next moment it faded, becoming no more than an ordinary star, and though she tried, she could no longer pick it out from among the multitude of others.

Imagination, she chided herself. She'd always had more than her healthy share. Feeling somewhat silly, she retraced her steps along the sand, then wended her way through the array of bathing machines until she emerged onto the Marine Parade.

As she crossed to the house she had rented, five more cats fell into step with her. *Fish.* The thought filled her mind, more an essence than an actual word. From several of the other gathering felines she received similar desires, for herring heaped high onto platters, for bowls of the rich cream she set out for them every night. Then a sensation of warmth enveloped her, of cats satiated with their repast and snoozing gently in her lap.

She stooped and gathered the nearest into her arms, where it proceeded to rub its chin against her hand. *Sausage.* The desire filled her mind, accompanied by *chicken* from another who pressed between her feet, nearly tripping her. *Cream,* came another. Emma stroked the soft head. How could one ever really be alone or lonely when one could "hear" these demanding little beasts?

TWO

From where Emma stood before the row of fashionable shops that lined the Steine, she could just catch a glimpse of the gloriously blue ocean, gleaming in the brilliant morning light. The salt tang in the air refreshed her, and if she closed her eyes and concentrated, she could hear the squawking and crying of the gulls, even above the incessant clop of hooves and the squeaking of carriages as they paraded along this main street. And a very bustling parade all these people made, too. She decided she wouldn't risk the dangerous feat of crossing here, but would proceed along this side all the way to the Marine Parade.

She shifted the book she had just obtained from Donaldson's Circulating Library and resumed her stroll, enjoying the pleasant sensation of sun on her upturned face. She would turn as brown as a berry, she supposed, but that mattered little to her, not compared to the sense of freedom it gave her. Her abigail would take a very different view, of course. Ignoring Emma's objections, the conscientious Mifton would ply her face with a mask of crushed strawberries, or worse, a mustard lotion, and—

A terrified feline cry filled her mind, wiping away every other thought. Startled, she halted, and her glance darted back and forth, seeking the source. A long-haired tabby stood at her side, but its mind held only curiosity as it gazed fixedly into the street. Emma followed the direction of its stare, and a gasp escaped her as she caught sight of a calico kitten, cowering in the midst of the barrage of carriages. She darted into the traffic before she considered, and a high-perched phaeton driven by an outraged gentleman narrowly missed running her down. Ducking between two riders brought her abreast of her quarry, and she stooped to scoop the petrified bundle of fur into her protective arms.

A horse neighed, penetrating her absorption, and she looked up to see the shod hooves of the rearing animal, barely a foot above her head. She spun to safety as its forequarters crashed to the paving. Behind her, shouts filled the street, of protest, of alarm, of anger. She didn't dare look at the chaos she'd created. She'd saved the tiny kitten, which clung to her upper arm with all claws extended, and that was all that mattered.

Except for the gentleman who had been driving the curricle to which the rearing horse was harnessed.

He swung from the vehicle and descended on her, fury in his dazzling green eyes, his tight-lipped mouth closed. It didn't remain that way for long. "You damned little idiot!" he declared through clenched teeth. "What the devil do you mean, diving under my pair like that? You might have gotten yourself killed!"

Emma stared at him, dumbstruck, aware all in a moment of the thickly waving dark hair, the well-remembered aquiline nose that jutted out from beneath the wide-set green eyes, the brow that had always furrowed so easily, whether with laughter or irritation, the generous mouth that could melt hearts when he smiled. Not that he'd ever smiled at her. During that one tumultuous London Season when the dashing Nicholas Radlett, Viscount Breydon, had been the center of her world, he'd been completely oblivious to her existence.

Abruptly, his brow furrowed deeper than ever. "Are you listening to me?" he demanded.

She swallowed, regaining her composure. She was not, any longer, a green and tangle-tongued miss of seventeen, but a capable widow of four-and-twenty. It only annoyed her that she had to remind herself of this fact. She glared right back at him. "Had you not been driving at a pace quite reckless under the circumstances—"

"Reckless?" His mobile eyebrows flew upward. "And just who was it who dashed into the street without so much as a glance at the traffic?"

"At the very heavy traffic," she confirmed, holding the kitten closer. "Which made your pace quite ineligible."

"*My* pace? You are quite getting away from the point, my girl, which is your reckless darting into the midst of the traffic—which," he added, holding up his hand to silence her, "is progressing at a very decorous pace. Or at least it was, until you invaded it. I—Good God." He stared back the way she had come. "Isn't it enough you risk yourself? Must you endanger them, as well?"

Emma, who had extended a soothing hand to stroke the quivering muzzle of the carriage horse nearest her, tensed. "I was trying to save it—" she began; then the plurality of the pronoun he had used sank in to her. "Them?" she asked, her voice quavering.

She didn't need to look. Now that her own alarm had settled, she could "hear" the feline voices, at least half a dozen of them, plaintive, protesting, alarmed, hungry. Longings for herring, for chicken wings, for saucers of cream and warm laps filled her mind. And every one of the cats made unerringly for her as a certain source of warmth, safety and food.

Emma hugged the kitten, which only made the poor little thing tighten the grip it had begun to loosen on her arm. "I didn't bring them," she protested, but it sounded feeble even in her own ears. Of course she brought them. She always drew cats to her, as if she made her gowns of catnip. And here came seven of the ill-assorted beasts, scrawny specimens with scarred ears, fat ones with sleek, gleaming fur, black ones with white paws, orange ones, tabbies, all parading unconcernedly through the disrupted traffic, tails high, as if the only thought on their little minds was reaching her.

And chaos surrounded them in the street. Riders tried to restrain their nervous mounts. Gentlemen drew rein on the sidling and stamping cattle pulling their carriages. Even pedestrians had come to a halt to watch the spectacle. She—or rather the cats—had brought the Steine to a standstill.

Her cheeks burning, Emma stooped and called the wayward line of felines. A couple of them broke into a trot, hurrying toward her. The others continued to saunter at their own leisurely paces, sniffing the intriguing odors of the street, eyeing the massive hooves of the horses with fastidious unconcern.

"That's not getting us anywhere," Breydon snapped. He strode between several horses and began herding the uncooperative cats toward Emma. She called softly, and several feline ears perked up. Between her beckoning and Breydon's shooing motions, the last of the ambling animals finally made it to the safety of the curb.

"Whatever possessed you to bring so many out with you?" he demanded as he joined her at last.

"I didn't. They aren't mine. And unless they came because of this poor little thing," she indicated the calico kitten, "which you nearly ran down, I haven't the faintest idea what they're doing here."

"I nearly ran down?" He stared at her, exasperated. "You created all this havoc to save a kitten in the street?" His vexed expression softened, and gently he stroked the little animal behind the ear, setting up a purr that caused the tiny animal's entire body to vibrate.

"Yes." She met his accusing gaze with defiance.

"Good God," he said again.

"M'lord?" A gruff voice came from just beside her.

Emma turned to see a wiry little man standing at the heads of the pair. Beautifully matched chestnuts they were, too. The groom cast an uneasy glance along the street, where the traffic had begun to move once more, then returned his attention to the viscount.

Breydon's lips twitched. "Try to keep your entourage out of trouble," he told Emma. With a dismissive nod, he returned to his curricle, swung onto the bench, and set his pair in motion. The groom jumped to the viscount's side, and they left her standing beside the street as they vanished along the Steine.

For a long moment she stared after them, until the insistent thoughts of the cats recalled her attention, and she met their direct stares. "That was Lord Breydon," she informed them, quite unnecessarily. The animals merely continued to regard her with their wide, plaintive eyes, and wistful thoughts of cream nudged at the edge of her mind. With a sigh, she resumed walking, wishing without any real hope that the cats would take themselves off to their own various homes.

A little over six years had passed since last she'd seen Lord Breydon. He hadn't changed much. His shoulders might appear a trifle broader, but that would be the natural result of the muscle he'd added with age. He must be just past thirty now. His eyes remained the same. They still looked at her without actually seeing her. No, he hadn't changed. He still had no interest in her.

She reached the Marine Parade, and her accompanying felines took off across the expanse of beach to where four fishermen drew an ancient dinghy, laden with the morning's catch, onto the wet sand. There would be tidbits galore, she wagered, and eyed with speculation the kitten she still held. It seemed such a tiny thing, certainly too young to be fending for itself. Patches of white, orange and black fur fluffed out, turning it into a puff ball. With a sigh, she resigned herself to adopting it.

She mounted the steps to the front door, but before she could turn the handle, the ever efficient Beecher, whom she had hired along with the house, swept it wide for her. With only the flicker of an eyelid, for during the course of her short inhabitance he had become inured to the cats that gathered about her, he let her into the hall.

"Mr. Dauntry has called, m'lady," he informed her in the regretful tones of one who, try as he might, could not avert a calamity.

Emma bit back her exclamation of vexation. "Where is Miss Sophie?"

"She has accompanied him to the bench across the street. You may just glimpse them, m'lady, if you turn around."

A sigh of relief escaped her. "Thank you, Beecher. Would you see to the kitten? It will only be for a few minutes, I promise."

Her majordomo eyed the little animal with resignation. "I believe the kitchen maid is free at the moment."

Emma rewarded him with a warm smile. "That will be the very thing. Betsy is so good with them. And this one is terribly hungry, I fear. Cream," she added with certainty, "and perhaps a little bread torn up in it?" Handing her mewing burden over to the man, she turned her mind to the more vexatious problem of Sophie's undesirable suitor.

At least the girl had shown the excellent good sense not to receive him alone. Even the strictest of chaperons could find little in which to object in a young lady sitting on a bench facing the ocean in the company of a gentleman. That Emma had a strong suspicion the gentleman was in fact a fortune hunter, she knew enough to keep to herself. Sophie, at seventeen, still regarded the world and its inhabitants through the starry eyes of one who had never yet been disillusioned.

The couple must have noted her arrival. They crossed the street now, and Emma opened the door to them as they reached it. A soft flush colored Sophie's cheeks, Emma noted in dismay. In her light blue muslin, and with no more than a riband threaded through her golden ringlets, the girl looked impossibly lovely. Almost as appealing, Emma reflected uncharitably, as her handsome dowry.

Mr. William Dauntry bowed low over her hand, his charming smile a natural part of his classical features. If possible, Emma liked him even less for his undeniable good looks. What hope did an innocent, idealistic young lady have in the face of so much seeming perfection?

A soft hiss sounded at her feet, and a fleeting image of something unpleasant pressed against her mind. The tip of a tail brushed her ankle as one of the cats who had taken up residence in the house beat a hasty retreat. Such thoughts and behavior were the animals' usual response to the presence of William Dauntry, and she found that fact significant.

Oblivious to the antagonism of both the cat and Emma, Mr. Dauntry beamed at her. "Sophie—Miss Stanyon—has told me you will be present at the Pickerings' *soiree* this evening." His gaze strayed to Sophie's softly blushing countenance. "I shall look forward to seeing you there." With that, he bowed to Emma, clasped Sophie's hand and gazed at her in a very speaking manner, and took his departure.

The door closed behind him, and Sophie sighed. "His manners must always please, must they not?"

Emma, with creditable restraint, held back her acid comment. "He certainly seems anxious to please you," she said with care.

Sophie's flush deepened. "Do you think so, indeed? I have hoped—" She broke off, her expression one of pretty confusion.

"I am so very glad we have come to Brighton," Emma said, and Sophie beamed at her, apparently misunderstanding the portent of the remark.

Emma drew her stepdaughter down the hall. She was glad they had come. Of course, had they returned to Stanyon Park, Sophie could not have encountered her importunate suitor so often. Here, though, she stood a chance of meeting some other gentleman who might oust the undesirable Dauntry in her affections. On the whole, Emma decided this latter to be preferable.

The door to the kitchens opened, revealing the competent, middle-aged Betsy, and Sophie came to an abrupt halt. "Oh, Stepmamma, you haven't! Oh, it's so little, and so sweet!" Sophie took the calico kitten from the maid, who bobbed a relieved curtsy and retreated to her own labors. "Where did you find it?"

"In the middle of the Steine," Emma admitted, and with a forced nonchalance, recounted an abridged tale of her encounter with Breydon, seeking out what humor she could find.

Sophie laughed, but eyed her stepmamma with a sparkling eye. "What a perfectly delightful gentleman this Lord Breydon sounds. I wonder if we shall meet him tonight?"

Emma blinked. To see Breydon again. . . . That thought hadn't occurred to her before. But now that it had, it lingered, teasing her, one moment an intriguing possibility, the next an uncomfortable threat of renewed embarrassment.

THREE

After the formality that characterized the entertainments during the London Season, the relaxed atmosphere in the drawing rooms of Sir Henry and Lady Pickering refreshed Emma. The crystal drops of the chandelier might glitter from myriad candles as they did in the city, cascading a shimmering, colorful light over elegantly attired guests, but the laughter here sounded less brittle, the conversations more eager. Sofas and chairs had been dragged to the sides of the apartment, leaving the center of the room open for dancing to the music provided by a string quartet.

Emma greeted her hostess, saw Sophie into the company of her dear friend Miss Isabel Abingdon, then went to seek out the company of a fellow chaperon. Her gaze, which roamed restlessly about the room, did not seek out Lord Breydon, she assured herself, and the double beat of her heart when she at last caught sight of his unmistakable broad shoulders and thickly waving dark hair was the merest of coincidences. She looked away, blaming her sudden breathlessness on the heat of the rooms. A glass of lemonade would set her to rights.

Armed with the beverage, she found a seat in a corner that commanded an excellent view of the dance floor. The musicians struck up a country reel, and William Dauntry appeared as if from nowhere, making his purposeful way toward Sophie. Even from a distance, Emma noted the betraying flush that tinged the girl's cheeks. In dismay, she watched as Sophie gazed up into his handsome face as he led her into a set with three other couples.

Satin skirts rustled as someone took the seat next to Emma, and she looked away from her stepdaughter to behold a dragon of a woman, with iron gray hair all but hidden beneath a purple turban boasting three ostrich feathers dyed a startling pink. Ells of purple satin swathed her ample figure, and a shawl of Norwich silk hung about her elbows. She regarded Emma down the commanding beak of her nose, and a snort of satisfaction escaped her. "Lady Stanyon?"

Emma blinked, barely hiding her surprise at this unprecedented condescension on the part of so great a personage. "Lady Seagrave," she managed.

The dowager Lady Seagrave gave a curt nod. "Don't think we've met more than once or twice, m'dear, but I made certain you wouldn't object to a word of warning."

"On the contrary." Emma recovered, but an awareness remained of the immense honor the great lady bestowed upon her. "A warning from you would be well worth hearing."

A chuckle escaped the formidable woman. "From the way you were looking just now, there may be no need for it. But you don't seem to me old enough to take on the chaperonage of a chit just making her come-out. Not all that up to snuff yourself, I'll wager."

Warm color touched Emma's cheeks. "I am far too well aware of it, ma'am."

"What you may not be aware of is the reputation of young Dauntry."

Emma's heart sank. "I've a few suspicions, but indeed, they have no foundation. I've heard nothing against him."

Lady Seagrave nodded. "But you don't like him? Sensible gal. He's been living on expectations for so long, he's run through 'em. Owes more than he's ever likely to inherit. So now he's hanging out for a rich wife."

"A fortune hunter." Emma clenched her hands. "I've suspected it, but I haven't wanted to say anything to Sophie when I had nothing but my unfounded feelings to condemn him."

Lady Seagrave nodded. "It never pays. Young chits are just contrary enough to try to prove how wrong you are by flying to Gretna Green. Not that your little Sophie looks a fast piece. But good-hearted and loyal. That can prove a fatal combination for some cunning scoundrel to play on. Best to distract her with someone else rather than set up her back."

"If you see any young gentlemen of sufficiently polished address and perfection of feature," Emma sighed, "I should be grateful if you would introduce them to her."

Again, Lady Seagrave's rumbling chuckle sounded. "I'll just drop a word in Augusta Pickering's ear. She won't care for Dauntry's making a green girl such a blatant object of his attentions." And with that, the formidable dowager took herself off.

Emma watched her departure with a growing sense of unease. Lady Seagrave, a member of the Prince Regent's set, an unquestioned leader of the *ton*, did not drop hints lightly. For her to have condescended to such kindness underlined the seriousness of Sophie's situation.

The dance seemed to go on interminably, but at last the music ended and another gentleman claimed Sophie's hand. Mr. Dauntry ignored the hopeful glances of two partnerless young ladies and went to lean against a wall, his brooding gaze following Sophie's every move. His behavior, which provoked precisely the sort of gossip Emma most dreaded, might have continued indefinitely had not one of Dauntry's friends induced him to join a game of whist. Emma watched his departure for the card tables with relief, then scanned the room, not quite idly. She didn't see Lord Breydon, and the intensity of her disappointment that he might have left forced her to admit, at last, that she very much wanted to see him.

The music ended, and the dancers drifted off to join friends. Sophie stood irresolute, her gaze traveling about the room in a manner far too marked to escape attention. The tongue wagging would commence in earnest, Emma feared. Yet before she could rise to intervene, Sophie strolled, ever so casually, toward the card room.

Emma waited a couple of minutes, then followed. She spotted the girl at once, standing to one side of the room, watching the play at one of the tables. Dauntry sat there, but Emma paid him no heed, not after her gaze fell on another of the players. Lord Breydon shuffled the deck and dealt the next hand.

The others at the table picked up their cards and began arranging them. Breydon, though, gave his no more than a cursory glance. His gaze moved from one to the other of his fellow players, resting at last on Dauntry. "I believe you have just notched the edges," he said in a purely conversational tone belied by the cold glint in his eyes.

Dauntry froze. "And I," he said after a moment's silence, "believe you to be blessed with a highly vivid imagination."

"Can't go about accusing a man of cheating without reason." A young fop, who had stood nearby watching the play, shook his head in disapproval. "Not at all the thing."

An elderly gentleman of military bearing set down his cards. "Not like Breydon to make idle accusations. Let's see 'em." He reached across and neatly extricated the cards from Dauntry's rigid fingers. He ran his thumb along the edges, and his heavy brow rose. "Notched," he pronounced, and fixed Dauntry with a glower. "I find your presence offensive, sir."

All conversation in the room ceased. In the sudden silence, a gasp sounded, unnaturally loud. Emma stepped to Sophie's side and laid a cautioning hand on her arm. With an effort, the girl remained still.

Dauntry looked about the table, meeting the implacable expressions of his confronters, and his lip curled. "It seems you are ready to believe the worst. I see no point in trying to convince you of my innocence." He hesitated a moment longer, as if awaiting an apology, but none came. With a carefully unconcerned shrug of his shoulder, he rose, bowed to those seated at the table, and turned to exit the room only to come face-to-face with Sophie.

She stared at him, her countenance beseeching. His lips tightened, and he swept her a deep, mocking bow. Without another word, he strode from the room.

Conversation exploded about them, but Emma paid the exclamations of shock, disbelief, and occasional satisfaction no heed. Sophie needed no words to express her distress; her countenance spoke far too eloquently. Emma could only be glad the girl's idol had been thus exposed, but she would have preferred it to have happened in a more private manner. She had to get poor Sophie out of the room, away from the prying, quizzical eyes of the *ton*, before her patent distress provided further fodder for those who delighted in creating scandals.

"Good God." Breydon's voice broke across the din. His gaze rested upon Emma, his eyes widening and his lip curling in an expression that held mocking humor. "It's the cat lady."

A great guffaw, accompanied by tittering laughter, greeted this comment. Emma's cheeks burned; for a long moment she glared at Breydon across the few heads that separated them; then she turned on her heel. Let the *ton* enjoy his latest witticism; they certainly seemed to regard it as a rare jest. That it was at her expense bothered no one but herself. At least it took their attention from Sophie's distress.

She guided her stepdaughter through the door and across the hall; yet she had no desire to reenter the drawing rooms. She cast a rapid glance about, searching for some unoccupied apartment where both she and Sophie might recover their countenances in peace, but no likely door presented itself. For a long moment she hesitated, uncertain.

Sophie, in a voice made rigid with her attempt at casualness, said, "Would you mind terribly if we went home? I have the headache."

"Of course." After leaving Sophie to send for their wraps, Emma found their hostess and made their excuses. Within a very few minutes, they stood on the entry porch as their barouche pulled up in the street before them.

Sophie hurried down the steps, reaching the carriage door before the groom could open it for her. She clambered inside as Emma descended to the pavement, and sat with her head bowed and hands clenched in her lap. A sniff escaped her, the prelude to what Emma greatly feared would be a tempestuous storm of tears.

As Emma laid her fingers on the carriage door, a wet nose nudged at her ankle. She looked down quickly to find not one, but four cats milling about her skirts. One already had its front paws on the step. In a moment it had jumped lightly inside and was making itself very much at home on the seat.

"Shoo it out," Emma begged Sophie, and stooped to prevent a second cat from joining the first.

Even as she spoke, two of the others sprang inside. The groom, who had been long in Emma's service, knew his role. With his right arm he relieved Sophie of one cat, and with his left he scooped up another. He had barely deposited these beside the two Emma had ushered to the walkway when two more stuck their noses out from beneath the undercarriage and three more sprinted down the street to join the commotion.

A rich, masculine chuckle sounded behind them, and an unfamiliar voice asked, "Putting them in or out?"

Emma turned to see a young gentleman, tall and dark, his elegant figure resplendent in evening dress. Amusement crinkled the corners of his eyes, lighting his angular countenance with a pleasant, humorous expression. Emma stared at him, aghast. He looked exactly the sort of young man she'd been hoping would catch Sophie's fancy, and here they were, up to their carriage wheels in cats.

"Want them in?" the gentleman inquired. "Not that I mean to interfere, you understand. Just thought I might be of some help." His gaze, which had strayed to Sophie, lingered there.

"No." Emma pulled herself together. Five cats had jumped in while she'd been distracted by this man's arrival. She resumed the unequal battle of ridding the vehicle of its furry occupants.

To her surprise, the gentleman waded in, cheerfully shooing cats aside, loading his arms with four of the indignant felines. The groom drew out two more, then bid Emma mount into the barouche before any more of the pesky critters beat her to it, and abruptly they were moving forward. The groom swung into position, and Emma, turning to call her thanks to the gentleman, saw him still standing at the edge of the street. He had rid himself of the protesting animals, but they had left their inevitable mark. His expression had changed from one of humor to one of acute distaste as he tried to brush stray hairs from his previously impeccable coat.

A soft exclamation escaped Sophie. "Oh, Stepmamma!

Those horrid cats. No gentleman in his right mind will ever brave the—the army of them that surround you."

Emma covered her hand. "Truly, I'm sorry."

Sophie sniffed. "Only Dauntry didn't seem to mind them. And that was because he cared so very much for my fortune. That was it, was it not?" She raised her misery-filled gaze to Emma.

Emma squeezed her hand. "I'm so very sorry, my dear."

"And you knew, didn't you?" Sophie pursued.

"I had a suspicion," Emma admitted. "It was the way the cats disliked him so much."

A hollow laugh escaped Sophie. "My protectors. One way or another, they will keep the gentlemen away from me."

"The right man won't let a few cats deter him," was all Emma could think to say. Fervently, she wished she could think of some way to comfort the girl. For that matter, she wished she herself could be comforted from Breydon's slight. All in all, it had been a very long while since she'd endured so singularly disagreeable an evening.

FOUR

Emma strolled through sand already warm from the early morning sun. Not far away, four small children, under the watchful eye of an indulgent nursemaid, played a game with the waves, shrieking in pretended fright and running each time one broke on the sand, then turning in pursuit with shrill laughter as it retreated into the sea. Emma watched for a moment, but those carefree days when all troubles could vanish with the cries of the gulls lay far in her past.

A stray cat rubbed its head against her ankle, and she resumed her walk with her new companion at her side. Ahead stood one of the bathing machines, submerged to halfway up its ladderlike steps. The horse between the wagon's shafts stood placidly, one fetlock cocked, as the waves lapped about its knees. Two male dippers stood in watchful attendance on a white-haired gentleman, whose grim expression denoted he submerged himself in the chill waters for his health, not pleasure.

Perhaps she should engage the services of one of the machines; she'd always loved swimming in the ocean. But today, the prospect failed to please her. Today, nothing did. Memories of last night haunted her, of Breydon's slight, of Sophie's muffled sobs when the girl thought her stepmamma could not hear. She could think of no cure for Sophie's broken heart that could penetrate the army of cats that continually surrounded them.

A deep sigh escaped her. She'd rather liked the look of that young gentleman who had helped them herd away the persistent felines after they had left the *soiree*. He, though, had definitely not liked the look of the innumerable hairs shed over his impeccable coat.

Fish. The longing filled her mind. *Cream.* The feathery, furry touch of a tail trailed up the back of her leg. Three of the self-satisfied felines now ambled along with her; she could "hear" each of their different voices, detect the slight differences in their thoughts and desires. Breakfast, of course, was uppermost in their minds. In hers as well, she supposed. She might as well turn back and see if Sophie had awakened yet.

As she neared the road, the cats— five of them, now— emitted a sensation of curiosity. Down the Marine Parade, from the direction opposite to the Steine, raced a tiny blur of mixed colors, orange, black and white. Behind it ran the all too familiar figure of Lord Breydon. The kitten turned up the steps leading to Emma's front door, where it placidly settled on its haunches and attempted to lick the tip of a tail that refused to be still.

The viscount lunged for it, but it made no attempt to escape his grasp. Straightening, he turned the unprotesting kitten over in his hands and poked at its front paws. Emma, with a startled gasp of outrage, broke into as rapid a run as she could manage, hampered both by her narrow skirts and by her accompanying feline entourage.

Breydon looked up as her footsteps sounded on the paving stones, and his gaze narrowed. A slow, rueful smile tugged at the corners of his mouth. "I should have known," he said, exaggerated resignation in his voice.

She slowed to a stop at the foot of the steps; his massive form filled the tiny porch. "What are you doing to Penelope?" she demanded.

"Examining her. She seemed to be in some frightful pain after she jumped into my breakfast parlor."

"Jumped—" Emma reached up to stroke the furry head, her alarm evaporating. "Perhaps you had better tell me, though she seems all right now." She sensed nothing but a purring satisfaction from the exasperating little animal. That, and a wistful desire for the remnants of sausage. Breydon repositioned Penelope to a more comfortable spot in the crook of his arm. "She scrambled through the open window while I was eating breakfast, then set up the most dreadful screech. While I was trying to catch her, a footman came in to see what was toward, and she took off out the door."

"And you followed." The first stirrings of amusement crept into her voice.

"Well, of course I did. I thought she was hurt. But all she seemed to want to do was lead me a merry chase. Directly to you, as I should have guessed she would." He eyed Emma with an unreadable expression. "I had no idea we were such close neighbors."

Memory of their last encounter flooded over her, and she stiffened. With an attempt at cool dignity, she took the kitten from him. "I shall try to keep her from bothering you in the future."

"There's no need." He stroked the kitten's nose, and allowed it to lick his finger with enthusiasm. "Penelope, did you say?"

A defensive note crept into her voice. "She earned her name. She spent last evening raveling my favorite shawl."

An appreciative grin began in his eyes, lighting their somber hue to a vivid green. "She's a classical scholar, I see. I suppose you will call her first offspring Telemachus?"

"The thought had occurred to me," she admitted, cautious.

He chuckled; then abruptly his brow snapped down,

and his expression underwent an odd change. He glanced toward his feet, and Emma, following the direction of his gaze, saw a very long bodied orange tom—a stray—and a particularly well rounded black and white specimen—her own Brutus—with their front claws digging into his breeches just above the knees.

"I'm so very sorry," she exclaimed. Setting Penelope down, she reached for the closest cat.

Breydon waved her aside and set about extricating himself. "Actually," he said, as he freed the orange tom and gave it a hopeful shove, "I am the one who should apologize to you."

Emma, who had her arms full keeping the other cats away from him, looked up, startled.

"Last night," he explained. "I meant no offense. I intended my calling you the Cat Lady as a private joke, just between the two of us. I hadn't expected it to wound you, or for it to afford such ill-natured amusement among the other guests."

She lowered her gaze to the cats. "I—I'm afraid I enjoy somewhat of a reputation where it comes to felines. I believe you can see why."

"I doubt 'enjoy' is quite the right word," he murmured.

"No." A heartfelt sigh escaped her. " 'Endure' is closer to the mark, I suppose. People can be so—" She broke off, a flush warming her cheeks.

"People always make fun of what they don't understand."

She looked up, startled, to encounter an expression of gentle warmth in his eyes. For a long moment she simply gazed back, lost in an unfamiliar sensation of affinity, of fellow feeling. He could be a friend, the thought strayed through her mind. He might not be driven off by the cats.

Fish, came an urgent desire in her mind, followed at once by several echoes of *herring,* and *sardines* and *sausage.*

Breydon blinked, stooped to detach the persistent tom from his leg, then tickled the purring Penelope behind the ear. "My errand seems to be completed. I shall return to my breakfast, and allow you to go to yours." With a smile and nod for her, he descended the three steps and set off down the street, with two of the cats in pursuit, their tails high.

Emma stared after him, bemused. Had he sensed the cats' yearnings? If so, it had not been at any conscious level, not the way they assailed her. Still, his own recollection of his morning meal had certainly followed hard upon the cats' desires. She gathered up tiny Penelope and let herself into the house.

Several of the cats she delivered to the kitchen to be fed from the scraps, but Penelope she carried with her to the breakfast parlor. There she found Sophie, pale and disinclined to converse. Emma considered her a moment, noting the mostly untouched array of delectable items on her plate.

"Will you watch Penelope for me?" she asked, handing the ball of calico fur into Sophie's surprised hands. Briefly, she related the tale of the kitten's morning exploits, ending with, "She's not in any pain now. I think she mostly wants some breakfast."

"So I see." Sophie, who had offered Penelope a fragment of egg, watched as the little kitten devoured it. She applied herself to the task of selecting tidbits for several minutes, then looked up as Emma turned from the sideboard, her own plate filled. "Lord Breydon. Was he not the gentleman—" She broke off, flushing.

Emma chose to misinterpret the words Sophie omitted. "He apologized, and quite politely, for labeling me the Cat Lady. And he was certainly kind to little Penelope."

Sophie forced a smile. "Then I suppose I shall stop

considering him in the light of a villain. For the moment, at least."

Encouraged by these signs, Emma asked Sophie what she might like to do that day. The girl's spirits sank at once, and Emma might have found herself in a quandary had not a message arrived from Miss Isabel Abingdon, Sophie's particular friend, inviting her to make up one of a party bound for Hove. As Miss Abingdon's younger sisters and their governess would also be making the trip, to keep them occupied while their parents prepared for the card party they would give that evening, Emma greeted the invitation with relief. She had only to help Sophie dress and see her to the carriage when it pulled up at the door a short time later. Life, she mused, went on. Sophie would recover from her disappointment in William Dauntry.

Sophie's departure left Emma on her own for the day. After a brief, losing battle with her conscience, she tended to a variety of chores she had managed to postpone. She was just settling down with her mending basket in the late afternoon when Beecher entered the sunny salon, announcing the arrival of a visitor. But Emma had already seen the imposing figure of Lord Breydon standing in the hall behind him. Flustered, she stuffed out of sight the chemise on which she restitched a hem.

"Do I disturb you?" He advanced into the room with three of the cats trailing at his feet. He halted, and Alcibiades, a half-grown gray with white paws, rubbed its face against his booted leg.

"You save me from my mending." She rose, feeling suddenly gauche and uncertain, dislodging Tabitha, the pale orange matronly cat who had been slumbering in her lap. It vociferated its complaint, and soothing its ruffled fur provided Emma the opportunity to recover her composure. When she looked up to her visitor again, it shattered once more.

He remained where he stood, but seven cats now surrounded him, standing on their hind legs and pawing at his elegant inexpressibles. His gaze rested on her, humor glinting in eyes warmed to a sea green. "I have brought a peace offering." He held out a paper-wrapped bouquet.

She took it, and the cats followed, the tips of their tails twitching, their sensations of delight filling her mind. The closest sat on their haunches, tapping at her skirt with their front paws. Drawing off the covering, she revealed several sprays of fresh catnip.

A soft laugh escaped her. "I can't think of anything more delightful," she declared. She selected one of the sprigs and waved it gently through the air, barely above the cats' noses. They leapt for it, in ecstasy, and she strewed the other sprigs across the floor where the cats proceeded to roll in it.

Beecher entered the room, stepping with care over the gyrating cats, and placed a tray laden with cakes, biscuits, two decanters and crystal glasses. Aware suddenly she had left her visitor standing, Emma flushed and apologized, and begged him to take a seat and partake of a glass of wine. This he did, along with several of the cook's best almond macaroons, all the while watching the feline antics.

"You will quite spoil them." She looked up and caught a broad grin on his face as his gaze remained fixed on the cats.

"They certainly like to play." He looked back to her, and his smile warmed. "Which reminds me, do you go to the Abingdons' card party this evening?"

"Why, yes." An answering warmth rushed through her, and she found she couldn't think of a single other thing to say.

He didn't appear to notice. "Then, I shall look forward to the pleasure of seeing you there." With that he rose and took his leave of her to keep an appointment with a friend.

Emma returned from seeing him to the door, her heart singing. Well, why shouldn't she be happy? she demanded of herself. It had nothing whatsoever to do with the light that had glinted in Breydon's eyes. It was just that she rarely remained in low spirits for long, she quite looked forward to playing cards, and she enjoyed the Abingdons' company.

She sank once more into her chair and drew out her mending, but her needle remained idle in her still hands. All right, she wasn't being entirely honest with herself. Breydon's presence at the party did have something to do with her soaring spirits. And after all, why shouldn't it? The viscount's approval might open new and exciting opportunities for Sophie. He would know any number of young gentlemen whom he might introduce to them. One of these, surely, would be so moved by the girl's sweetness of nature that he could overlook the cats—especially since it wasn't Sophie the animals haunted.

But Lord Breydon, Emma realized, had begun to haunt her. His sudden smile—no, more than that, a sense of his presence—lingered in her thoughts in a most disturbing manner, long after she should have turned her attention elsewhere.

FIVE

Emma peered into her mirror, surveying her appearance with a critical eye. With her gown she could find no fault. The peach-colored silk suited her dark hair and fair complexion, just as its simple but elegant lines set off her slender figure. The décolletage might be cut a trifle low, but a wide band of blond lace rectified that fault. She turned her attention to the riotous ringlets in which her abigail had arranged her hair, and frowned.

Her door opened, and Sophie peeped in, a brave, defiant smile on her pale face. "There you are, Stepmamma. Whatever is keeping you? Why, you look all the crack!" She advanced into the room, eyeing Emma with approval.

"I don't." Emma looked up from where she sat at her dressing table. "Why did I ever agree to let Mifton dress my hair in curls?"

"Because the effect is delightful." Sophie stooped to catch Penelope before the kitten could scramble up the hem of Emma's gown.

"It makes me look absurdly young." She studied her reflection a moment longer, then came to a decision. "I shall have Mifton smooth them out."

"Why not just cover them with a turban? No." Her smile, for a fleeting moment, became genuine as Emma opened her mouth in protest. "You will leave them exactly the way they are, or we shall be unconscionably late.

Do come," she continued with determined cheerfulness. "I've never known you to worry so about your appearance." She opened a drawer in the dressing table, drew out a single peach-colored silk rose, and pinned it in Emma's hair. "There, now let us go."

Emma cast a last, uncertain glance at her reflection, but surrendered. She had an uncomfortable feeling that nothing she did with her hair this evening would please her. With a sigh, she followed Sophie down to the waiting carriage.

They did indeed arrive late at the Abingdons', as Sophie had predicted. Normally, Emma would have been gratified for Sophie's sake at the stir their arrival created, but not tonight. After the laughter at her expense the night before, she would rather have slipped in unheralded and taken up a place in a corner where she could see everyone without being observed herself. Denied this, she brazened it out, striding forward with assumed confidence to greet her hostess, then turning to survey the guests already at play. Sophie stood at her side, head held high and proud, only her eyes betraying the heaviness of her heart.

Several acquaintances greeted them, yet even as Emma acknowledged them, her gaze continued to scan the room. Only when she spotted Lord Breydon, seated across a small table from General Radleigh, did she realize that she sought him. More than that, she had dressed for him as well. The realization mortified her—or was it responsible for the strange, tingling sensation that swept through her?

The viscount glanced up from his cards and met her uncertain gaze, and a sudden smile gleamed in his eyes. The peculiar sensation she experienced intensified, racing along her flesh, then settled in the pit of her stomach. An answering smile trembled on her lips, and hurriedly she looked away.

"Lord Breydon seems pleased to see you," Sophie murmured in her ear.

"Does he?" Emma struggled to achieve an incurious tone. "I'm sure I don't know why he should be."

"Perhaps your presence merely assures him that Penelope still enjoys excellent health. But you would know best." Again, Sophie's smile wavered on the genuine, then threatened to crumple completely. "Pray—pray excuse me. Isabel is attempting to start a game of charades. I shall help her." And with that, and before Emma could come up with any word of comfort, Sophie took herself off.

Emma watched her join her particular friend, and knew the girl would find some measure of solace there. But with her immediate concern for Sophie relieved, her thoughts returned to Breydon. If the viscount were indeed pleased to see her, he gave no further indication of the fact. A full hour passed before he approached her as she rose from the loo table, and then he came in the company of another gentleman. Emma blinked as she recognized the young man who had assisted them the previous evening with ridding their carriage of superfluous cats.

"Lady Stanyon." Breydon's deep voice seemed to contain more than a hint of warmth tonight. "I do not believe you are acquainted with Lord Linwood."

His companion made her an exquisite bow, and Emma eyed him with interest. If Linwood had requested this introduction, then perhaps he'd taken more notice of Sophie, and less of the cats, than she'd thought. She inclined her head. "This gives me an opportunity to thank you again for your kind assistance."

A boyish smile brightened his entire countenance. "A pleasure, I assure you."

"Even the cat hairs?" she couldn't help but ask.

"Even," he assured her with suitable gravity, "the cat hairs."

And then Sophie was beside them, the introduction made, and Emma had the satisfaction of watching her stepdaughter whisked off for a hand or two of piquet. With a mixture of relief and pleasure, she watched them settle themselves at a table. Linwood shuffled and dealt, but the game progressed no farther. Sophie made some comment as she picked up her cards, Linwood answered with obvious animation, and piquet was forgotten. The heads bent closer across the green baize cloth, and both seemed oblivious to the rest of the world.

A soft chuckle sounded near Emma's ear. "You are beaming on them like the most hardened of matchmaking mammas," Breydon informed her.

Heat flushed Emma's cheeks. "You are being absurd," she declared, then spoiled it the next moment by adding, "But only see how taken he is with her."

"And so he should be," came Breydon's prompt agreement. "She does you credit. And speaking of which, that's a very fetching way you have of doing your hair. It suits you."

Emma looked down. "You are determined to put me to the blush, my lord."

"Successfully, it seems." The chuckle was back in his voice. "Come, let us see if we can do better at playing piquet than they do."

The rest of the evening passed in a blur for Emma. She played several hands with Breydon, then left to join another loo table before the gossips began to link their names. Sophie joined her, but if the other players had to recall the girl's wandering attention once or twice, no one but Emma seemed to notice the soft glow that infused her.

The following evening proved every bit as satisfying. Both Breydon and Linwood attended the musical *soiree*,

and it was not long before the two gentlemen joined
Emma and Sophie, taking seats at their sides, and con-
versing with them or fetching them refreshments during
the interludes. Despite her eminently practical nature,
Emma could not suppress a welling of joy. She might concentrate her hopes and dreams on Sophie, but she still
had to admit to herself that despite the comforts of her
situation, she did secretly long for the love of someone
other than the cats.

The morning of their *al fresco* breakfast dawned three
days later, clear and bright. Emma had originally invited
twenty-four guests, but their friendships with Breydon and
Linwood had emboldened her to invite these two gentlemen, as well. Both had accepted with pleasure, leaving
Emma suddenly nervous that something might go wrong.

The caterer had erected a gay pavilion on the sand, its
sides open to allow an unhindered view of the ocean. Six
round tables laid with crystal and silver occupied most of
the space, while several smaller tables lined the area,
heaped with chafing dishes and urns. A thick carpet covered the ground, making walking as easy as if they were
indoors. Overhead hung baskets of brilliant flowers, while
outside the waves crashed on the shore and the seagulls
emitted their plaintive cries. Nothing, Emma decided,
could be more perfect.

Even the guests arrived on time, with elderly General
Radleigh, who had agreed to act as her host, one of the
first. The servers circulated among the tables that filled
rapidly, supplying an array of delicacies certain to please
every palate. Emma breathed a sigh of satisfaction and
ventured to seat herself at last.

And then the uninvited guests arrived. They came sin-
gly at first, then in groups of two or three, tails high,
whiskers atwitch, eyes bright, thoughts firmly fixed on the
aromas of sausages, herrings, and cream sauces. Emma,
who had anticipated just such an occurrence, signaled to

the footmen who stood on guard. At once they produced bowls of scraps from beneath the serving tables and carried their bribes a safe distance from the pavilion before setting out the plates of treats.

"Only you," came Breydon's voice from behind Emma, "would invite the entire feline population of Brighton to her *al fresco* breakfast."

"I didn't," she protested. "But it was obvious they would come."

"Of course it was," came his prompt response. "*You* are here."

"They don't always flock to me," she said, but her tone lacked conviction.

A giggle sounded from one of the young ladies seated near her, accompanied by a chuckle of disbelief from one of the gentlemen. Emma stared back at them, meeting their amusement with a bright, if somewhat forced, smile. Before she could make any suitable comment, though, the tiny Penelope strolled into the pavilion, making straight for her.

Breydon intercepted the kitten, scooping it up in his arm, settling it in his lap, and selecting a tidbit for it. "What they flock to," he said, "is food. It doesn't take them long to discover Lady Stanyon is too tender hearted to refuse them sustenance."

Emma let that stand. She could see no point in explaining that they came because some indefinable bond existed between them. She "heard" them, certainly, but it was more than that. She understood them, and they seemed to understand her.

Except they could be frustratingly obtuse when it came to understanding that she wanted to be rid of them once in a while.

Raucous calls from the gulls sounded overhead, and Emma looked out to see the huge gray-and-white birds with their wide wing spans swooping down on the cats to inspect the contents of the bowls. She sprang to her feet. "Where is the bread?" she called to her footmen.

With a laugh, she invited her guests to join her outside. The more curious followed her and received stale loaves and rolls, which she instructed them to tear and toss to the circling birds. Soon all joined in, scattering their largess to the winds.

"And now you're encouraging the gulls, as well," murmured Breydon, who had joined her in the commotion. "My dear Lady Stanyon, will you never learn?"

Emma tossed the last few crumbs and turned to see him, tall and immaculate, Penelope still cradled sleepily in his one arm. She raised her eyebrows. "What is there to learn, except that animals get hungry, too?" She couldn't possibly explain the clarity of their piteous longings, which made them impossible to ignore. "But then," she added, "it is obvious you never have anything to do with cats, do you?"

"I never said that." With a finger, he tickled Penelope behind the ears. She merely yawned and closed her eyes. "And there's no need," he added sternly, "to make comments about my encouraging her. I'm keeping her from being trodden upon in all this commotion."

"Of course you are," she agreed.

He cast her a rueful glance. "Do you know, I've been experiencing the strangest craving for cream, ever since I picked this little creature up. Do you suppose their desires are contagious?"

SIX

Never, Emma reflected, had she seen Sophie so happy. Her stepdaughter seemed to float through her days, her thoughts filled with Lord Linwood. Not even a chance encounter with William Dauntry in front of Donaldson's Circulating Library, in full view of the *ton*, ruffled the girl. She greeted him with a smile and friendly word, as she might acknowledge any old acquaintance, then moved on, serene in her inner happiness.

To an extent, Emma feared she herself suffered from the same complaint. Hardly a waking moment passed when Lord Breydon didn't occupy some corner of her mind. Dreams could be dangerous, leading to heartbreak, especially for a lady old enough to know better. Yet she greatly feared that should Breydon disappear from the scene, her life would be empty beyond endurance.

Still, common sense and prudence could be elusive, especially when attending a ball on a summer's eve at the seaside. The Castle Inn glittered with candles, and laughter mingled with the melodious strains of the cello and viola as they tuned to the violins. A magical night, Emma mused, as the sweet song of a flute rose in a trill.

Sophie, a vision in pale blue gauze, with matching satin roses cascading among her fair curls, moved from one group to another, greeting friends with an ease that Emma would have envied at her age. Across the crowded room, Lord Linwood spotted the girl. Emma watched in approval as the young gentleman continued his conversation with the officer at his side. His gaze might follow Sophie, but his manners and breeding prevented him from racing to her side, making a spectacle of them both.

Breydon, too, attended the public ball. Emma observed his entrance from where she sat demurely amongst the matrons and dowagers, her breath catching in her throat as he paused to survey the room. He never looked her way, though. At last he strode forward, pausing to speak to several acquaintances, until he stood at Sophie's side. He exchanged a word with the girl, then turned, idly scanning the chaperons. His gaze met Emma's, and a slow smile lit his eyes. A very minor reaction, when compared to the internal upheaval Emma experienced. He looked away the next moment, continuing his survey, then moved on to speak to General Radleigh.

Why was it, Emma wondered, that the very behavior of which she approved in young Linwood merely exasperated her in Breydon? Yet for him to have sought her out would have made her the subject of unwanted gossip—not to mention the tumult that would have taken place in her own heart as her hopes soared. No, he behaved just as he ought—and just as she must hope he would.

After that, with determined effort, she concentrated on Sophie and Lord Linwood, and pride welled in her at her stepdaughter's deportment. Twice Sophie danced with Linwood, but four dances came between, for which the girl bestowed her hand upon several other gentlemen. For the most part, she even managed to keep her gaze from resting on Linwood. Emma might catch an occasional betraying flush in the girl's cheeks, but she doubted even the highest sticklers noted anything to which they might object.

Linwood, too, displayed admirable discretion, but not for a moment did his casual demeanor fool Emma. She caught the possessive glances, the assured smile, those many betraying little details that declared him to be a man deeply in love and confident of its return. He would declare himself soon; and then she would have her dearest wish answered, and Sophie would be happy.

Then abruptly Lord Breydon stood before her, smiling, his hand extended, and all noble thoughts fled from her mind. The musicians, she realized, had just struck up the opening bars of a waltz. But chaperons didn't dance. She shouldn't stand, she shouldn't allow him to lead her to the floor, and most definitely she should not allow him to place his hand on her waist for the first of the closed steps. Yet she did all of these things, and did them while gazing into his eyes, a smile trembling on her lips. Tongues would wag, but at the moment she simply didn't care. She and Breydon moved as one through the intricate steps, the firm hold of his hand guiding her, spinning her under his arm, his smile only for her.

She wouldn't mind at all growing accustomed to this. She only hoped the cats would give her the chance.

Not that Breydon disliked the ridiculous felines who surrounded her. In fact, he seemed to like all animals. At least, she thought he did. Suddenly, it became a matter of extreme urgency for her to make certain of that.

She had a chance the following day. A number of gentlemen staying in Brighton—and some even at the Pavilion itself—had planned an informal racing meet, and Breydon had arranged to take a party to watch. He had thought of everything, she noted with approval as she and Sophie stepped down from their carriage to be greeted by their host. A large canvas pavilion stood near the track, promising protection from the brilliant sun that blazed in the cloudless sky. Liveried footmen passed discreetly among the guests, offering glasses of iced champagne and plates of delectable morsels.

Linwood appeared from the midst of the crowd and

begged the privilege of escorting Sophie to a vantage point where they could watch the saddling of the two horses matched in the first race. "Owners will be riding," he explained to Emma. "First-rate horsemen, both of them. Shame to miss a minute of it."

"Then, of a certainty it is a spectacle Sophie must see." Emma watched with a smile as Linwood grasped Sophie's arm and hurried her to where a crowd gathered some distance away.

"That should keep them awhile." Breydon offered Emma his arm. "Do you desire to see it, as well?"

"I believe I can safely miss the saddling," she assured him. She would be quite happy to simply stand here at his side, her hand resting on his sleeve, lost in the unfamiliar happiness that engulfed her whenever he was near.

"I doubt the race will be any great display, either, despite the undoubted ability of the riders." He strolled with her toward the pavilion, pausing only to obtain a glass of the sparkling wine for her. "There are four colts scheduled to run after that, and I am thinking of buying one of them. Do you care for horseflesh?"

"Very much, but you'll find me dreadfully untutored."

"As I am about cats?" His mouth twitched into a decidedly charming smile, and his fingers brushed hers where they rested on his arm. "Perhaps we can instruct one another."

She looked up, encountered the unexpected intensity of his expression, and dropped her gaze at once. Her heart beat with an erratic frenzy she found both stifling and exhilarating. She could think of nothing she wanted more than to be instructed by Breydon, and on any number of subjects.

A man who appeared to be in charge of the catering claimed his attention, and with a murmured word Breydon excused himself. Emma retired to a back corner of the shelter where she gulped down a revivifying mouthful

of champagne. She was as breathless and tongue-tied as
a chit in her first Season, which was ludicrous. She was
a widow of two years' standing, a chaperon with a stepdaughter to be successfully established. She had experienced two Seasons, both her own and Sophie's, and had
learned how to flirt in a discreet and well-bred manner.
So why did all this worldly wisdom fly out the window
when she stood face-to-face with Lord Breydon?

She took another sip from her glass and looked
around. 'To her surprise, the two ladies nearest her
averted their faces, but a telltale giggle lingered in an
atmosphere suddenly heavy with curiosity and gossip. A
sideways glance warned Emma that others watched her
and whispered, too.

General Radleigh, every inch the military hero despite
his civilian dress, strode over to her and took her arm.
"Come, my dear, mustn't stand in the shadows. Too beautiful a day for that."

Willingly, she accompanied him. "What are they saying?" she demanded as soon as they left the pavilion.

He gave a short laugh. "Now, don't be sly, puss. They're
all agog, and who can blame them?"

"About what?" Emma pursued, though she hoped she
knew. Or rather, she hoped not. To be the subject of *on
dits* was no pleasant matter—even if the stories did link
her name with Breydon's.

He merely winked at her. "You know your own affairs
best, m'dear. Ah, and here's Breydon now. I'll leave you
in his care." He awarded the viscount a slight bow, cere-
moniously bestowed Emma's hand on him, and took himself off.

Emma, her cheeks burning, tried to withdraw her fingers from Breydon's obliging hold, but he held them
tight. "My lord—"

"How formal." He tucked her hand through his arm.

"The race is about to begin. If we hurry, you may still find a place by the rail."

Emma dutifully took her position to watch the match, but her mind sped far from the spectacle before her. *Were* the gossips linking their names? If so, she and Breydon now provided them with fresh fodder for their delectation. Yet the general's comments implied more than that. Did speculation run high that Breydon might actually make her an offer?

The possibility stunned her. It had lurked at the back of her mind since the previous night, but she hadn't dared acknowledge it. Now, in the brilliant daylight, with her shoulder pressed tightly against his chest and his chin brushing the side of her head as he leaned forward to watch, the prospect thrilled her, leaving her weak, terrified, elated. She could think of nothing she wanted more. With every passing moment, her awareness of him grew. His merest smile or most casual touch sent her pulse skipping erratically.

"Well run, but much as expected." Breydon drew back and turned toward the pavilion. "Ah, they are laying out the nuncheon. Are you hungry?"

Food was the farthest thing from her mind. She followed, shaken, aware she had allowed her imagination and hopes to run riot with her. No gentleman contemplating making a lady an offer could possibly be so totally oblivious to the tumult he had just created in her.

He left her at the entrance to the pavilion to circulate among his guests, seeing to it that everyone found chairs and had everything they wanted. Emma retired to a corner where Sophie and Linwood joined her, bearing plates heaped with salmon mayonnaise and crab patties. Isabel Abingdon, accompanied by a young lieutenant in a dashing scarlet coat, claimed the remaining seats and began an animated discussion of the match they had just witnessed.

Emma leaned back in her chair and listened, amused and pleased by Sophie's enthusiasm. Linwood's gaze rarely left the girl's lovely face. Soon, Emma reflected. Very soon she would see Sophie happily established.

She reached for a crab patty, only to draw up short, assaulted by a scream of agony. She froze, looking about, as the cry sounded again in her mind. Her mind. And the anguish was feline. Penelope.

She sprang to her feet. She had to get home, rescue the poor little kitten. . . .

"Stepmamma?" Sophie stood beside her, her hand on Emma's arm. "Are you all right? What's wrong?"

"It's Penelope. She's been injured, and she's frightened." Emma's hand closed over Sophie's. "I must go to her at once."

"Of course. But the carriage isn't due back for us for several hours."

"I'll have to—" She broke off as she saw Breydon's broad-shouldered figure making his way toward them through the chairs. She hurried forward.

He caught her extended hands. "What's toward?"

She clung to him. "Is there a carriage I may borrow?"

"Take mine." He signaled for a footman and drew Emma away from the curious stares of his guests. He turned as the servant approached and gave his order. "Now," he went on as the man hurried off in search of Breydon's groom, "tell me what's upset you."

"It's Penelope." Her explanation tumbled out, disjointed, for the kitten's distress still tore at her mind. A stunned silence at the surrounding tables warned her that other guests overheard, but she didn't care. She had to reach the kitten.

Breydon listened, his expression intent as he studied her face. When she finished, he drew her from the canvas pavilion to where the groom already checked the harnesses. "I'm sorry I can't accompany you. The disadvantages of being the host. But Rigg will give you any assistance you need." He helped her into the curricle, then stood back as the groom jumped into the seat beside her and gave the horses the office.

They left the racing course in silence, Rigg concentrating on handling the frisky pair. Emma clung to the side of the carriage and concentrated on the kitten. As she sent it silent messages of reassurance, its frenzied screams faded to sensations of misery.

The journey to the Marine Parade seemed to take forever. At last, the groom drew up before Emma's house, and she sprang to the paving, scanning the street in search of Penelope. Then *fish* filled her thoughts, and a sleek, black feline ran toward her. Emma set it aside as it tried to rub against her leg, and pushed its culinary desires from her mind as well. And there, faint but persistent, she could hear the kitten's fear.

It had gone to earth beneath a massive shrub. Emma dropped to her knees before it, reaching as far back as she could, the twigs tearing at the flesh of her hands and arms. Then Rigg joined her, forcing his wiry body between the prickly bush and the side of the house until the toe of his booted foot could just nudge the quivering bundle of calico fur. The kitten hissed and darted forward, directly into Emma's outstretched arms. She caught it close, and the little thing hissed and scratched in its pain and fear.

"That's a wild cat, m'lady," Rigg declared with feeling. He inched his way back, unsnagging his coat with care.

"She's been hurt." Emma didn't need to follow the kitten's sensations to the center of its troubles; blood dripped sluggishly from a hind paw, and a nasty gash ran along the leg.

Rigg eyed the damage with professional interest. "Might need to set a stitch or two in that. I've had a spot of experience, but with dogs, mind. Never tended a cat before."

Emma's eyes brimmed, from relief that the kitten had suffered no greater harm, and from this unexpected kindness. She managed a shaky smile. "I've tended far too many. Thank you, but I should be all right."

Still, Rigg saw her to her door and into the hands of her majordomo before taking his leave. Beecher took in the situation at a glance, and in a very few moments the servants scurried to produce towels, hot water, and the basket containing Emma's emergency supplies of lint, herbal ointments, and the myriad other items she had found useful through her years of tending distressed felines.

She had just finished treating the wound, and now sat with the towel-wrapped kitten in her lap, when the door burst open. Sophie stormed into the room, her expression stony as she paced back and forth in open agitation. Emma, who had just begun to relax, felt every nerve tense once more.

"I was quite deceived in Linwood," Sophie exclaimed. She came to a halt before Emma, and her gaze fell on Penelope. The kitten lay curled with eyelids closed, and the faintest tremblings of a purr just sounded deep in her throat. "The poor thing." Sophie stooped to stroke its little head. "But she's better now? What happened? You went so very pale when it occurred, I feared the worst at first."

"No, but she tore her leg quite dreadfully. It must have been one of those hideous spiked points on the iron work." She studied the lines of distress that etched deeply into Sophie's lovely countenance. The girl's eyes glittered with an anger and unhappiness that tugged at her heart. "Tell me," she said simply.

Sophie choked on a sob. Sinking onto the carpet at Emma's side, she laid her cheek against her stepmamma's knee. "He was so—so unfeeling. He made a joke of your distress, as if you were some dreadful eccentric. And he must know perfectly well that you are no such thing! I was so furious with him, I—" She broke off and swallowed. "I told him exactly what I thought of him," she finished in a hollow voice.

Exactly what she *didn't* think of him, Emma reflected. She touched Sophie's gleaming curls, which had tumbled askew, and stroked her head. "You stood up for me, of course. But, my dear Sophie, I am so sorry I made it necessary."

Sophie sniffed and groped for her handkerchief. "Of course I stood up for you. He had no right to say anything so callous."

But that wasn't the problem at all. Emma murmured soothing words which she knew would provide little comfort. The real problem lay in Emma herself. Her behavior must have seemed extremely peculiar by any normal standard. How could she expect anyone else to understand her uncanny link to cats when she didn't understand it herself? And Sophie, inured to her odd ways, had come face-to-face with the manner in which the world viewed such oddities, and hadn't known how to handle it. She'd been confused, probably embarrassed, and she'd overreacted to what had probably been a relatively harmless jest on the part of Linwood.

And now the poor girl had quarreled with the gentleman she loved, and it was all Emma's fault. If she'd damaged that relationship, she would never forgive herself.

SEVEN

Emma and Sophie dined early that night, neither doing justice to the excellent meal prepared by the cook. Sophie toyed with each bite, her expression abstracted, her whole demeanor dejected. Emma's heart ached for her, and she reproached herself severely. There had been no need to make a scene; she could have left quietly.

Except the kitten's distress had become her own, and she had reacted with the kitten's panic.

She looked at the little animal, curled into a ball on the chair at her side, for once not scrambling into her lap to see what edibles could be snagged from her plate. Emma simply hadn't thought. She'd let her emotions rule her, and now Sophie paid the price.

For this once, they had no engagements; the long evening stretched before them, with nothing to break the monotony or raise their lagging spirits. Emma, racking her brain for ideas that might appeal to her stepdaughter, suggested a stroll along the sand. Sophie agreed, but without enthusiasm. At least it would be better than sitting in their drawing room, pretending to work on their stitchery.

While Sophie made her way to her room to change into half boots and fetch a shawl, Emma withdrew with Penelope to check the stitches and apply more ointment. As she dabbed at the wound with a damp cloth, Beecher opened the door into her sitting room and, with a note of triumph in his voice, announced Lord Breydon.

Startled, Emma looked up to see the viscount, tall and elegant in a black coat, black breeches, and white stockings. Involuntarily she drew the kitten close. It hissed, and at once she loosened her grip. It made no attempt to jump free of her hold, though; it merely squirmed into a more comfortable position and eyed the new arrival.

Breydon approached slowly, his gaze on the damaged leg. "How the devil did you know?" he demanded by way of opening.

Emma swallowed. "Good evening, my lord. We weren't expecting you."

At that, his eyebrows rose. "Weren't you? Why on earth not? You leave my party under circumstances like that and don't expect me to come to see what occurred? What an odd notion of me you must have."

Her lips twitched awry. "And now a very odd notion of me *you* must have."

He hesitated. "I admit, I would be glad of an explanation. You suddenly become convinced something has happened to one of your cats, you go racing off, and Rigg comes back and tells me one of them really is injured, and you knew exactly where it was hiding." He glanced down at the black-and-white Alcibiades, who rubbed against his stockinged leg, then back at Emma. "You must admit, it does sound a trifle unusual." He met her gaze. "I repeat. How did you know?"

She looked down, studying the fur she ruffled with nervous fingers. "It sounds too absurd," she said at last.

"Nothing," he said with feeling, "could sound more absurd than the thoughts I've been entertaining all afternoon. Will you not tell me?"

A shaky sigh escaped her. "I can hear them." Almost, it was a relief to admit the implausible truth. "Their thoughts, I mean. Or rather, I simply know what they want, since they don't think in words. I feel cravings for fish, or cream."

"And cries for help?" His voice held no expression whatsoever, nothing to give her a clue as to how he reacted to her absurd claim.

She kept her gaze on Penelope. "I feel when they're in pain, or afraid."

"Do you know in what way they're hurt?" he demanded.

She shook her head. "Only when I'm actually touching them. Then I can sense exactly where the problem is, though not always *what* the problem is." She hesitated, then forged on. "Do you remember my *al fresco* party, when you said you thought you knew what Penelope wanted?"

"But that was—" He broke off.

She looked up to see him staring at the kitten, an odd expression in his eyes.

His frown deepened, and he shook his head slowly. "No. All cats want fish and cream. There's nothing remarkable about me knowing that. And they certainly don't follow me around the way they do you."

"And for that you may be grateful," she assured him. "It is no great joy to be forever disrupting events and alienating people because there's an army of cats surrounding you, pleading for something to eat. And now that the subject has come up," she rushed on, "I owe you an apology. I know I must have created quite a stir at your party, and indeed, I am terribly sorry; but if you had felt her screams—" She broke off, choked by the memory of fear and pain generated by the injured kitten.

"There is no need to apologize," he declared, but a note of reserve crept into his voice.

She must have caused him considerable embarrassment, she realized. She apologized again, but he waved it aside, assuring her it was nothing and soon forgotten in the delights of the remaining races.

"You may see for yourself tomorrow afternoon," he added.

She stared at him blankly.

"The reception at the Pavilion," he prompted. "Have you forgotten?"

"Do you mean you still wish to escort me?"

He regarded her with a frown. "I do not issue invitations lightly," he said with a steadiness that gave weight to his words. "Nor do I withdraw them without good and sufficient reason."

"You don't consider the scandal-causing potential of your guest to be good reason?"

He stiffened. "Quite to the contrary. I can think of a good number of people who would only benefit from such a stir as you created this day." With that, he took his leave.

Emma, with a sinking heart, watched the door close behind him. Her revelations about her uncanny ability had made him uneasy, of that she was certain. Why, then, had he maintained his invitation to her for the reception the following afternoon? That he wanted her company seemed doubtful; he'd seemed anxious enough to escape her now. Did he want to proclaim before the *ton* that he held himself above the opinion of the gossips? She considered what she knew of him, and came to the disheartening conclusion that he intended to escort her to prove, both to himself and to the Polite World, that no one's opinion but his own determined his actions. He would escort her, prove himself an admirable host, return her home, and that would be that. It seemed highly unlikely she would see him again, after tomorrow.

She prepared the following day for the proffered entertainment with considerable trepidation. The thought had occurred to her during the night that perhaps Breydon intended to escort her not for his own sake, but for hers, to show the *ton* her odd behavior was of no consequence. If this were the true reason, it was a generous act on his part, and one for which she was truly grateful. She would see to it she gave him no cause to regret it.

She dressed with considerable care, her taste dictated by a desire for neatness and propriety. Everything about her, from her appearance to her behavior, must be beyond reproach for this one day. To her abigail's dismay, she decreed that her hair be swept back in a severe style suitable for a modest and circumspect dowager, then made her way down the stairs to await the arrival of Breydon.

The calico Penelope, the gray-and-white Brutus, orange Tabitha, and black Eustace lay in wait for her in the salon, descending on her with purposeful gleams in their eyes and shedding hairs in their glossy coats. For several minutes she fought a losing battle trying to keep the determined animals from her lap, until at last she gave up and went to stand by the window that looked out over the Marine Parade toward the sea. Penelope, still unsteady on her injured hind leg, pawed at her skirts, but the others leapt for the sill, Eustace going so far as to hiss at the others to claim the place nearest to Emma. Thoughts of warm laps and rubbed chins filled her mind, although a yearning for the playful chasing of a ball of wool played about the edges of her awareness.

She was on her knees, tossing a crumpled piece of writing paper for the cats to bat about, when Breydon strode in. She scrambled to her feet, her cheeks heated, only to stumble over the aggressive Eustace. Breydon caught her arm, steadying her, and drew her erect. "They—they wanted to play," she said, breathless and annoyed with herself for her embarrassment.

"I suppose they told you so."

She studied him for a moment, but couldn't tell

whether or not he mocked her. He certainly didn't sound at ease with the possibility. She stooped, collected the paper, and gave it one last toss. Eustace dove for it, but Brutus and Tabitha reached it before him. Penelope paid it no heed. She climbed onto the toe of Breydon's elegant shoe and patted his stockinged leg.

"Hasn't your mistress let you nap in her lap?" he demanded. He scooped the kitten into his hands, and the little bundle of fur purred in contentment.

Unable to resist, Emma asked in an innocent tone, "Whatever makes you think that's what she wants?"

He cast her a reproving glance and set the kitten on a chair cushion. "It's what every cat wants," he informed her. "Are you ready?"

With that, they left the house. Behind her, Emma caught wistful thoughts of laps; then the cats' sleepy attention turned to the afternoon sun that slanted through the windows. They would be perfectly happy while she was gone.

Breydon handed her into his curricle. The groom Rigg responded to her greeting with politeness, then ruined the effect by following it with a sideways glance. Still, to Emma's suspicious mind, he seemed more speculative than censorious.

They passed the drive to the Pavilion in discussing such innocuous topics as the beauty of the weather and the excellent manners displayed by his pair of matched chestnuts. Emma was groping desperately in her mind for another safe topic when they pulled in at the palace's West Entrance and made their way to the domed *porte cochère*. Breydon jumped down, handed Emma from his carriage, and while Rigg whisked the vehicle away, he led her into the opulent Octagon Hall. She gained the impression of a light, airy room, all floor-length windows and tent-like ceiling. She had barely a glance to spare, though, for she found herself facing not only the Entrance Hall beyond, but three of the guests who had been present at Breydon's gathering the preceding day.

Breydon's hand tightened on hers. "Courage," he murmured, for her ears alone.

"Why should I need it?" she whispered back, but even to her own ears it sounded like false bravado.

"Why should you, indeed?" He drew her forward, greeting his friends.

This first hurdle passed safely, Emma moved with more ease through the low opening into the long corridor, where a number of notables milled. Her fellow guests seemed content simply to be present amid the Chinese splendor of the Pavilion. Yet she couldn't rid herself of the suspicion that they were more anxious to be seen and to display their finery than they were in admiring the remarkable decor.

After exchanging a few more greetings, Emma allowed herself to relax. No one snubbed her. No one made unkind comments about the previous day's botheration. Perhaps she had exaggerated the reaction to her odd behavior. Or perhaps she should credit Breydon for standing by her, offering his protection as he showed his support of her before the *ton*. If she behaved normally, her indiscretion might well be forgotten. And she would—*must*—behave with complete propriety for Breydon's sake.

At least she could count on no stray cats roaming the halls of the Pavilion.

Prinny, elegant and affable, emerged from one of the doorways, passed among his guests exchanging greetings, then ushered them into the Salon. Emma moved with them, still on Breydon's arm, only to pause just over the threshold of the magnificent chamber. The Chinese wallpaper demanded her instant attention; then she allowed her gaze to travel upward to the chandelier suspended from the cloud-filled sky painted on the ceiling.

"Impressed?" Breydon murmured in her ear. He stopped a footman and obtained glasses of champagne.

Emma accepted one from him. "Words seem sadly inadequate to describe it, do they not?" She took a tentative sip, then added, "There are certainly a great many people here." She nodded to Lady Abingdon, who waved gaily, then continued her survey of the crowd. Most of those present she knew more by reputation than personal acquaintance. She didn't normally move in such lofty circles.

Lady Seagrave paused to exchange greetings with Breydon, bestowed a condescending smile on Emma, and moved on to join a circle of Prinny's more intimate friends. Emma wished she might have brought Sophie, or that Lady Abingdon would cease talking to that elderly roué who kept patting her shoulder. She felt alone, adrift except for Breydon, and even he seemed aloof since the previous day.

"Shall I fetch you a plate?" the viscount asked. "It could prove a long afternoon."

"A hot one, certainly, if we remain in here." She accompanied him to the side of the room, where tiered dishes, heaped with delicacies, filled a table.

A late arrival created a small stir by the door, and a formidable-looking matron, accompanied by Lord Linwood, made her way through the guests to greet Prinny. Linwood saw the lady settled amid welcoming cronies, looked around, and spotted Breydon and Emma with apparent relief. He threaded his way through the knots of people to join them.

"Beastly crush." He consoled himself with a frosted biscuit. "Wouldn't have come if my aunt hadn't demanded escort. Think it's allowed to escape to the gardens for the concert?" he added hopefully.

"Not only allowed," said Breydon, "but I should think highly advisable. Would you care to—"

If he said anything more, Emma didn't hear. Terrified wails filled her mind, blocking out all else. A wave of dizziness washed over her, then passed. Kittens, she realized. Five distinct voices assailed her, each crying pitifully.

"Emma?" Breydon clutched her forearms, supporting her. "Come, sit down. Are you all right?"

She shook her head, pulling away. "Where are they?"

"Who?" Breydon's grip tightened on her, keeping her on her feet. "What's wrong?"

"Can't you hear them?" But of course he couldn't. No one could, except her.

She turned away, blindly pushing her way through the crowds, only vaguely aware of the stares and startled comments that followed her. She had to find the kittens, discover what distressed them, soothe the poor little things. She burst through a doorway into the huge gallery that led to the Dining Room. Through here, somewhere ahead, she had to keep searching. She broke into a run, past the long table and fantastic decor and into the tiny room beyond.

She had reached the portion of the Pavilion ruled by the servants. She ducked through another doorway into a hall, then around a corner, only to stop short as she came face-to-face with a footman carrying a large, squirming sack. The wails, both mental and auditory, came from there.

"What are you doing?" she demanded. Tears filled her eyes, of fury, of the fear transmitted by the terrified kittens. "Give them to me!"

The footman stared at her, his expression bewildered. "It's only kittens, ma'am. I—"

"I know it's kittens. Just what do you think you're doing with them?"

"Drowning them, of course. Cook says the dratted things—"

"I won't allow it!" Emma grabbed the tied top of the sack, but the footman gamely held on to it. "Let go!"

The footman stared at her; then his gaze slid by, focussing beyond her shoulder. Emma tugged at the bag, but his grip remained tight.

"Lady Stanyon." A hand closed on her arm.

She turned her head to see Breydon at her side. "He says he's going to drown them," she hissed. "I *will* not allow it."

"Might I ask why not?" asked an amused voice.

Emma spun to find herself facing the Prince Regent himself. Behind him ranged a number of the other guests, among them Lady Seagrave and Lord Linwood and his aunt. Emma swallowed, her throat suddenly dry. But she wasn't about to let anyone, not even Prinny, interfere with her rescue of the poor little things. Her chin came up in defiance as she declared; "They are kittens, sir."

"So I apprehend," the regent drawled. "Drowning seems the most sensible solution."

The footman, taking this as a renewed order, tugged once more on the bag.

Except for tightening her own grip, Emma paid him no heed. "How could you!" she cried, turning the full fury of her outraged feelings on the regent. "Of all the cruel, thoughtless—" Words failed her, and the tears that had filled her eyes threatened to spill over her cheeks. Resolutely, she blinked them back. "I will not allow so terrible a deed. How you could even think to allow such cruelty! Give them to me!"

Prinny's eyebrows rose. "A lady of decided opinions, it seems. You." He gestured toward the footman. "Be so good as to give this lady that sack." With that, he turned on his heel. "Ah, Faversham," he went on, as if nothing untoward had just occurred, "I have particularly requested the musicians to play that work of Handel's we were discussing the other day.''

Emma didn't wait to hear any more. She snatched the sack from the limp grasp of the footman and blundered along the hall, not following the way she had come but seeking the nearest possible exit from the Pavilion.

EIGHT

The kittens mewed piteously, squirming in their fear. Emma murmured soothing words as she hurried from doorway to doorway, seeking a means of escape. At last she found the Entry Hall, which led in turn into the Octagon Hall and then to the *porte-cochère*. Ignoring the startled footmen, she darted out into the sun-filled afternoon, clasping the writhing sack before her in both hands.

Once free of the Pavilion, she broke into a run. She only slowed as she neared the Pleasure Gardens, with their crowds of people strolling the paths. The afternoon concert would begin shortly, she realized. A large number of Prinny's guests would come outdoors to listen. And to gossip. And to spread the word that the dowager Lady Stanyon had committed the most shocking *faux pas*.

Dear heaven, whatever could have possessed her? Her steps slowed even more. She had saved the kittens, but at what cost to Sophie—and to herself?

The kittens. Her horror faded beneath the pressing need of the little felines for reassurance. They didn't weigh much; she could only hope they were old enough to survive without their mother. Tentatively she scooped the bottom of the sack into her arm, and relief swept over her as she felt first four, then six solid little forms settle into place. Their clever mother must have kept them hidden for at least two weeks, possibly more. With proper tending, they would live.

The panic within the sack began to subside, to be replaced by feline bliss as, one by one, the little things drifted off to sleep. One pitiful thought of hunger lingered, faded, and finally lapsed. Their terror must have exhausted them, poor dears.

It hadn't done much for her, either. For the first time since their frantic wails filled her mind, she could think again, uninfluenced by the kittens. And the thoughts weren't welcome.

She looked about; her steps had carried her to the Steine. Other pedestrians strolled by, their curious glances resting on her burden. At least those on horseback or in carriages paid her no heed. Hugging the sack comfortably for the kittens, her head held high, she strode ahead, her one clear thought to reach the sanctuary of her house on the Marine Parade.

She had ruined herself socially, of course. She had better admit that at once, face it and accept it. To stand up to any host would have been disgracefully ill-mannered. But only she could have committed the unmitigated folly of offending the Prince Regent. She might as well pack up her cats and return to her dower house at once.

Perhaps, in time, Sophie would come to forgive her. And perhaps, if she could engage the services of another lady to chaperon Sophie for the next Season, the girl might make a social recovery and still make a creditable marriage. But Sophie loved Linwood, and Linwood had been present to observe Emma's unpardonable breach of etiquette.

One of the kittens stirred in the sack, setting several of the others to squirming into more comfortable positions. Emma hugged them close to her and knew she could have done nothing else—and nothing worse.

When she at last reached her house, Beecher opened

the front door to her, and took in the situation in one glance. His face resigned, he stepped aside and allowed her to head straight to the basement kitchen. Even as she called to him to send someone for a blanket, towels and a basket to make a nest, he was already signaling a maid.

Emma set her burden tenderly on the floor, and at once four of the resident cats crept forward to sniff. Emma boosted fat Alexander aside and untied the string that closed the sack. The sides dropped away, landing on the kittens inside, and Emma drew the fabric back to reveal the bundles of mewing fur. Two—no, three—brindle, one pale orange, another a darker shade, and one striped gray. She lifted the topmost kitten, one of the brindles, and subjected it to a gentle but thorough examination. Its eyes were open, but hadn't been for long.

"Aren't they little dears," breathed Betsy, the kitchen maid. She set a wicker flower basket on the flagged stone floor, then knelt beside Emma. Taking the pale orange kitten, she tenderly placed it on the soft folds of the blanket that lined their new bed.

Cook, a stocky, sensible man in his mid-fifties, eyed the proceedings with disapprobation. With a sigh, he set aside the tray of rolls he had just formed, covered them to rise, then poured a generous dollop of cream into a kettle. The bail he hooked over the iron rod in the hearth and swung the pot over the fire. Already, Betsy set to work mincing fish and tearing bread to add to the kittens' stew.

Emma picked up the basket and carried it to the salon, where she settled by the window through which the warm rays of the sun filtered. Penelope joined her, inspected the new arrivals, and crawled into the folds of the blanket with them. Emma closed her eyes, listened to the melancholy cries of the gulls, and wished herself safe at her home in the country, far away from Polite Society.

Betsy arrived some twenty minutes later with a china cup filled with the fish- and bread-steeped cream. Emma tested the temperature, found it acceptable, and selected the smallest of her new dependents. Readily it sucked at her little finger, and she kept a steady drip of the nutritious food streaming into the hungry mouth. When it fell asleep, she handed it to the waiting Betsy, who mopped it with a warm, damp towel, simulating the absent mother's giving it a bath.

Emma was on the final kitten when she heard the commotion at the front door announcing an arrival. With a guilty start, she remembered that Sophie was supposed to have joined her at the Pleasure Gardens for the concert. She'd forgotten everything, faced with her latest feline crisis. Which meant she'd left Sophie to face the brunt of any gossip.

The salon door opened, and her stepdaughter entered the room. No trace of emotion showed on the girl's face; not a good sign, Emma decided. Without a word, she took over Betsy's position, allowing the maid to return to her duties below stairs.

Emma watched in silence as Sophie stroked the kitten's face and stomach with the damp towel. That the girl knew the history of her stepmamma's latest and worst transgression was obvious. Emma gathered her courage and just touched Sophie's hand. "I'm so terribly sorry," she said, knowing it to be hopelessly inadequate.

Sophie, her expression unreadable, shook her head. "You did the only thing you could. I know that, dearest Stepmamma, so please, don't look so stricken. If other people can't understand—well, we don't need insensitive people like that. We're happier without them."

Why did such complete forgiveness only make her guilt worse? Emma struggled to maintain her composure, at last managing to say, "Most people would call us *too* sensitive."

"Most people must be thoughtless clods, then. I could

never be happy with anyone who could condone such cruelty to anything as sweet as these helpless little things."

"Oh, Sophie, he didn't! He couldn't! Linwood—"

Sophie sniffed, but the anger in her eyes denied the tears that glittered there. "He told me what happened, and how—how you stood up to Prinny himself, and—Oh, Stepmamma, he thought it a rare jest! Never have I been so angry with anyone."

Emma stared at Sophie, at a loss for words. For one moment she considered tying herself into the kittens' sack and jumping into the ocean. She'd do anything not to cause Sophie such pain. But heaping scandal upon scandal never did any good at all. If only Sophie could have been safely married, so the *haut monde* wouldn't associate her so closely with Emma's misdeeds. . . .

The salon door opened, and Beecher entered wearing his beaming, avuncular smile. "Lord Linwood, my lady." He bowed to Emma, but his smug gaze rested on Sophie's reddening face. He stepped back to admit the visitor.

Sophie, still cradling one of the kittens, rose shakily to her feet. Her chin thrust out, but her color receded, leaving her unnaturally pale. "I want you to know," she declared before Linwood could speak, "that I can only admire my stepmamma's bravery."

Linwood nodded. "I came here to tell you that, myself."

Sophie blinked, her rigidity melting in the face of this unexpected admission. "You did? I mean, you do?"

He nodded with vigor. "What I said—" He broke off and cast Emma an embarrassed, apologetic look. "Everyone was making jokes about it, you know. Not that anyone meant any harm, of course," he added hastily. "Unusual event, gave them all something to talk about. Amusing, don't you know. Relieved the boredom."

Sophie's gaze still held a touch of frost. "Indeed?"

Linwood, though, had himself under control. "Dash it,

Sophie, you can't tell me you don't know very well how it happens!"

Sophie had the grace to flush.

"Just so." He nodded knowingly, then turned to Emma. "Got to thinking about it, and dashed if I wasn't impressed. Showed real character. Don't think I know anyone else who would have risked Prinny's displeasure for the sake of what they believe in."

"And you'll tell people that?" Sophie regarded him with a touch of awe.

"Of course. Not that it may do much good, mind. Don't usually mix with the Carlton House set."

"But you do have a position in Society," Sophie pointed out.

He beamed at her. "Quite right. And dashed if I'll cut your stepmamma's acquaintance. My aunt won't, either. She agrees with me. Said it was about time someone stood up to the old—" He broke off. "Well, that's neither here nor there, is it? Point is, don't plan to let a gaggle of gossipmongers tell me what to think or who to know."

"Bravo!" cried Sophie.

He beamed at her. "Hoped you'd say something like that. Makes the next bit easier, don't you know."

"Next bit?" Sophie regarded him with a touch of uncertainty in her wide-opened eyes.

"Yes. Well, you see, I ought properly to be speaking to your brother, don't you know? Though Stanyon Hall is a fair journey from here. So I thought perhaps your stepmamma might be the best person to ask for your hand in marriage."

"My hand—" Sophie broke off, staring at him, her expression bemused.

"With your stepmamma's permission, of course," Linwood asserted. "But not if you shouldn't like it, though."

"Oh, I should like it of all things!" Sophie breathed.

"Perhaps you two had best discuss the matter, then let

me know what you've decided." Emma set the kitten she held in the basket along with its siblings and rose. "If you will excuse me? I fear I have a number of tasks awaiting me at present." She regarded the couple for a moment, then took the precaution of removing the other kitten from Sophie's trembling hands.

Neither Sophie nor Linwood returned any response. They stared at one another with what, in Emma's opinion, were rather fatuous expressions on their faces. Tactfully, she let herself out of the room and closed the door gently but firmly behind her.

She stood in the hall for a long moment, eyes closed, emotions churning. Linwood had proposed! She hadn't destroyed Sophie's chances and broken her heart, after all. That made everything all right.

Well, not entirely. There was still Lord Breydon to consider. She had publicly disgraced him, and when he had been so kind as to do his utmost to reestablish her in the eyes of Society after her *faux pas* of the previous day. She could not forgive herself for causing him embarrassment. Only the certainty that his credit must be good enough to withstand his brief support of her made the situation somewhat less odious.

But thoughts of him dampened her joy in Sophie's happiness.

He would not suffer, provided he had nothing more to do with her. Not that he'd want to, of course. But she wanted it, and quite desperately. Sophie's future might be assured, but without Breydon, Emma's own loomed very bleak and empty.

An urgent desire for herring assailed her, distracting her from the depressing thoughts of loneliness that threatened to engulf her. *Cream* thrust itself into her mind, and *chicken*. Well, at least she knew what Cook planned for her dinner that night.

A rope of fur wrapped itself about her ankle, caressing

and tickling, and orange Tabitha, with a rumbling purr, stepped her dainty way between Emma's feet. Black Eustace, looking distinctly like a furry brick with his front paws tucked neatly around his broad chest, watched her with hopeful eyes from his position on a chair cushion.

"All right," Emma sighed. "Let's see what sort of scraps we can persuade Cook to bestow upon you, shall we?"

Eustace stood and stretched, back arched low, tail held high. He jumped lightly to the floor and trotted along at her feet, bumping into Tabitha and rubbing against Emma's ankles. Two more of the cats joined them before she'd taken a half-dozen steps.

A lonely, empty life. Who was she trying to fool? No matter who else deserted her, she would always have a troupe of arrogant, demanding felines needing her.

NINE

Emma sat on the floor beside the blanket-lined basket, her jaw rigid, her back to her stepdaughter. "I cannot possibly go tonight."

Sophie, arrayed in a vastly becoming evening gown of peach-colored gauze, sank onto the edge of the brocade chair. "Stepmamma, you cannot simply withdraw from Society!"

"I am doing no such thing," Emma lied, her voice calm only through a determined effort. Gently she deterred the curious Eustace from pursuing too close an inspection of the sleeping kittens. "I am staying home to feed these poor little things. They'll be waking again soon, and someone must tend them."

"Then let Betsy do it this once," Sophie urged. "Step-mamma—"

The knocker on the front door sounded, and Emma rose. "That will be Lady Abingdon. Now, you run along and enjoy the card party."

Sophie remained seated. "If you won't go, then I shan't, either. I'll stay and help with the kittens."

"Don't be absurd. What would you ever tell Lady Abingdon, after she's been so kind as to promise to chaperon you for me?"

"That you are unwell, and I intend to nurse you."

"I am perfectly fit, and I will not have you keep her waiting. Linwood will be there," she added.

Visibly, Sophie wavered. "But how can I leave you—"

"I am not moped, for heaven's sake. What, do you intend to sit here all evening and try to rally me with anecdotes and *on dits*? I am quite all right, and if it weren't for them"—she gestured at the basket—"I should be going with you. Now don't keep Lady Abingdon waiting any longer."

Sophie rose, her expression uncertain, but Emma draped the elegant shawl of Norwich silk about the girl's shoulders. With a hand firmly in the center of Sophie's back, she propelled her stepdaughter out the door. As soon as she had seen her into the waiting carriage, she returned to the salon and sank onto Sophie's vacated chair.

She wouldn't give in to tears. She'd ruined herself, it was true, but she hadn't ruined Sophie, as well. That was cause for celebration, not this overwhelming melancholy that engulfed her. She stared moodily into the fire that crackled contentedly in the hearth, warming her infant charges.

A longing for comfort crept over her, of radiating heat, of peaceful slumber, of a lap and fingers rubbing her chin. Paws touched her knee, and the next moment the rotund Brutus deposited his considerable bulk on her muslin skirts. She cradled him close, welcoming the contented purr, and tried to capture the sensations of peace that emanated from him and make them her own.

Then Eustace joined them, his front quarters draped across her, the rest of his length hanging on to the chair. Her lap had never been designed for multiple cats. With a toe, she hooked the leg of a stool and pulled it to where she could place her feet upon it. Alcibiades at once positioned himself around her knees, and Tabitha settled across her ankles.

She behaved like a shocking coward, she knew, hiding behind the familiarity and acceptance of her cats. But she simply couldn't face the censure of Society. She hugged Brutus again and tried not to despair. Even if people would refuse to know her, she would always have the cats. Those lovable, beastly, impossible—

A wave of fury slammed into her mind, accompanied by lingering fear and an overwhelming sense of loss. Feline, she knew, but coming from where? She sprang to her feet, scattering her indignant, furry companions, and became aware that someone applied a knocker on her front door with a vengeance. The feline anger continued to rage through her; had she been a cat, every hair on her tail would have stood out, separate and rigid. She reached the door before she had consciously realized she'd moved.

In the hall beyond, she heard a deep voice she knew all too well, and froze. Breydon. The sensation of devastating loss that engulfed her swelled, as her own mingled with the unidentified feline's. She had barely time to retreat to her chair before the door opened, and Beecher admitted the viscount.

Breydon strode in, the calico kitten clasped tightly in one arm. "I was about to leave for the card party," he declared in tones of deep reproof, "when this damned silly animal came to my door to fetch me. Which is how," he added, "I divined you would be here instead of at the Marchamps'."

"Is she all right?" The sensations of distress continued, but they didn't, she realized, come from Penelope. In fact, the exasperating kitten purred, rubbing her tricolored head against Breydon's thumb.

He obliged with a gentle rub, and did not hand the kitten over. "She appears to me to be worried about you," he declared. "And from the look of things, she seems to have cause. What the devil do you mean by not going tonight?"

"Isn't it obvious?" Her own misery overshadowed the feline fury that continued to swirl through the edges of her mind.

He shook his head. "I hadn't expected such cowardice from you."

"You would rather I cause my hostess embarrassment by appearing where I wasn't wanted?" She turned away, staring with eyes uncomfortably blurred with moisture out the window toward the moonlit sea. A tickle along the back of her calf announced the sustaining presence of one of the cats, and she stooped to pick up the hefty Brutus. And still, the feline rage swirled through the edges of her mind.

"Are you quite certain it was Mrs. Marchamp, and not yourself, about whom you were concerned?"

The ache in her heart increased with the gentleness of his tone, overshadowing even the misery of the unknown cat. "Both of us, perhaps," she admitted, and hugged Brutus all the tighter.

"Emma." He stood directly behind her, his voice torn between amusement and exasperation.

The desire to turn, to feel his comforting arms close about her, almost overpowered her. She clung to Brutus and continued to look resolutely out the window.

"I brought you something," he said.

She didn't trust herself to move, or to speak. She could only stand there and wait, and cling to the cat for support and comfort.

Breydon set Penelope on a chair, where the little kitten set about licking her ruffled fur back into position. He exited the room, only to return a moment later bearing a basket from which a plaintive yowl emitted.

Emma tensed. This was the source of the distress that she'd been "hearing," that had been tormenting her since moments before Breydon arrived. He held the covered basket out to her, and, after a moment's hesitation, she set Brutus on the floor and accepted the surprisingly heavy burden. She lifted the lid. A brindle cat hunkered down inside, staring at her with wide, angry eyes. Sensations of discomfort emanated from it, mingled with fear and longing. It wanted— It wanted its kittens.

Enlightenment dawned on Emma, and she stared at Breydon, stunned.

"Aren't you going to reunite them?" he demanded. A touch of amusement lingered in his voice, and something much deeper, an emotion he tried to keep in check.

Emma lifted out the angry mother and knelt to set her among the kittens where they dozed in their folds of blanket, and had the satisfaction of seeing her sniffing, then licking, her litter. The tears that had threatened so often this day stung her eyes once more. "Just in time to save Cook from having to make more fish stew," she said, trying to make light of her emotions. "However did you find her?"

"That footman you assaulted at the Pavilion." Breydon sounded casual, as if approaching the Prince Regent's servants were an everyday occurrence for him. "He was surprisingly willing to help."

She regarded him with suspicion. "How much did it cost you?"

"Nowhere near what it is worth, seeing them reunited. And seeing you smile."

She looked away, back to the mother and her babies, too afraid to look into his eyes.

"You can't hide from me behind an armload of felines," he said, his voice low and determined. "I intend to have you. If that means taking them, also—well, I've always had a fondness for cats."

That proved too much for her. She turned then, her anguish a palpable force, and stared up into his face. But that was too dangerous, too tempting to gaze at him, to grasp at the proffered happiness. She loved him, she realized, far too much to allow him to be ostracized by the society he had been accustomed to lead.

As she did in all tight places, she returned her focus to the cats. The mother now lay on her side, her nurslings feeding themselves with enthusiasm, their tiny paws pummeling her stomach. "Pray, do not be absurd," she said when she could command her voice. "I have no intention of marrying anyone. I am quite content as I am." She rose and moved away, desperate to keep him from seeing the tears of anguish that filled her eyes. Rejecting his offer—rejecting everything for which she had longed—was more than she could bear.

The door opened, and Beecher stood there, at his most proper, studiously ignoring the orange Tabitha, who twined herself between his legs. "Lady Seagrave, my lady," he announced, and stepped back to reveal the leader of Society whom Emma feared most.

Emma froze, then desperately tried to force her features into some semblance of control. Breydon stepped forward, effectively placing himself in front of her, and mentally she blessed him for this consideration, among so many others. It gave her the precious seconds necessary to regain composure.

"Lady Stanyon," declared the new arrival, "I am so relieved to find you at home."

Distress swept over Emma, sensations of pain and fear. Feline sensations. It took her a moment to realize they came not from one of the many who lounged about the room, but from a bundled blanket grasped in Lady Seagrave's arms. An enraged growl emerged from its muffling depths. Emma's dismay evaporated; the cat needed help. She swept forward, relieving her visitor of her squirming, hissing burden, and opened the folds to reveal a tangle of long black fur. Baleful eyes glared at her from above a streak of white reminiscent of a mustache.

"Clarence is usually so very good." Lady Seagrave eyed her pet doubtfully. "An absolute lamb. I don't know what's come over him."

"They're always frightened when they're hurt," Emma said absently, her attention on the injured cat. "And here it is." Her fingers, following the cat's sensations, found a nasty abscess on the side of one hind leg. "We've been fighting, haven't we?" she asked the animal in a conversational tone. "Breydon, if you could ring for Beecher for me?"

The viscount, an odd half smile playing about his lips, pulled the decorative cord. The majordomo must have been lingering near the door, for it opened at once. Emma told him what she would need, then settled herself on a chair before the fire. Clarence submitted to being held. On the floor near her, the mother cat—heavens, she would have to find her a name—lay in the basket, her sleeping kittens surrounding her, and eyed the injured tom with withering contempt.

The experienced Betsy returned with Beecher, carrying a bowl of steaming water. This she placed on the table at Emma's side, then stood in readiness to restrain flailing claws or remove dirtied rags. Within minutes, Emma had trimmed away the matted fur, cleansed the ugly wound, and assembled and applied an herbal poultice.

Lady Seagrave, watching in awe, received the cat back into her arms with consternation. "Do you mean you have cured him?" she demanded. "Already?"

"Treated him, merely." Emma stroked Clarence's chin. "It will need to be bathed and dressed for several more days. He won't like it, of course. But in just a moment we'll have something for him which he will approve of."

With Betsy still in attendance, she made her way to the kitchens, where the maid chopped herring while Emma ground a mixture of soothing and healing herbs to stir into the pungent fish. This concoction Clarence accepted with relish, and Emma had the satisfaction of hearing a tentative purr begin deep within the animal's throat.

Lady Seagrave, holding her hefty pet, eyed Emma with approval. "Can't thank you enough, my dear," she said, as she rose, her cat once more wrapped securely in his blanket. "I couldn't have borne it if I'd lost my beloved Clarence."

Breydon, who had retired to a corner to play with Penelope, looked up. "Named, no doubt, for—?"

Lady Seagrave compressed her mouth, but couldn't disguise her reprehensible smile. "For the excellence of his disposition. And the number of his unofficial offspring, I fear."

"Don't forget this." Emma handed her a small bag containing sufficient herbs for several more poultices. Lady Seagrave accepted them.

"Though I may call on you for help if I have trouble?" She beamed on Emma. "Hope you don't mind becoming the pet doctor for the *ton*. Really, my dear, I'm afraid you're about to become all the rage."

"All—" Emma faltered. "But after what I did—"

Her visitor waved that aside. "Prinny has a good heart, you know. The story is all over Brighton, and everyone is quite agog with curiosity. Can you really understand what cats say?"

This Emma denied, but could tell Lady Seagrave didn't believe her. "And by morning it will be all over town that I can talk back to them!" she protested to Breydon when she returned from seeing Lady Seagrave and Clarence to the door.

His slow smile warmed his eyes. "So rather than making you an outcast, your ability is about to make you the toast of the *ton*."

She shuddered. "I will quickly disappoint them."

He shook his head, then set down the calico kitten and rose. "You couldn't. But at the moment, we have something else to discuss. What was all that nonsense about not marrying me?" Penelope batted his ankle with a paw, then attempted to scramble up his leg. He detached her claws from his knee and held her. "You can't be selfish, you know. You have to think of the children."

Emma eyed him with suspicion. "Children?"

"Think of poor little orphaned Penelope. She seems to regard me as her father every bit as much as she regards you as her mother. For the sake of keeping our family together, you have to marry me."

"For the children," she repeated. Her glance strayed about the room, taking in the mother and her kittens, Tabitha, Brutus, Eustace and Alcibiades, then returning to Penelope, who snuggled in Breydon's hold.

"And if they're not reason enough," he said softly, "do it for me. I can't imagine living my life without you." He deposited Penelope in the chair he had just vacated and took two steps toward her, holding out his hands. "Can you not find it in your heart to take in another stray?"

Somehow, Emma found herself in his arms, her cheek resting against his shoulder, his hand caressing her hair. Her eyes misted as she clung to him, more than half afraid that if she moved, if she breathed, he would vanish, taking with him all her hopes of happiness. But at last she had to draw a shaky breath, and he remained solid and substantial, warm against her.

Gently, he kissed the top of her curls, her temple, then found her mouth. For a very long while, all sensations faded except those created by him. Then his kisses progressed along her throat, until abruptly he paused. "There are at least a dozen pairs of feline eyes fixed on us at this moment," he murmured near her ear. "Does your entourage approve of our union, or will I have to win them over with platefuls of salmon mayonnaise?"

She allowed her attention to wander from him, which was no easy feat at the moment, and focused on the cats. At once, she was overwhelmed by their sensations of immense satisfaction—and one strong craving for fishes and cream. "There won't be any objections from any of us," she assured him, "though the salmon will be quite acceptable, too."

The gleam of humor she so loved sparkled in his eyes. "I suppose you will carry a bouquet of catnip at our wedding?"

She nodded with as much solemnity as she could manage. "And the cats may attend me down the aisle. St. George's in Hanover Square, do you think?"

For one moment he contemplated the scene, and his broad shoulders trembled with suppressed laughter. "The cats," he vowed with considerable feeling, "will be the only guests."

"Coward," she murmured, then was silent for a very long while.

TRIAL BY KITTENS

by
Valerie King

ONE

Miss Anne Tandridge carefully hooked the basket containing two abandoned kittens over her right elbow. With her left hand, she clung to the ladder and began her descent from the hayloft from which height she could hear the soft shuffling of the horses in their stalls below. Her shawl began to slip from her shoulders, yet she could do nothing except let it fall to the dirt floor. The kittens and their safety were her first concern.

"There, there, little ones," she murmured softly against their hungry mews. "We'll be down in a trice, never you fear, and then I shall be able to give you a little milk. Only, where is your mama?"

She clung to the ladder, which was quite rickety, and placed a careful, booted foot on one rung after another. So much of the manor was falling to pieces she would not have been surprised if the deuced thing simply split into two parts and sent her flying downward to land on her bottom.

"Just a few more steps," she cooed.

A man's warm voice intoned, "Just a few more after all these years."

Anne was so startled by the unexpected presence of a man that she let out a cry and whipped her head around. At the same moment, the third to the last rung gave way, and she fell abruptly into the waiting arms of a dark, sun-bronzed stranger!

"Oh, the kittens!" she cried. But the basket remained hooked on her arm, and except for a mite of jostling, the kittens were perfectly well.

The man, however, expressed his own sentiments. "Who the devil gives a fig about a litter of kittens when I've been waiting so long to see you again, to hold you and to kiss you? Dearest Anne!"

She stared at the intruder, dumbstruck. He wore a fashionable black beaver hat over sun-lightened brown hair. His eyes were a warm brown, and his smile was achingly familiar; yet she refused to let herself believe that the stranger cradling her in his arms was who he was.

His smile broadened, ostensibly at the shock written on her features. He released her, took the basket off her elbow, and settled it on the straw-strewn dirt floor. He whispered, "Tell me, Anne, that you have not forgotten me entirely." He then gathered her back up in his arms.

"Is it really you?" she whispered.

He nodded. "My darling, how long I have waited for this moment."

Memories flooded Anne in an instant. The stranger was not a stranger at all, but Richard Kingsley, her former betrothed. Only, how was that possible! She was so certain he had perished at sea . . . or, or been eaten by an Indian tiger . . . or, or—oh! He meant to kiss her, yet he shouldn't because she was no longer promised to him.

Oh . . . she had forgotten what his lips felt like pressed to hers, so soft and warm. She had forgotten the sensations kissing him could arouse within her, of longings and hopes so intense, so wonderful, that all of life seemed to take on new meaning and purpose. She had forgotten how strong he was, his body sinewy and shaped by the strenuous demands of his life.

She had also forgotten—just for the present, mind—

that in three years he had written only twice to her. Twice, oh, wretched man that he was!

She drew back, her hands pushing against his muscular arms. He seemed entirely disinclined to let her go. His expression was hazy. "Anne, do not deny me after all these years! I am like a man who has lived in the desert and thirsts for a drink. Anne! Anne! My darling! And to think I nearly forgot how beautiful you are. Looking at you makes my heart ache! I have missed you fiercely and dreadfully."

He again pulled her into his arms, and tried to kiss her once more; only this time her senses weren't quite so stunned.

She began to fight him, to push him away, and to call him to order. "Richard Kingsley, release me at once. *At once!* What do you think you are doing, coming back here after all this time and . . . and accosting me in this truly barbaric fashion! What rights do you think you have?"

"Anne!" he cried, sincerely shocked. "Whatever is the matter with you? Are you not pleased, delighted, even thrilled to see me, as I am to see you? And why do you ask if I have a right to kiss you, when I love you as I do, as very well you know?"

She was aghast. "I see you are just as arrogant as when you left England. *That,* at least, has not changed!"

"Arrogant?" he queried, appearing rather dumbfounded.

"Yes, and . . . and how brown you are! It is no wonder I did not recognize you at first."

A frown rippled his forehead. "You are changed as well," he said. "I would never have believed—and yet, when my lips first touched yours, I could have sworn you responded to me as you always did, as you did the day I left."

Anne lowered her gaze from his, and her spine grew quite rigid. She spoke quietly, "I will not deny that I was moved, but only for a moment, after which everything else, of honor and common sense, returned to me."

He took a step toward her, and she took a step backward, bumping into the ladder. "You are speaking in conundrums," he stated. "Speak plainly as you were always wont to address me."

She met his gaze and lifted her chin. "I am to be married in three days' time," she stated baldly. "You are come home too late to lay any claim to me."

His chin grew hard, and a red sheen darkened the sunbronze of his face. "The devil you are!" he cried. "You are betrothed to me! Before I left, you promised to marry me, to wait for me and to marry me. You said you'd wait forever . . . remember?"

She did remember, and painful tears burned her eyes. "I do remember, you faithless creature. I . . . I loved you, to the point of madness. I begged you to take me with you—"

His face filled with sudden hope, and he almost grabbed her up in his arms again, but she lifted a quick hand warding him off.

"Don't even think of kissing me again, you beast! I am only grateful that I remained behind to become the brunt of your thoughtlessness and inconsiderate conduct, for then I came to understand precisely the sort of husband you would be. I have since counted myself fortunate a score of times that I learned the truth of your character before ever wedding you."

Richard Kingsley was angry and confused. He didn't know what she was talking about. He could not think what he had ever done, or perhaps said in his numerous letters, to have offended her so completely. If anything, he had every right to be furious that in three years she had sent him but two letters. From the first, evidently, she had intended on forsaking him, and now she was to be married. Still, he didn't understand why she had a complaint of him. "You are making no sense at all. Only tell me what it is I am supposed to have done to have given you a disgust of me. Whatever it is, there must be some explanation, or something I can do to make amends."

He could see that she was caught by his words and pressed her. "Please, Anne, tell me what terrible thing I have done to you." He searched her face for some explanation, struck as he had been earlier by her beauty. Her blond hair was caught up in a charming knot atop her head and threaded with a light blue ribbon which perfectly reflected the color of her eyes.

She shook her head and appeared deeply pained. "You honestly can stand there and tell me you do not know, that you haven't even the smallest notion why I might not only have ceased to love you, but why I would be grateful to be marrying someone else?"

"No," he murmured. "I cannot."

She drew in a deep breath, and he watched her lip quiver. He could see that she was struggling to keep her composure, and some of his ire left him. This was not the return to Birchingrove Manor he had anticipated, or the reception of which he had dreamed for so long.

The kittens had clearly grown feverish in their need for milk and were presently calling out in long mews and cries. Anne reached down and picked up the basket. "I must give them some milk. Their mother appears to have abandoned them—two days now. If . . . if you wish for a cup of coffee, or tea, before you go, you may come with me."

"Thank you," he responded. He then took the basket from her and offered his arm to her. "But I don't intend to leave."

She ignored his protest and refused the use of his arm as she passed through the doorway in front of him.

Walking toward the manor, Anne found she was trembling. She had suffered a severe shock, and every nerve in her body was positively crying out in agitation.

She stole a glance at him, then quickly averted her gaze.

Richard had come home!

He had come home after three years, when it was far too late to be of any use. He had come home to Kent, home from his adventures abroad, home to marry her. Had he made his fortune as well, as he had promised to do? Yet, why had he not written but twice in the space of three years? She had sent him at least a hundred letters, and when she heard nary a word, she finally ceased to write altogether, her last and final letter having been sent a year ago.

From the fine cut of his clothes, the excellence of the tailoring and expensive nature of the superfine cloth of his coat, she thought it likely he had succeeded in his endeavors in India.

But it was too late!

She drew in several deep, steadying breaths. The kittens, fortunately, were setting up such a noise as to be of some distraction.

"You always were tender-hearted," he said, lifting the basket to inspect the two small creatures. "As for me, I should have thought it wiser to drown them."

She gasped and turned to glare at him. "What a dreadful thing to say!" she cried, grateful that he was giving her yet another reason to despise him.

He smiled crookedly. "Well, at least now you are *speaking* to me. In all the years I have known you, my love, I never found your tongue to fail you."

"I . . . it is just that you've given me a shock, a very bad one. And you should not be saying such things to me."

"I don't understand. Am I not permitted to remind

you that you were never at a loss for words in my presence?"

"Now you are pretending to be obtuse. You mustn't call me 'my love,' as you very well know."

He ignored her. "Are you really going to be married in three days?"

Something in his voice, a slice of hurt, struck a chord within her, and she found herself softening toward him. "Yes, I am," she murmured. She found, yet again, that she was perilously close to crying. For what reason, however, she didn't know, since she was no longer in love with Richard Kingsley. She had set him out of her heart and mind for nearly two years now. Well, perhaps only for the past twelve-month with any seriousness of purpose. Still, she didn't love him anymore. She didn't! She loved . . . that is, she was very fond of her betrothed, Sir Arthur Ide, whom she would be marrying in a private ceremony at his home, Flinthrall Castle, in the presence of his mother and her own Aunt Tandridge. She would be mistress of a fine property, whose chimneys were in excellent order, and which would provide her with a great deal of security—something she and her aunt had lacked for nigh on three years, nearly from the day Richard deserted her to go to India.

She glanced up at Birchingrove Manor, the tumbledown brick edifice which had been her home since she could remember. The chimneys smoked when the wind was in the east, or when it was not, come to think of it. The gardens had run riot with only one rheumatic gardener to attend to the small estate, and the rooms were in constant danger of sinking under a mountain of dust or succumbing to a constantly creeping mildew. There wasn't a floor that didn't creak ominously.

Yet, for all that, how she loved the manor.

Blast! Her eyes were filling with tears again!

She didn't want to leave her home, no matter how

drafty the place was, and she wished more than anything that Richard had not returned to England. But he had come home, and beyond that, Birchingrove had been sold at auction to pay off a passel of debts that her uncle had left behind. Uncle Tandridge had been a wonderful man whose hand had perhaps been far too generous to every needful request in a ten-mile radius of the manor. He had supported not just his wife and niece, but every farmer with whom he was acquainted, each of whom had suffered mightily during a string of failing harvests. He had perished in a ditch swollen from the rains nearly a fortnight to the day that Richard embarked on his ship.

For the past three years, her aunt had held the creditors at bay, but in the end, the manor and all its extensive, run-down lands had been sold off for a mere pittance of its real worth. The new owner would probably be arriving in the next sennight or so to take up possession of the manor, but by then, she would be married and, with her aunt, living in relative comfort at Flinthrall Castle.

Once in the kitchens, Anne found that the kittens, in true, infantlike manner, had fallen asleep. Rather than wake them, she decided to make Richard's presence known to her aunt and guided him toward the drawing room where her aunt habitually passed her mornings.

Arriving outside the doors, she insisted Richard wait in the hall so that she might prepare her beloved aunt concerning his sudden arrival. Mrs. Tandridge was a nervous woman, much given to palpitations, and Anne tried never to overset her if at all possible.

Placing the basket of kittens gently on the floor, she quietly entered the drawing room. She would have immediately launched into the extraordinary circumstance of Richard's sudden appearance in the stables, but the sight of her aunt, slumped forward on the sofa and a woebegone expression on her face, gave Anne pause. A letter dangled from the woman's fingers as she held a kerchief pressed to her eyes.

"Aunt Tandridge! Whatever is the matter?" she cried, hurrying at once to her aunt's side.

Mrs. Tandridge hastily began to wipe away her tears. "Nothing! I promise you!" she cried, sniffing loudly. "That is, nothing . . . to . . . *signify!*" She then burst into a fresh bout of tears.

"Dear Aunt, you must tell me what has happened. I have never seen you so distraught, not even when the creditors were hounding us day and night!"

Mrs. Tandridge lifted the letter, settled her gaze on it, and began to cry anew.

Anne sat down beside her and slipped a gentle arm about her shoulders. "There, there. Whatever has happened, I'm sure we can make it right—somehow."

"But we cannot, for if you must know, I begin to think Lady Ide is a cat, all claws and scratch with an entirely false purr. I always knew she was in love with my dear Henry and felt I'd stolen a march on her when he begged for my hand in marriage instead of hers, but I never supposed she would be so . . . so spiteful! Do but read *this!*" She extended the missive to Anne.

Anne thought she began to understand the nature of her aunt's distress. The letter was from Lady Ide who, in recent weeks, had begun to show her true nature, hissing and spitting in protection of her territory. With two adult females coming to live in the house she had commanded for over thirty years, Lady Ide was not a happy woman.

Anne quickly read the contents of the letter, and a feeling very close to chagrin settled over her. The letter enumerated those rooms that would be designated in particular to Mrs. Tandridge, and the hours at which she was expected to reside in *those rooms* so that *the family* might have exclusive use of the principal chambers.

Anne was mortified and wondered if Sir Arthur had

perchance seen the wicked letter before a pool of hot sealing wax had entombed so many hateful words. She thought it likely he was entirely ignorant of his mother's deeds—at least, she hoped so.

Another wretched thought occurred to her: was Lady Ide prepared to turn her home over to a new mistress which Anne was soon to be? By rights, Anne would be in charge of Flinthrall Castle once she took up residence there. She, alone, would be responsible for the general housekeeping of the ancient house. A faint shudder went through her at the very idea that she would likely have a battle on her hands with Arthur's mother.

"What is that sound, Anne?" Mrs. Tandridge asked. "Almost like a squeaking."

"Oh, the kittens! They have awakened, poor things!"

"So the mother has not returned?"

"No."

"How very sad for them."

"Yes, but Aunt, there is something I must tell you. Though I believe it will be a shock, we . . . we have a visitor today, someone completely unexpected." She knew her aunt had never approved of Richard and wondered how she would respond to seeing him now, after so many years.

"Indeed?" Mrs. Tandridge responded.

"Yes." She rose to her feet and moved quickly into the hall where she found Richard hunkered down beside the kittens and petting them with the tip of his index finger. The kind gesture had quieted them, at least for the moment.

"Richard, my aunt has regained her composure and can receive you now. I . . . I did not tell her that you had come home."

He stood up as she spoke. He had removed his shiny beaver hat and his gloves. Somehow, he looked much younger, and old feelings began to resurface of tumbling in love with Squire Kingsley's third son and knowing all the while that it was hopeless because between the pair of them they hadn't a feather to fly with.

She smiled because of the memories, and something in her expression must have betrayed her, for he quickly stepped close to her and possessed himself of her hands. "I see your heart in your eyes," he whispered. "You never could keep your thoughts from me. Only, tell me it is not too late."

For the barest moment she wanted to tell him of course it wasn't too late, that she still loved him, that she always would. Instead, however, she remembered his faithlessness—*two letters in three years!*—and withdrew her hands from his strong grip. "Please. Come greet my aunt."

"Of course," he responded politely. If he looked at her with hungry eyes, she ignored him as much as she ignored the answering hunger that rose so traitorously and so swiftly in her own breast.

She glanced toward the kittens and saw that they were wobbling about unsteadily. She promised herself she would tend to them as soon as she saw Richard settled in conversation with her aunt. She led him into the drawing room.

"Do you recognize our visitor?" Anne asked, trying for a light tone. "I vow I almost did not know him, for he is become so very brown."

Mrs. Tandridge squinted her aging eyes and blinked several times. "Come closer, sir," she commanded.

Richard obliged her and moved to stand before her.

Anne saw that his countenance had stiffened a little. He did not speak, but waited until Mrs. Tandridge had made her perusal of his face and person. After a minute, her mouth fell agape. "Mr. Kingsley," she murmured, astonished. "You are come home from India?"

Mrs. Tandridge turned toward Anne, her complexion paling to the color of chalk. "Richard is come home?"

she queried, astonished. Her eyelids fluttered, and she slowly fainted sideways onto the cushions of the sofa upon which she was seated.

"Aunt!" Anne cried. She raced to her side and searched in her workbox for a vinaigrette. Not finding one there, she opened her aunt's reticule, which was never far from her side, and found the small silver box within. She flipped open the lid and held the strong fragrance beneath the unconscious woman's nose.

Richard moved forward and began rubbing and patting Aunt Tandridge's hand. "What made her go off like that?" he asked. "Surely I cannot be that changed?"

"I daresay it is because she received unhappy tidings just before I first entered the drawing room. She was in a wretched state when I found her. Perhaps the two circumstances combined caused her to swoon."

"Humbug. She's afraid I'll cast a spoke in the wheel, something at which she excelled when I was courting you."

Anne would have remonstrated, but at that moment, Mrs. Tandridge moaned and tried to sit up. "Oh, my. Oh, my," she murmured.

"My poor aunt," Anne said gently. She once more sat down beside her and helped her into a sitting position.

"Did I faint?" Mrs. Tandridge queried.

"Yes, you did," Anne responded.

She held a hand to her stomach. "I believe I'd like a little of the cherry brandy," she said and gestured to a decanter near the pianoforte. Richard took up the hint and fetched her a small portion which, upon receiving, she sipped delicately.

After two or three sips, she took a deep breath and addressed Richard. "I wish you would go away," she said, not mincing words. "All is settled for my niece. She will live in comfort and enjoy a great deal of consequence as a result of her forthcoming marriage. You would only be doing a great deal of mischief were you to try to turn her heart toward you again, and I won't have it. I simply won't have it. So, I suggest you leave the county permanently."

Richard took up a chair opposite the old woman. He appeared to be entirely unmoved by her speech. "How unfortunate that these are your sentiments, Mrs. Tandridge, for I am already fixed in Kent and I shan't be going anywhere."

"What do you mean? I certainly hope you do not intend to remain in the neighborhood when Anne is very shortly to be wed?"

Richard glanced at Anne. "I'm afraid its a bit too late, you see: I'm the new owner of Birchingrove."

TWO

Anne stared at Richard in disbelief. Had she heard correctly? Was he telling her aunt that he was the new owner of Birchingrove Manor? "Y—you are?" she inquired, dumbstruck.

He sat back in his chair, and she had the strongest impression, given the satisfied expression on his face, that he felt he was the cat who had just swallowed the mouse. "Yes. I have come to take possession of my home. So, you see, I have every reason to stay, and none to leave, though for the present I am fixed at The George."

"In Headly Green?"

He nodded.

Anne chewed on the inside of her lip. Richard had just given her a second severe shock, and she was having some difficulty adjusting to his tidings. He was the new owner of Birchingrove. How extraordinary!

Possibilities rose to her mind, yet these she would not consider for a moment. After all, even if Richard had come home with enough blunt to purchase the manor, would that ever make up for all the letters he had failed to write to her?

She glanced at her aunt, who was making a strange whimpering sound, and found her staring at Richard wide-eyed and shaking her head. "You've made your fortune," she said at last.

Richard fixed a purely hostile gaze upon Mrs. Tandridge and merely nodded in response. Anne knew what he was thinking, that her aunt was a mercenary person with little true sensibility or even dignity. She knew better of course. Her aunt was doing as she had always done, approaching the subject with a practical turn of eye. Only with Mrs. Tandridge's careful management had they been able to remain at Birchingrove for as long as they had. Otherwise, the poorhouse might have claimed them both years ago.

And where had Richard been then? Where were his assurances that he would be home soon to love her and to take her to wife?

When the kittens began to cry again, Anne rose to her feet. "I must care for them," she murmured. "I have waited far too long as it is."

"Stay a moment," Mrs. Tandridge stated.

Anne was a little surprised by her aunt's firm tone and therefore had little recourse but to politely hear what she meant next to say.

Her aunt addressed Richard. "You must send for your bags at once. I vowed that the moment the new owner of Birchingrove arrived, we would extend every courtesy to him, for I will not have the entire neighborhood criticizing either my conduct or my niece's."

She turned to Anne. "Dearest, will you have Tom take the gig to the village and fetch Mr. Kingsley's belongings?"

Anne was reeling from her aunt's most surprising change of heart. Certain suspicions teased her brain as she stared down at her. Perhaps Richard's opinion of Mrs. Tandridge was not so far off the mark, after all.

For herself, she didn't want Richard to remain at Birchingrove, at least not while she was under his roof. She was entirely too susceptible to him to be in the least comfortable. She opened her mouth to utter a protest, but Mrs. Tandridge prevented her. "Please go at once, Anne."

There was a sternness to her eye which brooked no refusal. To argue with her would be to expose both herself and her aunt to Richard, and that she would never do.

"Very well," she acquiesced. She glanced at Richard and, seeing that he wore a rather triumphant expression, added, "First, however, I intend to care for the kittens."

She flounced from the chamber and picked up the basket in the hall. Making her way to the kitchens where she knew she would find the milk and perhaps a dropper with which to feed her mewing charges, she began to wonder if she was in the midst of a dream—or perhaps a nightmare. Richard had not only arrived entirely unexpectedly, but he had also proclaimed his ownership of Birchingrove. She still couldn't credit what was happening. And whatever was her aunt thinking to have actually invited him to move to the manor when, in her opinion, the far more proprietous thing would have been to have let him remain at The George?

With Cook's aid, she found a dropper, warmed a bowl of milk, and began the tedious process of feeding the little infants for the first time. Because they were starved, the first taste of the milk made them frantic. Every time the dropper emptied, the kitten in her hand would claw and struggle against her grip, trying to make its way to the source of the milk. Twice, she nearly dropped the little yellow-striped kitten, who had an eye that had almost opened, and once the black-and-white kitten slipped through her grasp to plop onto her lap, fortunately without coming to harm.

Cook said, "Once they're grown, I'll keep one o' them in the kitchens, miss, if it pleases ye. I found another mouse in the buttery—God 'ave mercy!" She clucked her tongue.

"It would please me very much," she responded. As she continued to squeeze the dropper, Cook gathered up a cutting basket and shears. "I'll be in the garden if ye be needing aught else."

"Thank you, Cook," Anne responded, then hastily added, "If you chance upon Tom, will you send him to me?"

"Aye, miss."

The black-and-white kitten had finally settled down to eat when Richard found her. He explained his presence in the kitchens, saying, "Your aunt professed the headache and retired to her bedchamber. I became so lonely that I decided I would seek you out, for I wasn't certain when, if ever, you meant to return to me." His gaze shifted to the kittens. "So, you mean to keep them after all."

"Instead of drowning them?" she retorted icily. "Of course I shall keep them and care for them. I am not so ruthless as you."

He glanced into the basket in which the yellow-striped kitten had presently fallen asleep. He reached in and stroked the animal. "He has a full belly now, I see."

Anne watched him touch the soft fur and wondered. For all his protests, he certainly did not seem disinclined to fondle the little creatures. She would have commented on the matter, but at that moment the door to the kitchen, which led to the herb garden, suddenly flew open and hit the wall with a bang.

"Good God!" a masculine voice called out. "Does nothing in this house function properly?"

Anne sucked in a breath. In a whisper, she explained, "My . . . my betrothed is come."

"I know that voice," Richard murmured.

Anne's betrothed, however, did not immediately appear in the doorway, but continued in a loud voice, "You there, Cook! Have you seen Miss Tandridge? Do you know where she can be found? I have been rapping away at the front door for this quarter hour and more with no one to attend me. So, please, if you would, tell me where I might find Miss Tandridge."

Richard's gaze suddenly shot to Anne's, and his brow drew together in a harsh frown. He whispered rather harshly, "Do not tell me, Anne, that you are to marry Sir Arthur Ide? Tell me anything but that! Was this your aunt's doing? Did she arrange the marriage in order to save herself from the poorhouse?"

Anne's cheeks grew very warm, indeed. "Of course not!" she responded hotly. "I . . . I happen to be very much in love with Sir Arthur and he with me." Oh, now she had taken to telling whiskers!

Richard's eyes narrowed. "Arthur Ide does not have room in his heart to be in love with anyone other than himself, unless, of course, he is greatly altered since last I was in England."

"How dare you!" she whispered hoarsely. The dropper had emptied, and she refilled it quite sloppily. The black and white kitten, however, did not seem to mind as he alternately sucked and licked at the dripping glass.

Sir Arthur darkened the doorway. "Miss Tandridge! There you are, my sweetest! I thought I heard voices."

Anne's blush deepened. Sir Arthur had never quite learned how to offer his endearments without sounding like a complete coxcomb. He proceeded to enter the kitchen carefully, guarding every step.

"Hallo, Sir Arthur," Anne responded. She dared not cast a glance Richard's direction. She could *feel* his smirks and sneers. "Only tell me, what is the matter? You are walking as though you are afraid the boards will break beneath your step."

"As to that," he responded in his crisp, nasally manner, "I wouldn't be in the least surprised were such an eventuality to occur. More to the point, however, Cook just informed me that the kitchen is overrun with mice."

Anne bit her lip to keep from smiling and ignored the faint, disgusted snort that sounded from the man next to her. "You cannot be afraid of a mouse," she returned gently.

"No, of course not!" he responded promptly. "But one does not enjoy the possibility of squishing even one of them beneath one's boots."

"Well, you shan't do so," she assured him. "Cook found a single mouse today, not in the kitchen but in the buttery, so I would not be overly concerned. By the way, I believe you are acquainted with Mr. Richard Kingsley?"

The black-and-white kitten had finished eating. Anne placed him in the basket with his litter mate, who woke up and attacked his tail. Richard leaned over the basket and offered his little finger as a toy.

Sir Arthur turned toward Richard and smiled politely. "I didn't recognize you, old fellow. You are turned so brown I had thought you were a fieldhand parading about, for some obscure reason, in gentlemen's clothing."

Anne was shocked by Sir Arthur's rudeness. She turned to glance at Richard, who now stood up to face the intruder. She knew him well, that he would not like being spoken to in so high-handed a manner.

"I have been in India for a time," he said.

"How delightful." A very long space followed before Sir Arthur finished with, "Indeed."

Richard remained silent. He held Sir Arthur's gaze, and Anne was immediately put in mind of ancient warriors meeting on a battleground. That she might be a prize over which they would fight gave her no comfort at all.

"Pray, do not begin brangling like a pair of tom cats,

else you will put me severely out of temper," she stated firmly.

When the men each relaxed a trifle and turned their attention toward her, she addressed Arthur. "Will you stay to nuncheon?"

"That would be lovely," he said, smiling tenderly upon her. "As it happens, I was thinking we might enjoy our repast *al fresco,* as it were, in the glade beyond the oak grove. I rode by earlier and found that the grass was not so high as to be unmanageable by half. What do you say, my sweet kitten?"

He seemed so pleased with his address, as well as by his suggestion for an *al fresco* adventure, that she found herself irritated. Everything about Arthur was so very studied, as though he practiced his speeches, his witticisms, even the very folds of his neckcloth a dozen times before allowing anything to be brought forth in a drawing room or even a humble kitchen.

She smiled and nodded. "I think you've a lovely notion, but I must inform you of a certain change which will affect the day's pleasures." She gestured with a turn of her wrist toward Richard. "Mr. Kingsley is at present residing with us," she said, but amended hastily, "by my aunt's insistence. He is, if you must know, the new owner of Birchingrove."

Sir Arthur was obviously shocked. "The devil—!" he cried, quite unlike his usual composed self, as he turned to glare at Richard.

For his part, Richard merely smiled in the most maddening fashion that would have sent even the mildest person flying into the boughs. Sir Arthur, not being particularly mild of temper, flushed a deep claret in color. Even his cool gray eyes seemed to turn a red hue.

"Will you not offer your new neighbor a proper welcome?" Richard inquired in a mockingly sweet tone.

"I would," Sir Arthur responded, "were that neighbor

to bring even the smallest amount of virtue or proper manners to our countryside."

Anne opened her eyes wide, unable to credit that Sir Arthur would have said anything so wickedly provoking to a man of Richard's stamp. In the past, Anne had seen Richard plant a facer for a mere insolent nudge, nonetheless a blatant challenge such as Sir Arthur had just delivered. What match was Arthur for him?

The two men were disparate in nearly every aspect of their persons, but in particular in physique and skill. Richard was solidly built and muscled, which even a one-eyed gudgeon could detect, while Sir Arthur was a lean fellow who held of little account the activities of sporting men. Richard, before he had left England, had boxed with Gentleman Jackson and had frequented Manton's shooting gallery. He was even known to have superb fencing skills. The only ability Sir Arthur possessed, to Anne's knowledge, was a quite accurate aim with bow and arrow. Were the fur to fly in this moment, she could not perceive how Sir Arthur would manage Richard on any playing field, nonetheless avoid having his cork drawn for so much insolence!

Before Richard had even a moment to bristle, however, she stepped between them and addressed her betrothed. "Arthur, you will apologize at once to Mr. Kingsley. Whether as the current owner of Birchingrove, or a guest in my aunt's home, he still has her permission to be in her house and as such deserves to be treated with courtesy for her sake."

Sir Arthur pursed his lips together and breathed heavily through pinched nostrils. "Of course, my dear. You were very right to have upbraided me. Beg pardon, Kingsley."

When Richard remained silent, Anne turned toward him and glared. He rolled his eyes. "Apology accepted, Ide."

The kitchen fell silent.

Anne remained standing between the gentlemen until every evidence of ill feeling melted away. Sir Arthur finally took a few steps in the direction of the door, and Richard resumed his place by the basket of kittens. She sighed gratefully.

"As to the *al fresco* scheme," she began, addressing Sir Arthur, "I shall lay the whole of it before my aunt, and she shall determine what would be proper. In the meantime, would you care to adjourn to the drawing room? I shall have Cook prepare some light refreshment for you both if that would be acceptable to you?" She turned to gaze upon each man, one after the other.

Sir Arthur nodded, and Richard smiled at her, catching her gaze and holding it for a second or two.

How unfortunate that smile was, for she found his display of teeth somehow caused butterflies to tumble about in her stomach. Old feelings! Drat!

After issuing orders to Cook to please search for Tom and tell him to bring Richard's belongings to Birchingrove and to then prepare a platter of fruit and biscuits for their guests, she escorted the men to the drawing room and afterward sought her aunt's counsel in her bedchamber. She scratched on the door and, upon hearing a sniffling sound, pushed open the door gently. "Aunt? Are you well?" she offered softly into the sunlit chamber.

She saw that her aunt was seated in a chair by the window and perusing what appeared to be a letter. At the same time, tears trickled down her cheeks. She did not seem to be aware that Anne had entered the room.

The bank of small-paned windows, which covered nearly the entire east wall, allowed a mass of golden sunbeams to fill the bedchamber with an amber glow. The effect was magical to Anne, who had spent many nights as a child cuddled beside the woman who had been a mother to her since she could remember. The sight of her now, with her cap bathed in sunshine and tears streaming down her alabaster cheeks, brought a warmth of affection filling her heart.

"Whatever is the matter, Aunt Tandridge?" she queried, entering the room fully.

Mrs. Tandridge lifted horrified eyes to meet Anne's sympathetic gaze. She quickly folded up the letter in her hands and stuffed it into a box which appeared to be quite full of letters, correspondence no doubt from the past fifty years of her existence.

"I . . . I . . . oh, dear. I didn't mean for you to see me in such a fragile state," she murmured. "It is merely that Mr. Kingsley's sudden return has overset me. I never liked him, Anne. Never. You must understand that. I felt he was arrogant and boastful and not nearly refined enough to husband you. Can you comprehend as much?"

Anne had never been ignorant of her aunt's opinions of Richard, even from the first, yet she couldn't help but defend him a little. "You were so deeply prejudiced by his lack of fortune and his inferior position as a third son that you never allowed him the virtues he does possess. I will concede that he occasionally appeared arrogant and even at times stubborn and willful, but he could be extraordinarily tender and kind, generous and quite amusing."

Mrs. Tandridge appeared to be very sad as she lowered her gaze to the box at her feet. "You sound as though you are still in love with him."

"Only a very little, for you must remember that he did not keep his promise to me, to write frequently so that I might always be aware of his thoughts, of the state of his heart, of how his activities were faring in India. I might still admire him and even feel an occasional surge of tenderness toward him, but I shall never forget that he failed me."

Mrs. Tandridge's eyes filled with tears anew. Her

mouth worked. She appeared wishful of speaking yet couldn't.

In order to spare her so much obvious distress, Anne presented Sir Arthur's notion of an *al fresco* nuncheon. Mrs. Tandridge wiped her cheeks one last time and said, "I think it an excellent notion. All of us ought to be out-of-doors, especially on such a beautiful day."

"I'll tell Cook, then. I'm sure she'll be able to prepare something for us."

Anne walked slowly down the stairs. She was grateful to have spoken so openly to her aunt about Richard, both of her aunt's dislike of him as well as her own paradoxical sentiments. She was growing more at ease with the notion that Richard had come home to stay, to take up residence as the new owner of Birchingrove, to live within her own circle of acquaintances.

She found the men engaged in a game of piquet and sampling a small platter of cut fruit and macaroons at the same time. Each was sitting as she would expect—Sir Arthur with one leg finely crossed over the other, Richard leaning forward with his elbows on his knees and scrutinizing his cards intensely.

She watched them for a moment, her heart caught up warmly in the image of each. Sir Arthur wore a black coat; Richard's was blue. Sir Arthur's neckcloth was simple perfection, Richard's an intricate layering. Sir Arthur had pursued her for the past eight years and kissed her only once. Richard's many kisses still burned on her lips.

When she finally entered the chamber, she moved in Sir Arthur's direction, smiling at him first as he turned to greet her. When she drew near, she laid her hand on his shoulder. He turned his head to regard her closely, and in his eyes she saw his immediate censure. She removed her hand and let it fall to her side.

Richard noted the exchange and didn't know whether to be furious that such a prosy old bore as Arthur Ide would spurn the affections of so glorious a female, or ecstatic that in his stupidity, Sir Arthur would actually open the door to the attentions of another man. His many unhappy opinions of Sir Arthur were once again confirmed, and to the man's conceit and arrogance, he would now add stupidity.

Richard let Sir Arthur win; he played his last few turns casually and loosely, fixing his gaze more often than not on Anne instead of the cards. He was content to watch her struggle to avoid his gaze, to observe how beautifully she blushed because of his silent attentions to her, to consider just when and how soon he could ravish her lips again.

The moment the game ended with Sir Arthur smiling with a great deal of undeserved self-satisfaction, Richard addressed Anne. "Is it settled, then? Are we to dine today in the *oak wood*? I can't tell you how many times I have longed to return there, especially to the rather gnarled tree by the stream. I wonder if the grass is grown *unmanageable* again."

Anne met his gaze and this time did not avert her own. She knew that a blush had covered not just her cheeks, but her neck as well, for she felt very warm all over. She knew precisely what he was referring to, and it was not at all to a picnic or even a stroll through deep grass. She had cuddled with him by that tree, nestled deeply into knee-high grass, kissing him as though her heart would break if she did not.

The memory of that moment flooded her mind and seemed to seep into every part of her body in warm waves of reminiscence. She had begged him either not to leave her or to take her with him, for she had felt certain something untoward would happen to separate them, and so it had—his character, his faithlessness in not writing but two letters to her in three years.

She was angry that he was reminding her of her loss,

and so lifted her chin. "I do not think very much of that tree," she said. "It is quite bent, unattractively so." She shifted her gaze to Arthur, who was refiguring his points of the moment, and added, "I much prefer to go to the glade as Arthur has suggested."

Sir Arthur laid down his pencil when he heard his name and said, "Has your aunt, then, decided she will permit us to dine out-of-doors?"

"Yes, *dearest,*" she responded. "Though I do believe she would do anything to oblige you."

At that Sir Arthur beamed. He was always pleased when others made an effort to place his desires above their own. He then rose to his feet and said, "Pray, however, don't disturb your cook. I shall return in a trice with fare from my own kitchens."

"Arthur, it really isn't necessary. Cook would be more than happy to make the preparations for a picnic, truly."

"You forget my delicate stomach. Though I know your cook is quite adequate in her own way, I really detest having to eat anything other than my chef's dishes. I'm sure you understand."

"But . . . but, do you have to leave so soon?" she asked anxiously. She knew Richard's mind and of the moment was frightened by the prospect of being left alone with him. She continued, "You didn't really get to see the kittens I rescued from the barn. Why don't you let me show them to you before you leave?"

"No, no, my pet. I am determined to go now." With that, he patted her arm and moved past her before she could protest. Arthur was not a man given to taking up a hint readily, so she truly could not have expected him to do so now.

From the corner of her eye, she could see that Richard was smiling as he sat back in his chair. Wicked man that he was, she knew what he intended. The moment Sir Arthur quit Birchingrove, he would assault her.

There was nothing for it, however. Sir Arthur apparently saw little in Richard Kingsley to be of any real threat to his happiness and quit the house by the back door having left his horse in the stables.

THREE

"Anne! Anne!" Richard called after her as she hurried down the hall, heading toward the kitchen. "Don't run from me. Besides, you know I shall catch you."

"I am not running from you," she called over her shoulder, telling yet another whisker. "I am merely hastening to return to the kittens. I daresay they will need to be fed quite often today. Besides, I must inform Cook that she needn't prepare nuncheon for the family."

He caught up with her. "Humbug!" he breathed over her shoulder, catching her by the elbow and forcing her to stop. He turned her abruptly toward him and, before she could utter even the smallest protest, took her in his arms. His lips were very close to hers as he said, "Tell me you remember better times beneath that twisted oak tree, hidden by the tall grass from any who might have chanced by."

"Don't," she pleaded, pushing at his shoulders and trying to force him away from her, but with little success. "That was a long time ago and best left forgotten."

"Never forgotten," he murmured. His lips touched the tender place at the very corner of her mouth. She moaned softly, for he was used to tease her in that manner in years gone by. He drifted his lips over hers and moved to the other corner of her mouth. For some reason, her hands ceased pushing against his shoulders and were now fingering the superfine fabric of his coat.

His lips drifted again, her own parted as though of their own volition. Her eyes closed, and her body leaned into his, reminding her of former times. He kissed her deeply, his tongue feeling familiar once more as he violated her mouth.

She knew she should tell him to stop, for in this very act she was betraying Sir Arthur. Yet, somehow the thought of Arthur made her arms slip about Richard's shoulders and hold him fast

He held her more closely still, his kiss deepening. After a time, he drew back. "Anne. Anne," he murmured. "All these years I have dreamt of holding you in my arms, longing for you, wanting to feel your dear, sweet self held against me." He kissed her eyelids and her nose, her forehead, her cheeks, her chin and at last assaulted her lips once more.

Anne forgot all about her present life. She was again beneath the oak tree, nestled in the embrace of Richard's arms, hidden by the tall grasses. She remembered his thousand gestures and promises of loving her forever. She remembered giggling and laughing and letting him taste of her lips for hours. She remembered her ankles getting sunburned where the shade of the tree shifted as the afternoon crept by. She remembered looking into his warm brown eyes and feeling as though she was disappearing into his soul. She remembered his promises to write often, at least twice a week.

The truth returned painfully. She slowly disentangled herself from the web of his arms. "I shouldn't have let you kiss me like this," she said.

He was still hungry for her and tried to draw her back into his arms, but she wouldn't let him. She averted her face, and some of his ardor began to dim. "So you would tease me," he whispered.

"And you would not keep your promises," she returned quietly.

He shook his head and appeared utterly confused. He still, apparently, hadn't the smallest notion what she was talking about.

"Never mind," she continued. "It doesn't signify, not by half. I shall be wed on Saturday."

"Not to Sir Arthur!" he cried vehemently.

She was taken aback and felt her knees begin to quake. "He is not so bad a fellow."

"You are not to wed him, Anne. I shall do everything in my power to make certain you don't. When I first learned, in the stables, that you were to be married, my initial instinct was to damn the fellow and take you to Gretna out-of-hand. But after a little while, I think when you were feeding the kittens, I began to believe I shouldn't make a push, that I had, for reasons I still couldn't comprehend, come home too late."

"You should continue to think in this manner, Richard. It is only proper."

"I might have," he said, gripping her shoulders hard, "except that you have chosen to wed the most ridiculous man in all of Britain. Sir Arthur Ide! The very thought of him makes my skin crawl. To think of him, *him*, touching you! Anne, can you stand there and tell me you look forward to becoming his wife?"

How could she lie to him; yet she must, else he would continue to kiss her and then trick her into marrying him somehow. "Of course I do," she said. "I would not have accepted of his hand in marriage had I not believed with all my heart that he would make me happy."

He appeared stunned. "You may strike me, but don't lie to me."

At that moment, Cook appeared in the hallway, her arms covered in flour up to the elbows. "I do beg yer pardon, miss, but the kittens are setting up a caterwaul, and I am presently kneading two loaves of bread."

"Thank you, Cook. I'll attend to them at once."

Anne said nothing more, but moved away from Richard.

An hour later, Anne walked beside Sir Arthur as they made their way along the path by the stream and headed toward the oak grove. In her arms, she carried the basket of kittens. Behind them marched three overburdened, red-faced servants from Flinthrall Castle, carrying blankets, serviceware, and a huge wicker hamper of food.

When Anne had first witnessed Sir Arthur's notion of a simple *al fresco* nuncheon, she was shocked and nearly inquired facetiously where the table and chairs were. She soon accustomed herself, however, to the formal nature of the occasion, especially since Richard forced her to meet his eye. She saw writ in his expression not only a great deal of amusement, but a harsh accusation as to the manner in which her future would be conducted. Never would she allow him to know how much in agreement she was of the moment.

She quickly averted her gaze, which she was finding she had to do very often, and turned to thank Sir Arthur for his obvious attention to every detail of their forthcoming nuncheon.

He had nodded in appreciation of her gratitude, then inquired gently why she felt it necessary to bring the kittens with her.

"Because, they need a great deal of nourishment at present."

"I can understand that, and indeed, I do praise you for your tender disposition; but I can't help but wonder why you would not turn over such a task to one of the undermaids."

He waited for an answer. She let him wait.

She wondered why he didn't divine the reason himself, that Birchingrove's two undermaids were far too busy trying to maintain the manor to have time to do anything else. As for Cook, she didn't have even a scullery maid to assist her in her labors. Nor would she think of asking the stableboy, Tom, who also helped work the small farm attached to the manor. All the servants spent long hours performing an impossible task given the shortage of hired help.

When Sir Arthur still seemed incapable of comprehending, she sighed, "Because it pleases me to care for the kittens myself."

He lifted a brow which fully expressed his disapproval, yet said no more. She felt her heart sink. Would this be the way of their marriage then, every decision, every activity of hers to be questioned and approved or disapproved?

She pondered these things now as the kittens began to mew. The jostling movement of the basket had disturbed them. She lifted the basket to cradle it better in her arms, which gentled the movement as she walked along the path, and the kittens again grew quiet.

"There it is!" Arthur exclaimed. "The very place I have chosen. There, on the far side of the glade beneath that large oak tree."

Anne paused in her tracks and felt herself pale. Oh, dear! It was the very tree beneath which she and Richard had at one time embraced.

Arthur continued his self-praises. "Did I not choose the most beautiful spot on the entire estate?" He marched forward, ignorant of Anne's distress.

Richard, however, was not in the least unaware of her discomfiture and drew very close. "A lovely tree, indeed! How happy your betrothed's choice has made me, for now I can at last say Sir Arthur and I agree on something. This is the finest spot on the estate."

"I remember that tree," Mrs. Tandridge said, joining them from behind. "My husband and I picnicked there many years ago." Her gaze took on a faraway aspect, and it seemed to Anne that her eyes grew misty with sweet remembrances.

"It would seem, then, we all remember the tree," Richard said.

Anne cast him a scathing glance, then moved forward quickly to catch up with Sir Arthur. Why did it have to be this tree, of all trees? Why?

Once arrived at the tree, Anne seated herself on a nearby stump while the servants busied themselves setting up the nuncheon according to Sir Arthur's explicit directions. The blankets, of which there were three, could not be laid down until the servants had properly trampled the grass. And then the baronet would not agree to their arrangements until perfect diamonds had been created juxtaposing each blanket with a corner toward the tree and a corner toward the nearby brook. She sighed heavily. All the servants were sweating profusely beneath Arthur's demanding and hurried commands.

She could not like him in this moment, behaving as though he were commanding a regiment of foot soldiers instead of three house servants. She rather thought he cut an absurd figure, pointing here and there and barking out his orders.

One thing she did approve of, however, was his solicitous conduct toward her aunt. He made certain she was quite comfortable, arranging several pillows just so until Mrs. Tandridge convinced him she could manage her meal without suffering a disabling cramp in any of her limbs. Mrs. Tandridge, a strong woman for all her nervous dispositions, finally glowered upon Sir Arthur, who took this as his cue to cease fussing over her.

As the servants were milling about and arranging a vast quantity of food, the kittens awoke and began crying for their supper. Only then did Anne realize she had not brought along any milk for them. She felt rather foolish and inquired of Sir Arthur if he had perchance brought milk or cream with him.

"Well, yes, but not for the kittens, I fear," he stated with some finality.

She smiled. "Arthur, they would each drink but a tablespoon or two." He shook his finger. "I'm sorry, my pet, for though I made certain a pitcher of cream would attend our little nuncheon, that cream is already designated to be enjoyed with some very fine raspberries for dessert. Your little charges will have to wait for their supper, I fear. Though I must say, and you know how much I dislike criticizing anyone, you should have thought of the milk before leaving the manor." He then commanded one of the servants to use separate plates for cutting up the apples and pears since he couldn't abide one of his foods touching another.

Anne tilted her head and watched and listened. Her heart sank farther still. She glanced down at her little charges and knew she could not possibly wait. She said, "Will you, then, send a servant back to fetch some milk for me?"

He seemed shocked by the idea. "I have everything planned, dearest. The servants are required here to make the *ladies and gentlemen* in the party comfortable." His voice was chiding as though he were addressing a child.

Even Mrs. Tandridge glanced up at Sir Arthur and said, "Do be reasonable. I should be happy to forego my portion of the raspberries and cream in order to see the kittens fed. Do but listen to how desperate they sound. Their mother abandoned them yesterday."

Sir Arthur, however, grew very rigid about the jaw and pretended not to hear what Mrs. Tandridge had just said to him. Anne felt the insult to her aunt quite deeply, though she realized Sir Arthur did not mean at all to be insulting. He was merely very specific about his life and about what he thought proper. She glanced at her aunt, to whom Sir Arthur handed a beautiful glass of champagne, and saw that her expression had grown inward and quite dark. Her imaginings, Anne could well comprehend, since only earlier that day she had received Lady Ide's horrid letter specifying her low position in what would be her new family.

All this time, Richard remained silent, and for that Anne was grateful. She knew him well enough to suppose that his opinions of the exchange might not be entirely happy. That he held his tongue, she found very considerate. When he approached her after a few minutes, he turned his back toward the tree and, picking up several pebbles, threw them one after the other into the brook.

"I am not feeling well," he said. "I have just developed a fierce headache and find I must return to the manor. I intend to lie down and rest until the pain disappears. Please make my excuses to the others." He turned toward her and gently dispossessed her of the basket. "Don't fret. I'll see that they are fed. Do you have the dropper with you?"

"It is beneath their blanket," she answered quietly. She found that her eyes were suddenly very wet. "And thank you, Richard. You're very kind to do this for me."

He didn't say anything, though she knew there were a dozen things he could easily have said. He merely smiled and looked down at the kittens. "I'm going to call the yellow one Wink, if you haven't any objection, for only one of his eyes is open, and whenever I look at him, I have the strongest impression he is trying to tell me a joke."

She chuckled. "I have no objection whatsoever."

He smiled at her, held her gaze for a long, significant moment, then headed back down the path.

"Now, where the devil is he going?" Sir Arthur inquired loudly.

"He has the headache from being in a new clime, I daresay. He wants to rest for a few hours."

"Well," Sir Arthur exclaimed, "what am I to do with his portion of all this food? I wouldn't have brought so much if I'd known Kingsley wouldn't be eating."

Anne glanced at the servants, who were still red-faced in their formal livery of blue and silver. "Give his portion to your servants," she suggested. "I daresay they are grown hungry from their labors."

He seemed aghast at the notion.

Anne glanced toward the servants and watched with some humor as they bit their lips and averted their eyes in order to keep from laughing. Sir Arthur would have been as likely to have shared his meal with the servants as he would have been to have cut off one of his legs.

Mrs. Tandridge met Anne's gaze and stated rather firmly, "Yes, Arthur, give Kingsley's portion to the servants."

"Well!" he cried. "Our nuncheon is all but ruined."

At that, Anne rose from the stump and cried, "Nonsense. Dear Arthur, you are a great deal too fastidious to be at all content in an *al fresco* anything. Here, give me that chicken."

Sir Arthur scowled as he handed the platter to her. Anne took it, as well as a bottle of champagne, and turned toward the servants. "You there, with the shockingly red hair," she said. "Come, take this fowl and this half bottle of champagne and enjoy yourselves." When he made no move toward her, she approached him on a swift step, thrust the food and the drink into his startled arms and turned to hold Sir Arthur's gaze steadily.

The servants remained standing rigidly obedient, waiting for Sir Arthur to approve of her decision.

She felt the matter ought to be addressed at once and

queried, "Is this how it will be, then? Will my word have no weight among your servants or in your house?"

Since his mouth fell agape and he could not summon even a single word to answer her, she addressed the servants. "If you do not obey me this instant, I shall set to screaming."

The red-haired fellow swallowed hard and glanced longingly at the chicken. She watched him deliberate for several weighty seconds, but in the end his appetite outmatched his fear of his master. He made an about-face and headed for a group of stumps some thirty feet away. The remaining pair of servants followed quickly behind in his wake.

Anne turned around and found Sir Arthur just as she had left him, with his mouth wide open and his eyes staring very hard at her. He said, "My mother warned me you might not be—" He broke off abruptly.

Anne understood everything at this moment. "Might not be what? Entirely governable at all times? Arthur, no woman is." She then sat down and began to enjoy what was an exceptional repast. Flinthrall Castle enjoyed the skill of a very fine chef, indeed.

Sir Arthur was silent for a full half hour, undoubtedly adjusting his sentiments, for his mouth, even while he ate, was quite turned down at the corners the entire time.

After he had completed his meal, however, he began to be more pleasant and entered into Anne and her aunt's conversation with considerable spirit. He even asked Anne to sing for him, during which time he reclined on a pillow at her knee and listened with some pleasure to her song.

When she was done, he said, "You've a lovely voice."

Mrs. Tandridge turned toward her host. "As do you, Sir Arthur. Would I be too presumptuous in begging a duet from you and Anne? I think nothing would be sweeter beneath this tree."

Anne suggested they perform the popular ballad, "My Mother Bids Me Bind My Hair." Sir Arthur, to her surprise, agreed rather enthusiastically.

The first verse began beautifully once they had agreed on a starting pitch, but the second verse ended with Sir Arthur letting out a yell and swiping at his hand and wrist. "Ants! Blast!" He stood up and immediately began to call for the servants and to hoist each lady to her feet completely without warning or discussion. "We must leave at once! At once!"

Anne wisely moved out of his way. When he began barking his orders at full voice once more, she addressed her aunt. "There is nothing for it, but to leave. We might as well go down the path now, for I vow I, too, am beginning to form a headache."

"Yes, let us return to the manor." She hooked Anne's arm, and together they walked side-by-side toward Birchingrove.

Mrs. Tandridge glanced back at Sir Arthur. "Do you know, I rather think that if Wellington had had Arthur in Belgium, the combined armies would have trounced Boney in half the time."

Anne giggled and gave her aunt's arm a squeeze.

Once Anne had bid goodbye to a much harassed baronet and three puffing, crimson-faced servants, she went in search of Richard. Cook had informed her that he had indeed fed the kittens once he returned from the glade, but didn't know where he had taken them afterward.

"You mean, he has the kittens with him?" she queried, amused.

"Aye, miss. He said he feared yer wrath were he not to keep them by his side until ye returned. And, if ye don't mind my saying so, miss, Mr. Kingsley is quite my idea of what a gentlemen ought to be, unlike some others as best not be mentioned."

"I don't mind you saying so in the least," she said, for in this moment she was quite of the same opinion.

Afterward, Anne began going from room to room in search of Richard. She did not find him in the dining room, the drawing room or the music room, all of which were located on the ground floor. Climbing the ancient, squeaking wooden stairs, she went to the library where she found him fast asleep on a sofa with the kittens snuggled on his chest and surrounded by a flannel blanket.

She was not unmoved by so homey a sight and could not help but recall seeing her beloved uncle in very much the same attitude and place, a favorite of his, during the warm summer afternoons.

She approached Richard slowly and quietly, not wishing to disturb his slumbers. He seemed very peaceful, as though he had come home, which, as the new owner of the manor, he certainly had. She found her heart swelling with affection for him.

He had shown her nothing but compassion and kindness in leaving the picnic to care for the three-week-old kittens as he had.

A deep yearning entered her heart as she gazed upon the face she had once loved so very much. "Richard," she whispered softly. "Why didn't you write to me all those years?"

In response, he began to snore quietly, a circumstance that made her smile and made her wonder about the future. When a terrible sadness threatened to overtake her, she silently quit the chamber.

FOUR

Anne made her way downstairs and found her aunt in the drawing room. She was sitting on the sofa nearest to the fireplace, a box beside her, the very box over which she had been weeping just a few hours earlier. She appeared somber as she met Anne's gaze.

"What is it?" Anne queried, trying for a light tone. She knew that the day had been a difficult one for her aunt, given that Richard had arrived so suddenly and both the Ides seemed to be intent on making her inferior position in their family clear to her.

Mrs. Tandridge laid a hand on the box. "I have something to tell you, which you will not like and for which hourly I am coming to regret more than I can say. I believe that I have made a serious error in judgment and can only defend myself by saying that I was doing what I felt was best for you." She had never seen her aunt's face so pinched with worry. Her eyes filled with tears as she continued, "Half of what is in this box belongs to you. The other half, I fear, belongs to Mr. Kingsley."

Anne's gaze dropped from her aunt's teary eyes to the black lacquer box settled beside her. She felt rather weak of a sudden, as though her body knew the contents of the box even though her mind couldn't seem to comprehend what her aunt was about.

She moved forward as one in a dream. Was this Pandora's box? she wondered distractedly. She could hardly breathe. "The box is full of letters, isn't it?" she asked.

Mrs. Tandridge nodded and her voice caught on a sob as she cried out, "Yes! Yours and Richard's."

"Oh, no," Anne murmured. She began to recall a dozen instances of her aunt's perfidy, of always insisting that the mail be brought directly to her, and offering quite generously to post Anne's letters to Richard.

She moved quickly to seat herself on the sofa. She pulled the box toward her and lifted the lid. She fingered through what must have been hundreds of letters, some from India, some that had never left Kent. "Oh, dear aunt! Whatever have you done to me, to us!"

At that moment, Richard appeared in the doorway, with the kittens crying from the basket. "They awoke fretting and mewing not a few minutes past," he said. "I think they need to be fed again. Good God! Whatever is the matter! What has happened? Anne, you are as pale as a ghost!"

Anne left her seat, tears of her own now streaming down her cheeks. She went to him and threw her arms about his neck. He surrounded her with one arm while still holding the basket of kittens in the other.

"You never said a word when you arrived," she cried.

He patted her back as she began to weep into his neck. "There, there, my darling. Have you had bad news from the post? Come, sit down and tell me!"

Anne pulled back. "Oh, Richard, you will not like it at all!"

"Why is your aunt weeping as well? Has someone met with an accident?"

"No! No! It is worse, I think. No, I don't mean that. Oh, Richard." She left the circle of his arm and searched frantically in her pocket for a kerchief. Finding one, she blew her nose soundly, then beckoned him forward. She faced her aunt and said, "You must tell him what you told me."

Mrs. Tandridge tearfully explained her traitorous conduct and begged forgiveness. Anne remained silent, her eyes downcast and the only words Richard spoke were, "In due time, Mrs. Tandridge, I may find it in my heart to do so. Of the present, however, I think Anne and I have some reading to do."

Mrs. Tandridge rose to her feet still wiping her eyes. "Yes, of course. By all means. Let me also relieve you of the burden of the kittens. I'll see that they're fed."

"Thank you, Aunt," Anne responded quietly.

An hour later, Anne was still horror-struck as she knelt on the carpet beside Richard and stared at the sea of letters spread out over the sofa. She leaned back on her heels and murmured, "I can't believe that this has happened. I don't know if I'll ever be able to forgive her."

"Was this what you meant," he asked softly, "when you told me I had been faithless? Had you believed I had not fulfilled my promise to you to write very often?" His hand grazed her cheek tenderly with the backs of his fingers.

"Yes, precisely. Only now what am I to do? I am betrothed to another man." She turned to look at him, anguish boiling within her heart.

"You must break off the engagement. I am sorry for it, but I had a prior claim to your hand."

Anne swallowed hard. She had never known so much turmoil as this. He drew close and slid his arm about her shoulders. "When I heard from you so little, at first I remember being terribly distraught. You were my reason for going to India in the first place, for enduring the heat and dirt of that place, that I might secure our future. Not having even the closeness of your letters was almost more than I could endure. But after a time, the absence of your correspondence fired me. I became absolutely driven to complete what I had come to India to accomplish, and that without loss of even a breath of time. I daresay had I not been filled with such a fervor, I would not be here now. I might have remained in India for three, five, even ten years longer to achieve all that I was able to achieve. I knew something untoward must have happened to have prevented you from writing. I knew you, Anne. I knew that you would have written every day—"

"Many of those first weeks, I did. But after two years— oh, Richard, I thought you had forgotten me."

"My darling, why did you think me so faithless?"

She shook her head and met his gaze with a sob welling up in her chest. "Men are not always able to adapt to the pen."

"Then, you have little faith in us *generally.*"

"I suppose so. But you have to understand that within a fortnight of your departure our situation here at Birchingrove became absolutely desperate as you will soon read in these letters. When my uncle died, he left scarcely a farthing of his inheritance unencumbered. You see, he had helped so many farmers in these difficult times, believing, of course, that one day prosperity would return to England, that he had acquired a mountain of debts— you cannot imagine! I needed the comfort of your assurances that all would be well—"

"And I would have given them. Indeed, I would have sent you whatever you needed."

At that, she collapsed on him and let her tears flow freely. He cradled her for a long time, promising her that all would be well.

After a time, Anne drew back and once more blew her nose soundly. The day was on the wane, and long evening shadows had begun to darken the drawing room.

"Feeling better?" he inquired.

"Yes, much. Thank you. I didn't mean to become a watering pot, but this, all of this, completely overwhelms me. I still cannot credit that my aunt felt compelled to separate us in this manner."

"You mustn't blame her. She never allowed herself to know me, only that my prospects, by her calculation, were not precisely what any mother would want for her daughter. I'm sure that once your uncle died, she felt obliged to direct your future down a different path."

"You are a very forgiving man," she said.

He slid his hand down the length of her arm. "How can I be anything else when I am at last home and you are here, flesh and blood, and not just some vague dream I was used to conjure up in order to fall asleep at night."

The touch of his hand caused a rippling of gooseflesh to travel down her neck and side. He was holding her gaze quite fiercely, so that it seemed but natural that he should lean forward and place his lips on hers.

She closed her eyes and permitted herself to feel the warmth and softness of his kiss as though for the first time. She tasted of India in that kiss, of the roar of elephants, the pounding of seasonal rains, the cries of monkeys. Richard had come home. He was here now kissing her, reminding her why she had tumbled in love with him in the first place.

Her pulse began to race. Images of sailing ships rolling over vast seas began to pound within her. His kiss deepened. He drew her onto his lap again, only this time not to cradle her but to crush her against his chest.

"Anne, my love," he murmured. "I have waited so very long for this day."

"Richard," she breathed against his lips.

He slanted his lips over hers and kissed her maddeningly. She slung her arm about his neck and clung to him. Desire raged within her, forgotten passion now surging forward like heavy surf after a storm. She felt wild and very young. The years betwixt had stolen her youth and her happiness. Kissing Richard was restoring both to her. How happy she was now, deliriously so, content beyond words.

Arthur had never kissed her like this!

The thought was like ice water cast over her. She drew back from him on a gasp.

"What is it?"

"Arthur," she whispered.

"No," he said, smiling. "He is not here."

"I know that. I was thinking of him."

"While you were kissing me?" he asked teasingly.

"No, not precisely. I was thinking he never kissed me as you have just now."

Richard chuckled. "I should think not," he said. "He would need a thousand years of practice to begin approaching anything near to passion."

Anne lowered her gaze and let her arm fall away from his neck. "I am betrothed to him," she said quietly.

He took her chin in hand. "That doesn't matter, not one whit, especially in light of these!" He swept an arm toward the letters strewn over the sofa.

"He and I signed a marriage contract," she stated.

"It is not an uncommon thing, nor is it improper, for a woman to break such a contract. A man might not, but a woman can and generally will do so if she has a good reason—and you do!"

"I don't believe it's so simple. I agreed to become his wife. I have an obligation to him."

She watched his gaze darken and his jaw grow stiff. "You have an obligation to me," he said, "to our love and our future. You were betrothed to me before I quit England."

"Yes, I was."

"So, shouldn't you consider my claim as paramount? It would be only logical."

"I don't know how to view the situation," she said. "At first, when you returned, I could only think of how you had never written to me and for that I was loath to forgive you. However, now I realize the matter is not simple. Sir Arthur made several loans to my aunt once we were betrothed, which was a year ago. Our engagement has been celebrated by dozens of our mutual friends; we have received any number of gifts. Sir Arthur has been incredibly kind to me and to my aunt."

His expression had grown quite serious. She supposed he was beginning to understand that she could not simply jilt Sir Arthur as though he was only useful to her while Richard was absent.

"You do not love me as you once loved me," he stated, looking at her somberly.

She stared at him for a long moment, wondering why a protest did not immediately rise to her lips. Perhaps he had spoken the truth. "I don't know," she said slowly. "Your unexpected return has given me such a shock. Of the moment, I'm not certain what I am feeling."

"You've changed," he said.

"The three years since you left have been almost unbearably difficult."

"I wish more than anything that I had taken you with me."

She smiled faintly. "I wish that you had as well. Do you remember how I begged you to do so?"

"I nearly agreed. But India would have taken something from you as well. It is not a clime agreeable to most Englishwomen. Oh, Anne, what is to become of us?"

"Richard, I must have time to think about all that has happened. I . . . I want to read your letters, to try to make sense of the past three years in light of them. And . . . I don't want to act hastily."

"I understand," Richard murmured. He stroked the nape of her neck with the back of his fingers. "What a strange homecoming this has been."

"Indeed."

* * *

Later, when the sun had made its final descent, Anne dressed herself in a simple country gown of embroidered white muslin, then ordered the carriage brought round. She donned her dark blue silk pelisse and bonnet, the latter of which was decorated fashionably in white ostrich feathers and satin ribbon.

Within a half hour, the traveling chariot drew up to the front door of Flinthrall Castle. She knew that Sir Arthur would not like that she was calling without having set the engagement previously. Despite his sentiments, however, she knew she must speak with him tonight, to inform him of the odd turn of events Richard's letters had wrought.

The butler took her bonnet and pelisse and announced her formally and gravely at the threshold of an elegant drawing room decorated *en suite* in yellow silk damask. Sir Arthur had guests; therefore the room numbered five in all, six, then, including Anne. Unfortunately, she was woefully underdressed for the occasion. All the guests wore full evening dress as befitted a formal dinner.

She was slightly taken aback and had not been aware that either he or his mother was entertaining anyone this evening, else she would not have imposed. At the same time, the thought nagged at her that she ought to have been included.

Sir Arthur greeted her with a dull flush along his jaw and cheeks. "Dearest," he proclaimed as he came toward her wearing a black coat, black silk breeches, white stockings and black, silver-buckled shoes. "We . . . we were not expecting you. Marsden," he called to the butler, "there will be one more for dinner."

"No, I would not dream of imposing, Sir Arthur. Marsden, you will not need to set another place. I only wanted a word with Sir Arthur."

"I see," Sir Arthur murmured. He inclined his head toward his butler, dismissing him and his former command at the same time. "First, let me make you known to my mother's guests."

"I should be delighted," she said, moving forward beside him.

Lady Ide greeted her with a veiled expression and a rather cool smile. The guests were distant cousins, Lord Dunstall and his wife and daughter.

Lady Dunstall greeted her by extending two fingers, and the daughter dropped a quite formal and elegant curtsy. She was a young woman, perhaps nineteen. "I am very pleased to make your acquaintance," she said with precision. "I cannot tell you how happy I am that my cousin"—here she smiled upon Sir Arthur—"is to be married. We have been friends for such a long time, he and I, that I told Mama I must go to Kent to congratulate him"—here she turned to meet Anne's gaze again—"and offer my very best wishes to you for your future happiness."

Anne was a little taken aback by this speech. "You are very kind, Miss Dunstall." She remained and chatted for several minutes with them all. She had not conversed for very long before she gained a strong impression that Miss Dunstall had been hopeful of quite a different outcome concerning Sir Arthur's future. The chit positively doted on him. Another fact became obvious: Lady Ide positively doted on Charlotte Dunstall, for she nodded approvingly at nearly every word the young woman uttered.

She began to comprehend why Lady Ide's treatment of both her and her aunt was decidedly frosty. Miss Dunstall was her choice for her son.

After a polite passage of time, Sir Arthur made his excuses and drew her across the foyer and into his office. Before she could speak, he broached his own concerns.

"Anne, this will not do. Not now and certainly not after we are married."

She didn't know to what precisely he was referring. "I beg your pardon, Arthur, but whatever do you mean?"

His brows rose in considerable surprise. "Arriving here so unexpectedly!"

She found this slightly amusing. "So, when we are married, you would have found my arrival tonight unacceptable?"

"No, of course not. Oh, I see that you are funning, only I wish you will be serious. I am most in earnest."

"I can see that you are, though I am unable to understand why. If anything, I am a little distressed that I was not invited to meet your relations. Really, Arthur, it is quite unsettling. Was there some reason why my aunt and myself were disincluded from tonight's festivities?"

He narrowed his eyes. "Just who, might I ask, informed you that we were entertaining? I don't care for it one whit that someone has been gossiping about the affairs of my household."

She watched him closely, wondering if he realized he seemed to be more concerned with having been discovered than whether his actions had in any manner hurt her. She addressed her question in a different manner. "Did your mother not wish for my presence here tonight?" she asked quietly.

Sir Arthur blinked, and a quick flush darkened his cheeks.

"I see," she murmured. She then addressed his suspicions. "As to your previous inquiry, no one told me you were entertaining this evening. As it happens, I knew nothing about the Dunstalls' arrival until just now. I came for my own reasons. I felt I had to speak with you on a quite serious matter which has arisen unexpectedly in the past few hours."

He lost some of his disapproving stiffness. His brow

crinkled. "Indeed?" he asked. "Pray tell me what has happened."

"Mr. Kingsley insists he has a prior claim to my hand and is suggesting my betrothal to you is invalid."

Sir Arthur paled. At the same time, she heard a gasp from beyond the door. Spies!

Anne turned away from Arthur, her heart sinking yet again. She had little doubt that her conversation with Arthur was being listened to. She had more than once suspected as much when she would visit in private with her betrothed. Now she was certain it was true. She wondered, were they to wed, whether she would ever be free of such encroaching conduct.

Until this moment, she had believed that Lady Ide's somewhat reserved manner toward her was merely an extension of her rather formal demeanor. Now she began to construe darker reasons.

She moved toward the window which was framed by deep blue velvet draperies and stared out at an immaculate lawn and tidily groomed hedges. Flinthrall Castle was exquisitely, if unimaginatively, maintained. Even now, she heard the rasp of pruning shears and noticed the wiggling of a large shrub as one of Sir Arthur's discreet gardeners hacked away at the excess growth.

She felt Sir Arthur's approach.

"But we have been betrothed for a year now," he said quietly. "You cannot possibly be thinking that you would break our engagement."

"I'm not certain what to think or to do."

"Even if Kingsley's claim was legal, do you wish to marry a man who ignored you for three years? What manner of husband would he make as you have told me often and often?"

At these words Anne relaxed and remembered why it was she had accepted of Sir Arthur's hand in marriage in the first place. When he forgot his rank as the premier gentleman in their small neighborhood, when he humbled himself, when he spoke from his heart, he could be utterly endearing. "Arthur," she said, touching his cheek with her hand, "you and I have known one another a long time, and what I value most is your sense of fairness. Richard does have a claim—of sorts. No, please, let me finish. You see, my aunt withheld his letters all these years. Only a few hours past, she told me the truth and returned all of his letters to me. There were over a hundred in all."

"I see," he murmured faintly.

"From her perspective, she was acting on my behalf, for she had no opinion of Richard when he left for India. I can't say what precisely moved her to reveal the truth at this eleventh hour, probably because sooner or later I would have discovered the truth from Richard himself."

"What she did was unconscionable," he said quietly. His face had grown drawn and sad. "Do you . . . do you still love him?"

"I don't know how to answer you, for you must remember we were betrothed at one time. Yet, three years have passed since I last saw him, and if anything, I feel very confused, though he did say he found me different somehow, changed I suppose."

Sir Arthur met her gaze. "Yet he still wishes to wed you?"

She nodded. "He does have a right, I think, to press his claim, just as you have a right. Arthur, I'm not certain what I should do."

"You must choose between us, I suppose, though I must say I feel my claim is much stronger than his. We— you and I—signed marriage contracts! You did not do so with Mr. Kingsley."

"That much is true, which is why I wanted to tell you what was going forward. I need time to think, to consider what I ought to do. I need to read his letters. I think then I will have an even greater understanding of him, of his character which I have misconstrued these past three years. Were the situation reversed, were you the one to arrive home after so long an absence, believing yourself promised to me, only to find I was about to wed another man, would you release me so readily from our betrothal?"

He grew very grave. "Of course I would not. A promise is a promise." He was silent apace. "Very well. What is it you mean to do?"

"At present, I'm hoping that a good night's sleep will provide the answer. Will you call on me tomorrow at eleven? I promise you, no matter what, I shall have a decision by then."

"Yes, of course I shall, but Anne, let me say at least this much. I know I haven't the sort of bravado that defines a man of Kingsley's stamp, but I believe I should make you a most excellent and loyal husband as well as a good, upright father for our children. I beg you will ponder this very odd circumstance most carefully, and choose, through the sound judgment I know you possess."

She had never heard him present his case better and for that reason slipped her arms about his neck and embraced him. "Thank you, Arthur."

He seemed nervous, however, and drew back from her, his color heightened. "Yes, well, you are most welcome. I daresay, however, that I ought to be returning to Mother and our guests. I do wish I could ask you to stay."

"I need to return to Birchingrove," she responded quietly.

"Yes, yes—all those letters. My God, what a muddle!"

"Don't fret yourself. Enjoy your evening with your cousins, and I will see you tomorrow."

Once Sir Arthur had seen his bride-to-be settled in her

carriage and the horses trotting down the drive toward Birchingrove, he returned slowly into the house.

He was met by his mother, who awaited him in the entrance hall. Her hands were clasped to her bosom, and her lips were compressed into an uneven line. "I knew how it would be," she said crisply, "once you followed your impulse to align yourself with one of the females of Birchingrove. Did I not tell you from the beginning that something would occur to upset the apple cart? Anne might be charming and beautiful, but you see what her manners are, disrupting our party as she has! But that wretched *Brasted* female! She has been a blight on our neighborhood since she wed Henry Tandridge. I, for one, am grateful that the alliance is ended. And you should be, as well—"

At that, Arthur felt obliged to stop his parent's tirade. "The betrothal is not ended," he stated firmly. He was angry suddenly with his mother, who seemed horror-stricken that he would contradict her. "And as for that *Brasted* female, you are only jealous that Penelope Brasted was able to steal Henry Tandridge from beneath your nose, and I don't wonder why, for you are uncommonly petty besides being horridly spoilt. Now, please, let us return to the drawing room and tend to our guests." He offered his arm to her, and though tears were sitting on her lashes quite putting him in mind of Mrs. Tandridge, he added in a lower voice, "Besides, you know very well indeed it was a wretched thing not to have invited Anne in the first place. I never approved of your decision. I wince at the thought of how this whole evening must have appeared to her."

He turned and watched his mother's lip quiver. He felt only a mild degree of disgust. He could not remember a time when she did not manipulate him through her tremblings and tears.

"Yes, Arthur," she responded in weak accents. "I suppose you must be right; you always are." She sniffed loudly. "Only do but consider, if Anne jilts you, then we shall not be crowded together under one roof, which I could never endure, at least not without succumbing to a fit of the vapors every day. You know what my nerves are, and—"

"Oh, Mother! Please, I beg of you, stubble it for once!"

FIVE

Richard broke every wax seal first, then arranged the letters according to date. For a long time, he stared at them, laid out as they were on his four-poster bed, a hundred or so faded vellum missives covering a threadbare burgundy bed cover, Anne's fairest copperplate curling on and on, lovely Anne, beloved Anne, Anne whom he might lose to her aunt's misguided machinations.

He drew a chair forward next to the bed and positioned it just so. He had brought up a decanter of brandy and poured himself a small portion in a snifter. He removed his coat and hung it in the wardrobe. He would have sat down and begun to read, but at that moment, the kittens, which were in a basket on the hearth, began to cry.

"Hungry, again, eh? Well, it seems I will have to feed you, since your mistress has not yet returned." He gathered Wink up in the comfort of a square of flannel, held him in the crook of his elbow and began the tedious process of using a dropper to get a sufficient amount of milk down his poor little throat. "You are adorable, aren't you? But don't tell Anne I said so. Wouldn't want her to think I've gone soft. She needs a man right now, not a moonling. Do you think she intends to marry that ridiculous jackanapes?"

Wink tried to bite the glass end of the dropper. His

tiny paws and even tinier claws pulled and tugged at the glass.

"My sentiments exactly."

At eight o'clock, Anne scratched on Richard's door. Receiving no answer, she rapped lightly and called his name. "Have you fallen asleep?" she called to him. "I've just now returned, and my aunt said you've the kittens with you. I'll take them off your hands, if you like. I brought some fresh milk with me. Richard?"

The door opened slowly. Anne met Richard's gaze, and for the barest instant she thought something terrible had happened to the kittens, for he appeared utterly anguished.

"Anne," he whispered.

"Richard, what is it? Have the kittens . . . I mean, did something go amiss?"

"No," he said slowly, opening the door a little wider and allowing her to enter. "They are sleeping."

"Then, why . . ." She got no farther. She saw that her letters were scattered all over his bed. A branch of candles burned low, and the brandy stopper was removed from its decanter. "Oh."

"Come in," he murmured.

She advanced into the chamber and moved to the hearth. The kittens were fast asleep, curled into one another. Except for the distinctive difference in each coat, she would not have been able to tell where one began and the other ended.

One large trunk and several portmanteaux were scattered about the chamber. "I see that your things arrived from The George."

"Yes. Anne, please look at me."

She turned toward him. "I can't stay long."

He took a step toward her, his heart in his eyes. "I read

your letters from the earliest date to the most recent. My heart is breaking. The last several letters were a plea that I respond. I can't bear that you were suffering so, both because you thought I was silent and because of your penurious circumstances following your uncle's death. Dearest Anne! How much I wish I'd known what was going forward all that time!"

Anne clasped her hands tightly together and averted her gaze. She wanted desperately to throw herself into his arms and sob away the pain of the past three years, but to do so would be to discard Arthur as though he were of no value to her, as though she had no obligation to him. "Please," she murmured. "Don't speak of it, not yet. There is something I must say before this truly difficult dilemma between us is broached." Only then did she dare look at him.

He looked as though he wanted to say something, but she lifted a quick hand. "Please, Richard. You must understand. I will not deny that my feelings for you, once my aunt made known to me her part in our separation, returned in full force. I will not deny my love for you. And yet, I refrain from ending my betrothal to Arthur not solely because I feel a certain obligation to him. Richard, much is changed within me since we last loved and planned our futures together. I am not so innocent as I was then. Life crashed down about my ears when you left, and when I accepted of Sir Arthur's hand in marriage it wasn't solely because of my need for his ability to provide for both myself and my aunt. I do hold him in some affection—no, I don't love him as I love you; I did lie to you earlier about that. Yet, there is more. When I accepted of his hand, I believed he would make an excellent father for our children and that he would be a dutiful, faithful husband to me. You have been gone a long time. You've lived where life is conducted quite differently from

England. You cannot tell me you have been untouched by your adventures in India."

"That much is true," he said solemnly.

"Then, you can understand me in part."

"Yes, I believe I can, though I must say, I don't agree with you at all."

"Will you respect that my view of our situation is different from yours and that I must have time to make a decision about my future?"

"Of course, Anne. Yes, of course."

He seemed properly subdued in her opinion, so she felt safe in approaching him and kissing him on the cheek. She was not prepared for the sudden embrace that followed, how he drew her close to him, holding her tightly about the waist, and kissing her full on the lips.

Oh! She had no breath in her lungs.

All the strange events of the day seemed to coalesce in that moment. Her soul felt drawn from her body as she slipped her arms about his neck and gave herself to his rough embrace. Whatever happened, in this moment she belonged to Richard, and the pain of the past collapsed and disappeared. All was forgiven, since there was nothing to forgive.

His lips became a warm search upon hers. She permitted him to enter her mouth, to join himself with her. No matter what the future would hold, Richard would always be part of her life, in the rich remembrances of his early courtship of her, of promises made beneath a gnarled oak tree, of falling into his arms when the ladder in the stables disintegrated, even of this moment when he held her roughly to him.

When at last she drew back from him, she found that tears of real regret were burning her eyes. She wanted to tell him that there was no true decision to make, that her heart had always belonged to him and always would;

but three years had passed, and she was not the same woman he had left behind.

Reason returned to her. She disentangled herself from his arms, which seemed not to want to let her go. She couldn't speak to him; indeed, what more could she say? Instead, she turned, picked up the basket holding the kittens, along with the small container of fresh milk, and quietly left his bedchamber.

Taking a deep breath, she closed the door behind her with a firm snap.

A half hour later, her bed appeared in much the same state as Richard's had when she left his chamber. Every letter, of which there indeed numbered over a hundred, had had its seal broken and was now lying about on the bed waiting to be read. She, too, arranged the missives by date. She reclined on her side, a branch of candles settled on a nearby table which cast a warm glow over the multitude of letters. Resting her head on her pillow, she began to read.

She laughed at the first twenty or so letters which were full of anecdotes and any number of sailing adventures, written in just that tone that put her fully in mind of the man who had parted from her for India three years past. The next twenty or thirty expressed a concern that he had received only two letters and was anything amiss? Was she in need of funds? Did her aunt still disapprove of him as severely as when he had left? Was she not suitably impressed that he had kept his promise to write so very frequently?

The remaining letters had lost a great deal of joy and animation. Though the accountings of his life in a hot climate and the daily success of his enterprises were skillfully written, Anne could detect his mounting concern.

The final five letters were a promise that he would be home before the summer of 'seventeen in order to determine for himself what had gone amiss.

And so he had.

Anne summoned her maid upon reading the last letter, and after having her hair brushed out carefully, tied up in bits of cloth, then stuffed under a mobcap, she climbed gratefully into bed. She was drifting off to sleep as the maid quit the chamber and closed the door. One last thought kept running swiftly through her brain—however was she to choose between Richard and Arthur?

Anne awoke before dawn to the sound of the kittens crying for their milk. She was greatly fatigued as she slid from bed, donned a robe and slippers, and made her way to the kitchens. She procured a new cup of milk, which had been kept on ice through the night, and carried it back upstairs. By the dull light of a candle she fed Wink and his littermate.

"What shall we call you?" she asked, letting her gaze run over the black and white patches.

The kitten paused in his licking of the dropper and stretched. "That's it," she murmured. "I shall call you Stretch. Wink and Stretch."

When at last the cuddly pair had returned to snuggling in each other's paws, she blew out the candle and crawled back into bed. She remembered Richard telling her he would have had them drowned. She smiled knowing full well Richard had only been trying to get her to rise to the fly. His every action since had belied his harsh words. With these thoughts she fell asleep once more.

Later, somewhere between waking and sleeping, as her bedchamber filled with morning light, Anne awoke knowing what she had to do with such clarity that she wondered at the inspiration. She lay in bed pondering the unusual solution to her dilemma. She glanced toward the hearth, where the kittens were still sleeping, aware that somehow they had provided her with the means of choosing between her beaux. With all the nurturing each kitten required, she had become attuned to the patience a gentleman would need once his nursery began filling with children. Did either Arthur or Richard comprehend just how much understanding, affection and care a family required?

She wanted to believe that Richard was the sort of man who would be a loving and patient father, yet how would she really know? If she were to judge his capacity as a parent by the many kindnesses he had shown the kittens since his arrival, he would score well. On the other hand, his overt concern for Wink and Stretch could easily be set down to his desire to win her away from Arthur. As for Arthur, he showed every likelihood that he would be consistently annoyed by any intrusion into his daily regimen. Yet, what if he held deeper qualities she had not discovered? What if he had hidden potential in the realm of fatherhood?

At the very least, she owed both men the opportunity to prove themselves.

Only, would they agree to the sort of contest she had in mind? To own the truth, she wouldn't blame them if they scoffed at her scheme and she ended up without a husband after all.

Oh, well. There was only one way of discovering their respective sentiments.

At eleven o'clock, the two gentlemen stood before her in her aunt's, or rather Richard's, drawing room, and spoke in unison. "What do you mean a contest?"

"I mean precisely that," she responded. "I have created a sort of contest for you, and the winner of it will have my hand in marriage." At this juncture, she found it necessary to choose her words quite carefully. She needed the men to think the contest was a race solely against the clock and that the winner would be the one with the best time. The truth was, time would be the deciding factor only if both Arthur and Richard made the wrong choice at a critical point in each respective drive—

the point at which the drive back to Birchingrove had three quite different routes.

She intended for that moment in the drive to decide her future—whoever chose on the side of consideration and concern for her well-being over speed and winning the contest would have her hand in marriage. Of course the failsafe was simple: if neither man showed the sort of consideration she was hoping for, then she would allow the man with the best time to marry her after all.

She supposed it wasn't entirely fair not to advise them of the exact nature of the contest, except that if she were to do just that, each man would be on his very best behavior, and that was not what she wanted in the least. She wanted both Arthur and Richard to conduct themselves just as they would if there wasn't a contest at all.

She began, "You will each take me on a drive of equal length in order to accomplish one or more tasks along the way. Speed is a critical factor, though my safety cannot be entirely ignored. Either of you may choose not to participate, in which case my hand shall be forfeit." Since both men appeared quite astonished, she felt obliged to add, "I would not blame either of you for refusing to engage in the contest, for by its nature I realize it cannot be entirely pleasing."

She watched the men turn and look at each other quite squarely, as though each was taking the measure of an opponent.

"Will you agree to the contest?" she queried, glancing from one to the other.

She could see their respective reluctance, but in the end each agreed with a firm nod.

"Excellent," she responded, smiling. "The event will be timed by the clock on the mantel. I have already determined that Arthur shall be first, since we would have been wed tomorrow had Richard not returned. Richard, you will wait here in order to determine the time of our departure as well as the exact minute of our return."

"So the quickest time wins, then?" Richard inquired.

How was she to answer this? She merely met his gaze fully, but neither nodded nor shook her head in response to his query.

"Very well, then," he said, taking her silence to mean she agreed with him. Having crossed this hurdle, she breathed a little easier and continued, "I have laid out each course with a meticulous eye to terrain and distance. I feel that each route is roughly the same in terms of difficulty and distance and should be accomplished in about three hours' time. I will direct each of you along the way. Oh, and one last thing, since I am still caring for the kittens, hoping to see each of them safely through the next few days, I will be bringing them along."

Richard immediately protested. "The deuce take it, Anne!" he stated harshly. "We are each of us fighting for your hand. Must we be saddled with the kittens as well? Cannot your aunt care for them? Must they come with us?"

"I'm sorry, Richard, there is no other way. The servants are terribly busy, as you very well know, and my aunt is suffering from a dreadful headache this morning. No, no this is best, and I promise you, the kittens won't have the slightest effect on the contest."

He grunted both his acceptance and his displeasure.

Arthur merely lifted a brow as she turned and picked up the familiar basket. The kittens were crying again.

Anne again addressed Richard. "You may make a note of the time. Arthur's feat begins now."

Richard glanced at the clock and said, "Eleven twenty-one and thirty seconds."

"Thank you. You may make yourself comfortable in the library. When you are ready for your nuncheon, just let Cook know. She has been forewarned of the contest."

He bowed to them both, then quit the chamber.

Arthur walked quickly forward. "Is the carriage brought round?" he asked in some agitation. "Anne! What are you doing? You don't mean to feed them now?"

Anne sat down on a chair near a table upon which was placed a cup of milk and the kittens dropper. "Yes, I must."

"Dear God, no! This isn't in the least fair! Richard was right. We shouldn't be saddled with these, these ridiculous cats!"

"Richard will have to contend with them as well," she responded composedly, "so in that sense it will be fair. However, I must and will feed them now, before we leave."

Arthur groaned and began to pace the floor. Twice he asked if she was almost finished. "No," she replied calmly, each time.

Finally, the kittens were quiet once more. "I am ready to go," she announced. "Will you see the curricle harnessed and brought round?"

"What?" he fairly shouted. "Why did you not tell me the horses hadn't been put in harness? Am I now to lose even more time because you did not have the foresight to send for the carriage?"

Anne smiled faintly. "I'm sorry, Arthur, but everything will be all right in the end, I promise you. Just do your best."

He left in a huff. Twenty minutes later, still quite agitated, he helped her and the kittens to clamber aboard the curricle. When he set the carriage in motion abruptly, she laid a hand on his sleeve. "Gently, Arthur, the kittens can't bear a great deal of motion. They are so young and still rather feeble. Pray, slow down."

He strove to calm his rising temper. "Richard was right. If you expected each of us to perform well, you shouldn't have saddled us with these invalids!"

She scooted close to him and put her hand in his pocket. "But they are adorable *invalids,* aren't they, and think of all the time you have just with me."

Arthur glanced at her and then the kittens. "I have never cared for cats, though I believe they are useful in the barns and in the attics."

Anne sighed.

"What is my first task?" he inquired. "Where am I to go?"

"You are to drive to Greenhill Farm and procure some milk for the kittens."

He gasped his frustration. "Milk for the kittens!" he cried. "Are we at that again?"

"Yes. Our poor cow has stopped giving milk entirely, and though my aunt and I both might survive without milk, the kittens will not."

"Very well," he mumbled between tight lips.

Anne remained silent during the journey, which, since the route was circuitous and involved several rutted country lanes, became a trial of patience for the long-suffering baronet. Anne kept her attention fixed on the kittens, holding the basket aloft quite frequently when the wheel would plummet into a deep rut, so that they would not be disturbed overly much.

When at last the farm was reached, Mrs. Henley came running out bowing and exclaiming over their unexpected arrival. Anne explained their need for milk to be delivered to Birchingrove.

"Aye, miss, whatever ye be needin'. Yer uncle were a fine man and helped us often and often. We be more than happy to return the favor. Won't ye come in? I've a pot of tea on and some fresh macaroons."

"Thank you very much. We would be delighted—"

"But, Anne!" Sir Arthur interrupted.

She turned to him. "Don't worry. We shall return to Birchingrove in plenty of time, I've little doubt. Come!

You will enjoy Mrs. Henley's biscuits, for they have won prizes at the local fair. Besides, I daresay the kittens need to be fed again."

He looked down his nose rather sharply at the farmwife, compressed his lips, and finally descended the curricle. Once inside, Anne requested that Sir Arthur help her feed the kittens, for they were crying again. He glanced about the chamber, and noting that a young girl of about ten was sitting quietly on a stool by the hearth, offered her a tuppence to care for Wink and Stretch while he drank his tea.

The young lady, though shy, obliged him readily.

After a half hour, when Mrs. Henley's marvelous biscuits had been consumed and her perfect English tea imbibed, Anne bid her farewell and directed Sir Arthur to take up the reins once more.

He helped her gain her seat, then handed the basket of kittens up to her. "Why don't you make a present of Wink and, er, Stretch to the child who fed them? She seemed much taken with them, and I daresay we shall make much better time if we do not have to concern ourselves any longer with their care."

"Arthur, they are important to me. I don't wish to give them away, at least not until I've seen them fully recovered."

He looked into the basket and frowned severely. "I hope once we are wed," he said firmly, "you do not mean to bring a passel of cats into the house."

"What about children, Arthur? Would you feel the same way were I to give you a dozen or more? Would you tire of them running about the house, always underfoot and demanding our love and attention?"

He grew rather pale as he rounded the curricle and took up his seat next to her. "Children are quite a different thing, surely. You can't mean to compare these furry beasts to our own offspring? At the same time, do you truly intend to provide me with a dozen heirs?"

She chuckled, but didn't answer him. He picked up the reins and encouraged the horses forward.

"Where to next?" he inquired heavily.

"Crown Wood Farm," she said.

"What?" he cried. "That is nearly five miles distant and through rather difficult country."

"Yes, but my aunt wished me to secure some oat seed for the northwestern field. I thought it an excellent notion."

"What on earth, then, do you have planned for Kingsley?" he cried, much astonished.

"Something worse, I fear. There is a farm to the northeast of Turvin's Wood which has some fine, composted manure for sale. I think he shall have to take the larger wagon for that chore."

At that, Arthur smiled for the first time since the journey began. "Yes, the wagon would be absolutely necessary."

She saw the workings of his mind, that he believed himself to have the advantage. He was not of so sanguine a temper by the time they reached Crown Wood Farm, however. Drawing the horses to a halt in front of a ramshackle farmhouse, he said, "I will not be surprised if after all that jolting, we lose a wheel on the return trip."

The kittens were mewing. "They will need to eat again and rest, I think."

Arthur did not protest this time. He merely sighed heavily, having come to resign himself to the strange test Anne had placed on him. He helped her descend and fairly glowered upon the kittens. Once inside, at the enthusiastic request of the farmwife, Mrs. Crockham, he ignored Anne's request to again assist her in feeding the kittens. He sat silently at a clean kitchen table and pretended to sip another cup of tea, at least until three cats raced into the kitchen chasing a mouse. One of the cats, most unfortuitously, caught sight of Sir Arthur. Something about him seemed to appeal to the scruffy feline, who immediately began to rub about his legs, depositing all manner of long, gray hairs on his fine, polished boots.

Anne ignored his discomfiture and fell into a lengthy conversation with Mrs. Crockham while her husband fetched the promised sack of seed oats. They discussed her youngest child, a babe of nine months, who was miserable with his teething. Anne suggested she bring the child to her, that perhaps the kittens might amuse the suffering little one.

Mrs. Crockham was grateful, and the child was indeed amused, if but for a few minutes, after which he set up a pitiful wail. Anne expressed her sympathy, and when Mr. Crockham arrived in the doorway informing her that the seed was strapped quite tightly to the back of the curricle, she took her leave. Sir Arthur said nothing, but offered a very faint bow in response to the farmer's heartily expressed hope that he would live a long and prosperous life.

When he took up his place once more in the curricle, Anne directed him to the village. "I took the liberty of ordering nuncheon at The George."

"Thank you," he murmured.

The journey down the hill from Crown Wood Farm was not nearly so tedious as the journey up. The outskirts of Headly Green were reached within a short half hour of leaving the Crockhams' farm. Once at the inn, Anne turned the kittens over to a maid and saw Sir Arthur's countenance visibly relax.

He chuckled. "For a moment, I thought you meant to feed them yourself, in here."

"Would that have been so very bad?" she asked, smiling.

Arthur frowned as he looked at her. "I can't believe

you would even pose the question," he responded. "Animals do not belong in a dining parlor."

"No, of course not," she responded kindly, thinking about the long-haired gray cat who had rubbed about his boots earlier. "Which was why I gave them to the maid."

"As well you should have."

When the nuncheon of fresh trout, cauliflower and small potatoes was consumed, the kittens retrieved from the maid, and the horses put to, Anne turned to Sir Arthur. "And now, you may choose the route by which we return to Birchingrove Manor. The King's Highway is the quickest; the route through Drane Hill quite beautiful this time of year; though not quite so short as the highway; but the smoothest road by far, though the longest, is the lane which goes north of Rook's Nest, for the rock is freshly laid." She found that her heart was racing. What would Arthur choose? Would he see beyond the contest into her heart and her desires? Would he see something more than just making good time?

He did not seem to hesitate as he flashed her a contented smile. "We will, of course, take the King's Highway, for I have no intention of losing this contest."

Anne smiled, yet her spirits drooped. For all his faults, she did hold Arthur in some affection and had hoped, for the sake of their betrothal and the promises they had made to one another over the past twelve-month, that he would choose the route by way of Rook's Nest. That he did not even question which way he should go was daunting. Yet, in fairness to Richard, she could give him no hints and merely smiled in response. "As you wish, Arthur."

As he set the team in motion, he seemed exhilarated.

A half hour later, when she stepped across the threshold of Birchingrove, she was covered in rock dust from head to foot, and the kittens were crying.

Arthur bolted into the drawing room and, not finding

Richard, raced upstairs to the library. Anne heard him from the entrance hall. "Pronounce the time, my good man, and by God I'd like to see you do better on the journey Anne has planned for you!"

A few moments later, Anne met Richard's rather astonished gaze as he stood at the top of the stairs and scanned her up and down. "Traveled on the highway, eh?"

Anne only chuckled and began to climb the stairs. "I will need a few minutes to change my pelisse and bonnet. However, your time must begin now. Will you be so kind as to feed the kittens while I am dressing or you can wait until I am done and I shall see to the task myself?"

He frowned, but drew in a firm breath. "I shall be happy to feed them," he said, taking the basket from her as she reached the landing.

Arthur stood in the doorway of the library and smirked. "That is all you will be doing for the next few hours, Mr. Kingsley, I promise you that! I tried to give them away to a schoolgirl at one of our stops, but Anne would have none of it. Perhaps you may persuade her otherwise."

Richard ignored Arthur's acerbic comments and headed downstairs. Anne watched him go, wondering what his choice would be. If he chose, as Arthur did, to take the quicker route, she would have to award her hand to the man with the best time after all. What would Richard's choice be?

SIX

Anne met Richard in the kitchens and found him cradling Wink in the crook of his arm. He lifted concerned eyes to her. "Do I have even the smallest chance?" he queried.

She merely chuckled. "All I ask is that you do your best, be patient, and we'll see what happens."

"But was it really fair to begin the time when Arthur returned? He's the fellow who got you covered in white dust."

"Do stop complaining. Wink has fallen asleep. Bring him along. By the way, we'll need the wagon, I'm afraid, for our second stop will be at Turvin's Wood for some manure."

"M-manure!" he cried.

"Oh, now you've wakened Wink. That was very unkind of you."

"There, there, Wink," he reassured the infant kitten.

"Look!" Anne cried. "He will not be Wink much longer. His other eye is opening!"

"So it is," Richard responded. "Now, how is it I grew to be a man without knowing about kittens and their eyes?"

"I daresay it is because kittens, by their soft, cuddly nature, are more naturally the property of little girls."

He settled Wink into the basket, and the kitten immediately curled up close to Stretch. "Do we need to bring some milk for them?" he asked.

"No. We shall get some at one of the farms."

"Oh," Richard responded quietly.

"Don't be blue-deviled. You will have me with you the entire way."

At that, he truly brightened, and Anne's heart melted. She wondered, however, whether he would make the same choice as Arthur. If he did, well, she would no longer reside at Birchingrove. She already knew, because of the wagon, he couldn't match Arthur's time. So, all that was left was his choice.

Concerning speed, however, Richard disproved her immediately. When she told him he was to go to Hollow's End Farm, he lifted a brow and said, "May I choose the route?"

"I don't see why not."

Richard remembered the country well and took every shortcut he could find. Though he slowed down for any deep rut that might send either her or the basket of kittens flying aloft, he still made excellent time. She, however, had begun to question the wisdom of her contest. Her posterior was becoming grievously sore.

At Hollow's End Farm, Anne entered the kitchen of Mrs. Drane and accepted her tea with gratitude. Richard, unlike Arthur, and much to Anne's pleasure, drew a chair forward to match hers and entered into Mrs. Drane's conversation with genuine interest. The kittens remained asleep in the basket on the table.

As at Greenhill Farm, she professed to be in need of milk and requested that Mr. Drane send some to Birchingrove.

"That he will, Miss Tandridge. Never let it be said that we be forgettin' the help Mr. Tandridge gave to anyone in need whilst he was alive. I heard tell he left the pair of ye ladies in dire straits, and fer that I do be sorry. I daresay he gave away all he had."

Anne nodded. "He was a great man and we miss him sorely. Our affairs, however, are in tolerable order of the present."

Mrs. Drane winked. "Aye, that it would be, what with yer marriage so soon to Sir Arthur Ide."

"Yes, indeed," Anne responded sincerely.

A few minutes more and she took her leave. Once settled in the wagon, she directed Richard in a northerly direction toward Turvin's Wood to fetch the manure. Once again Richard availed himself of as many shortcuts as he could discover, and the short journey was made in good order.

Upon arriving, Richard grimaced at the nature of their chore. "Are you certain this is necessary?" he asked, his nose wrinkling as he stared down at the well-dressed pile of powdery compost.

"Yes," Anne responded firmly.

He glanced at her. "I don't like at all the thought of seeing you driving about at the head of a load of dung."

"It's not dung, precisely," she explained. "The earth has processed it quite nicely, and Cook will be most grateful for the addition to her kitchen garden."

He merely chuckled and helped her to take up her seat once more. "We've made good time," he said, glancing up at the location of the sun. "Two hours, I'd say."

At that moment, however, the kittens began to cry. "They will need some milk before we leave," she said.

"So they will." He did not complain, at least not precisely, as he said, "Anne, I am troubled that the contest turns on this. Can we feed them along the way?"

She shook her head. "No. They would become ill. The traveling is difficult enough as it is."

He shrugged his shoulders. "I wish you had suggested

a shooting match instead of a jaunt about the country-side."

"Do you think my contest ill-conceived, then?"

Since Richard had set the horses in motion, heading them toward the farmhouse where they would feed Wink and Stretch, Mr. Turvin was well out of hearing range. Even so, he spoke in a low voice. "Anne, I don't profess to know the depth of Sir Arthur's attachment to you, but the very notion that I might very well be forced to live the rest of my days without you and all because Wink and Stretch must eat, I tell you it is nearly more than I can bear."

Anne laid a hand on his arm. "All I ask is that you do your best. Perhaps, in a way, I am asking Fate to make the decision for me."

He met her gaze and shook his head. "You should have let me decide for you. I would have known precisely what to do with Sir Arthur."

Anne smiled. "I have little doubt of that," she said, chuckling.

After the kittens were fed, she directed Richard to Headly Green where she had bespoken a dinner—roast chicken, a fine plum pudding, potatoes and broccoli. She watched him make a conscious effort to keep from rushing the meal. She ate slowly and deliberately, treating Richard just as she had treated Arthur. The moment, however, that she pronounced the meal at an end, he was on his feet. He summoned the kittens nearly at the exact same time, ordered the horses harnessed as well, then swiftly extended his hand down to her.

Anne could only smile as she gained her feet. She could tell that he was restraining himself and felt strongly that if he was given permission, he would break into a run.

With the kittens in hand, and her posterior settled yet again on the hard, uncomfortable seat of the laden wagon, Anne found that her heart was beating in odd spurts. The time had come for Richard's choice, and she truly had no way of divining what his decision might be.

Though her knees trembled, she informed him of the particulars, just as she had told Arthur earlier that day. "And now, you may choose the route by which we return to Birchingrove Manor. The King's Highway is the quickest; the route through Drane Hill quite beautiful this time of year, though longer than the highway; and the smoothest road, though longer still, would take you north of Rook's Nest. The rock is freshly laid."

She held the basket of kittens tightly to her chest. She waited and waited. Finally, she turned to look at him and saw that he was struggling within himself as to what he ought to do. She knew by the slapping of the heels of his boots against the floor of the wagon that he wanted to be going fast and furiously back to Birchingrove.

Richard did not look at Anne. His thoughts were full of indecision, something to which generally he was entirely unaccustomed. Because both Anne and the kittens ought to be taken home at a leisurely pace, he wanted desperately to choose the latter route, by way of Rook's Nest. But, damme, if he did so, he wouldn't have the smallest chance of besting Arthur's time.

The King's Highway was the only way. He had indeed made excellent time through judicious selection along the way, and if he drove at a spanking pace, he felt in his bones he could win the contest. The compost was tied down snugly with canvas and rope, so he had no concerns there of causing turmoil on the highway with a loose, noxious cargo; and the horses, as fatigued as they were, had had a brief rest at the inn and could certainly make a tolerable show from the inn to Birchingrove.

He glanced at Anne, who was sitting composedly beside him. She didn't seem in the least interested as to which route home he chose, in which case she was giving him permission to take the highway. Yet, he couldn't forget the dreadful sight of her as she returned with Arthur, covered in the typical white rock dust so familiar to the better-maintained roads all over the kingdom.

He picked up the reins. He would go by way of the highway. More than anything, he wanted to marry Anne. More than anything.

"I know it will be a sore trial for you, Anne," he said gently. "But I really must take the highway."

"As you wish," she responded with a smile.

Anne held her face immobile and cast her gaze into the distance. She forced herself to take deep, even breaths. She didn't want him to see even the smallest distress his decision had cost her.

"There is no argument that we should go by way of Rook's Nest," he explained. "You will be jostled to pieces on the highway and so will the kittens. But damme, Anne, I will go on the highway if to do anything else would mean losing you!"

"The choice is yours," she said, turning at last to him and smiling once more.

He met her gaze and murmured, "I'm sorry, but you'll forgive me once we are enjoying our honeymoon."

"So, you believe you can best Arthur's time?"

He nodded and gave the horses a light slap of the reins.

She glanced at his hands and at the leather straps wound in and out of his gloved fingers. He should have slapped the horses hard along their flanks, even used his whip, yet he refrained from doing both.

"You must do what you feel is best," she offered, curious as to when he meant to take charge of the team.

He frowned and whistled to the horses quietly.

Hope began to rise in Anne's breast.

He clicked his tongue and called to his team, but still did not pick up his whip or in any other way encourage them into a faster pace. As it was, they walked sedately out of the inn yard.

One of the horses stumbled slightly, then regained its pace.

Anne watched as Richard's shoulders slumped a little. "I can't do it," he confessed. "Not even to wed you. My father's teachings are too strongly burned into my head. I would be torturing these poor horses, you and the kittens were I to push to the end. I'm sorry, Anne, but we will go by way of Rook's Nest, your contest be damned."

Anne felt her eyes fill with tears, and her throat grew quite constricted.

He glanced at her. "Please don't cry. I can bear anything of this moment except that. Only, tell me you understand."

She turned and smiled up into his face. She saw him through a watery haze. "I do understand, and you will never know how much your consideration of me in this moment, as well as of Wink and Stretch and our unfortunate horses, will always mean to me."

By way of answer, he sighed heavily. Moving past the village green, he took the lane to the right and began the journey back to Birchingrove quite safely north of Rook's Nest.

"Then, I have won!" Arthur cried as he rose from his chair and marked Richard's time. "What a whipster you've proven yourself to be—a full half hour beyond my time."

Richard smiled faintly and bowed to Sir Arthur. "My congratulations," he said. "And my hope that you will be very happy, indeed. And now, I intend to retire that you may have a few moments alone with, er, Miss Tandridge."

Anne watched him go, her heart singing out a strong yet silent song. Richard had made the choice that had won him the contest, yet how and when to tell the men?

She turned to Arthur, who was preening in his victory.

"By God," he said, "I thought this notion of yours a fairly wretched one, Anne, I must say. But now that it is over, I find I am light-headed—with happiness, of course." He approached her, smiling.

She offered her cheek, and he gave her a swift peck. "Well, thank God that is all settled!" he cried, drawing back from her. "I am not fit to remain here a moment longer, however. I had one of the maids brush my coat, but the dust of the road is sunk to my skin. I know you will understand when I say I must take my leave."

"Please do so," she said kindly, unwilling to address the matter of the contest when she was so tired and Sir Arthur so intent on leaving. "And I shall call on you to-morrow at ten."

"Whatever for?" he asked. "We shall meet at the church at four as agreed upon."

"Why, I mean to boast of your victory to your mother, of course," she teased.

He paled. "No, no! Pray do not say anything to her of this. She will not comprehend in the least why I was put through my paces."

"I was only funning a little, Arthur. Of course I would never breathe a word to your mama. The fact is, there are a few things about our nuptials I'd like to discuss with you."

"Whatever your heart desires, my pet."

"Thank you. Ten, then?"

He nodded and was gone.

Anne did not see Richard that night or even the following morning at breakfast. He had left Birchingrove quite early, and she felt certain she understood why since she had let him continue in his belief he had lost the contest. However, she was reluctant to say anything to him until she had settled the matter with Arthur.

She arrived at Flinthrall Castle on the hour and was shown into the morning room where he was seated by the fire reading *The Times*. He rose upon seeing her and appeared genuinely happy.

"Arthur," she began calmly, "I've come to tell you that you lost the contest yesterday. I didn't say anything at the time because we were all so very tired and I didn't want to have to explain things to you without my head being quite clear."

"What the deuce!" he cried, his brows drawing together in a hard snap. "But that's not possible. I had the better time. I won quite fairly and handily I might add."

Anne regarded him for a long moment, wondering how she was to make him understand the true nature of the contest. "Time would only have been an important factor had both you and Richard made the wrong choice. Yesterday, however, you, alone, made the unfortunate choice that decided the contest."

He seemed utterly confused. "What choice was that?"

"To take me home by way of the highway instead of Rook's Nest."

"What?" he exclaimed. "I still don't take your meaning. To travel by way of Rook's Nest would have required at least twenty minutes additional to accomplish."

"Yes," she said pointedly, "but the route was far easier on me, the kittens and the very tired horses."

He shook his head and began to pace the room. "This is nonsense. Utter nonsense. I absolutely refuse to accept what you are telling me. If you are going to construct a contest, Anne, I must say it would be at the very least a matter of honor to inform the participants of exactly what the contest was about."

"Yes, but had I told you both that what I wanted to see was which of you would be a more caring husband

and father, you would each have been on your best behavior instead of acting in a normal fashion."

"Then, you are saying because I chose to travel the highway, I would not be a fit husband for you?"

"I suppose so," she murmured. "Do but think? Do you recall how loudly the kittens were crying and what I *looked* like once we had returned to Birchingrove?"

He grew very somber. "Even your cheeks were white with dust," he mumbled. "But I should have been given some warning." His gaze jerked to hers. "Is that it, then? Did you give Richard some hint? Is that how he chose his route?" Anne lifted her chin.

"In no manner did I reveal what I felt he should do," she retorted firmly. "Though I will tell you he first chose just as you did and truly meant to take me home by way of the highway. Only after one of the horses stumbled a little did he tell me he couldn't bring himself to subject me or the horses or the kittens to such a punishing trip."

"I've little doubt that he is parading about the manor even now boasting to any who will listen of his victory."

"That would not be possible. He is still ignorant of the true outcome of the contest. I felt I needed to explain the situation to you first, before venturing to address Richard."

At that, some of his pique left him. He begged her to seat herself in a well-cushioned chair of violet silk beside the fireplace. He took up a chair opposite her, crossing a leg over a knee in his fastidious manner. "This cannot be the end of it," he said, staring at the Aubusson carpet at his feet and again shaking his head.

Anne had had the entire night, which had been rather sleepless, to ponder the extraordinary situation. She had rehearsed just how she would tell Sir Arthur the truth, and so she had. At the same time, other more pertinent issues had arisen which she now addressed. "Do you know what I expect of my husband?" she queried softly.

At that, he lifted his gaze to meet hers yet remained silent.

She continued, "I expect my husband to be more concerned about my comfort, health and safety than anything else in the entire world. I expect him to set me above everyone and everything else in his life—above his closest relatives, his wealth, his club, his lands, his friends or any other obligation he might have."

He stared at her, his mouth falling slightly agape.

"We have never spoken of such things, Arthur, which I believe was my fault. From the beginning, mostly because I felt compelled to do so because you were saving my aunt and myself from the poorhouse, I kept silent about what I expected of our marriage."

"I see," he said. She had hoped he would have offered more, something in the nature of a wish that she had opened her heart more fully to him. Instead, she saw a familiar glint of censure in his eyes.

She added, "You would have expected me to have deferred to you in everything, wouldn't you?"

"Yes, of course. As your husband, yes, of course. It would only be seemly."

"And to your mother as well?"

"Naturally."

In this moment, Anne felt she understood Sir Arthur Ide completely. "Well, then, I shall explain my own views more fully to you so that perhaps, in this way, you might believe yourself to have been the victor of the contest after all. Arthur, you are much mistaken if you think I should have been a gentle, *silent* wife. Had I come to Flinthrall as your spouse, I would have early on asserted my claims as mistress of the house. Your mother would have had to turn the housekeeping keys over to me once and for all, without discussion. I would not have allowed her to continue ruling the castle, and I certainly would never have permitted her to relegate my aunt to a low, demeaning station in the household."

She watched him pale visibly. She drew in a breath and flayed him a little more. "In every situation, my wishes would have been above your mother's, and I would certainly never have allowed her to entertain guests without my permission. Flinthrall would have been known among the neighborhood as my house—not hers. Ultimately, were your mother's manners not to improve, I would certainly have insisted she be removed to the Dower House."

At that, he gasped and sank back into his chair. "I've never known you before," he said, aghast.

"No you have not; but I alone am to blame for not having revealed myself to you sooner, and for that I do beg your pardon."

"And you are not just saying these things in order to soothe my pride?" he asked, suspicious.

At that, she laughed outright. "No, Arthur, I'm afraid not. I'm certain that one day you will agree we do not suit, though I will always be flattered that you wished to make me your wife. But I've come to believe I'm sparing us both a great deal of pain. Might I suggest, however, that before you offer for another female, she understand precisely how you expect your household to be arranged once you are wed? You have treated my aunt quite shabbily, as well you know, in setting your mother over her as you have."

He did not answer her, but instead pursed his lips disapprovingly, a gesture which brought her to her feet.

Holding her hand out to him, she said, "I will say goodbye to you now. I am sorry that Richard returned to overset all your plans, but I am persuaded what has happened was just as it ought to be."

He rose to his feet and shook her hand politely. "I'll have your horse sent for," he said coolly.

"That won't be necessary," she responded, smiling.

"One of your footmen is walking my mount about the front drive for me."

Anne returned at a gentle trot to Birchingrove with a light heart and a more secure understanding of herself. She had dreaded the interview with Sir Arthur, but somehow, once she had begun her speech, she lost all fear of him and felt emboldened to speak her mind.

She realized now that she had kept herself blind to Sir Arthur's faults during the year of her betrothal to him. Yet how unhappy both of them would have been after several months of marriage, for she had spoken truly when she said she would not have been a silent wife. She had little doubt that within weeks of tying the connubial knot, she would have been engaged in a serious battle with both the Ides for supremacy at Flinthrall. How relieved she was that she no longer had to concern herself with either Sir Arthur's dictatorial manner or his mother's manipulations.

At Flinthrall Castle, Lady Ide listened in rapt wonder to the news that her beloved son was not to marry that Tandridge female after all. Silently, she blessed herself a score of times, for she knew what Anne Tandridge was—a horrible cat who would not be satisfied until she had removed her mother-in-law to the Dower House!

She said, as much to Arthur, which brought a light to his eye. "She very nearly said the exact same thing to me," he stated in some wonder.

"There—you see! My poor boy, though I've little doubt that she has bruised your innocent heart, I cannot help but feel you are well out of it; well out of it, I say!"

Sir Arthur drew in a deep breath through pinched nostrils. "You may be right, Mama. Indeed, I begin to think you are!"

Lady Ide smiled and nodded. She was silent for what she felt was an appropriate length of time, then said in her most innocent voice, "Isn't our dear Charlotte in excellent looks these days?"

Sir Arthur lifted his gaze from his copy of *The Times.* "Why, yes. Now that you mention, I recall thinking that she has become quite a handsome young woman. Handsome, indeed."

"Oh, yes. Very handsome, indeed!" She sipped her tea and sighed contentedly in response to this promising beginning.

Anne found her aunt in her bedchamber. She had not been entirely well for the past two days after confessing her misdeed in keeping the letters locked away from their rightful recipients for so many years. She was seated on a chaise lounge in her bedchamber, a warm, peach-colored cashmere shawl over her legs and a vinaigrette in her hand.

Anne drew forward a chair to sit beside her, intending to tell her about the contest.

Before she could speak, however, Mrs. Tandridge said, "Have you yet forgiven me, my dear?" Tears brimmed in her lovely blue eyes.

"Yes, of course I have," Anne said, placing a hand on her aunt's arm. "You meant only the best for me. I know your heart, that you are devoted to me as deeply as any mother could be."

Mrs. Tandridge smiled waveringly. "Very sweetly spoken, my dear. Only tell me, have you gotten rid of that awful man yet?"

At that, Anne chuckled. "Yes, of course I have."

Mrs. Tandridge shuddered elegantly. "I never liked Arthur. Not one bit. Always on his high ropes about, well, about *everything*."

"Very true, but what a hypocrite you are in having professed to adore him all these years."

"I know." She took a gentle sniff of her vinaigrette and without meeting Anne's gaze, queried, "So, tell me, just how much does Richard have?"

Anne gasped and rose abruptly to her feet. "You would ask that question!" she cried. "I, however, refuse to give you an answer. Even if I knew, I wouldn't tell you, for to own the truth, if he had come home a pauper, I wouldn't have cared. I would still have loved him and somehow married him."

"Anne, don't say that! Without at least a competence, life can be so incredibly troublesome."

"You are being absurd, as well you know, and I will not continue this ridiculous conversation. Besides, I have something very important to discuss with Richard."

"I am merely being practical, my dear, as always."

Anne leaned down and placed a kiss on her cheek. "I know, Aunt. How well I know."

When she quit her aunt's bedchamber she returned to her own room and changed into a summery frock of patterned lavender muslin which she thought quite set to advantage her blond hair. Besides, Richard had always told her how much he loved her in lavender.

When her hair was tidy as well, she gathered up Richard's letters into one of her paisley shawls and ventured downstairs. She found that Richard had just returned, looking quite handsome in his several-caped greatcoat, his brushed beaver hat and a snowy neckcloth folded in a style unfamiliar to her.

"Would that be the Mathematical?" she queried, gesturing to his cravat.

He appeared very grave as he shook his head. "No. The *trone d'amour*."

"Ah. How very romantical," she murmured, smiling.

"Please, don't do that. You almost appear to be flirting with me. You will break my heart if you smile in that manner while under my roof." When Anne continued to smile, he barked, "Are you listening to me?"

"No, not especially."

He grunted as she moved into the drawing room.

"What are you carrying in your shawl?"

"Your letters," she sighed. "I intend to read each one today, quite slowly, savoring every syllable. I'm going to begin by reading them aloud."

He removed his greatcoat and threw it over the back of a nearby chair. Before she knew quite what was happening, he had caught her arm roughly. The letters flew out of the shawl and slid into a heap on the floor.

"Why do you torture me in this manner? How dare you flaunt my letters in this, this cruel fashion? Have you no idea how much your fine little contest has destroyed my life?" His face was horribly twisted with anguish.

She let him gather her up in his arms. "Have I destroyed your life?" she asked softly.

"In a most brutal manner. I couldn't sleep last night. I have determined to leave England and return to India. I booked passage on the next ship—"

"I will follow after you, Richard," she said quietly.

"What? Anne! Anne! Why are you doing this? Teasing me as you are when you are to be married today?"

Her eyes filled with tears. "Because, you simpleton, I'm not marrying Arthur. You both were mistaken yesterday. He did not win the contest at all."

"What?"

"You won my ridiculous contest. The moment you chose to take me home on the gentler but more circuitous route near Rook's Nest, you won."

"I don't understand."

"Are you as obtuse as Arthur? Don't you see? It wasn't

a contest of speed unless you both chose to take me along the King's Highway. Only then would I have been forced to wed Arthur or whichever of you had achieved the best time."

He stared at her, bewildered. "This makes no sense at all. Are you saying that because I took you home by way of Rook's Nest, that I won your ridiculous contest?"

"That is what I've been trying to say."

He shook his head in obvious disbelief. "Yet you said nothing to me yesterday. Have you even the remotest idea how blue-deviled I've been? A pit of hell could not have been worse. You can have no idea."

"Yes I can," she responded quickly. "For I have felt the same way the past year—no, the past two years. I didn't mean to torture you, and I would have said something last night; but I knew I had to inform Arthur of his mistake before I did anything else. I just wasn't sure how to go about it."

"You saw him today, then?"

"Yes, earlier."

"Poor fellow."

She chuckled. "Only his pride smarts, I'm persuaded. I am convinced he never loved me, not really, and when I suggested the possibility that once I had become his wife I would not have been quite so sweet and demure, he appeared rather horror-struck, especially when I mentioned the possibility of his mother moving to the Dower House."

At that, the expression on Richard's face lightened. "He would not have liked that—nor would his mother."

"Not one whit."

He looked deeply into her eyes, and all the pain of the past two years melted away. Anne was caught up in the supreme sensation of loving and knowing she was loved beyond measure.

He kissed her wildly and passionately, as though he had

never kissed her before, as though he feared he would never kiss her again. She received his tender assault, basking in the beauty of his love and affection for her, returning kiss for kiss, embrace for embrace.

After a long moment, she heard a clucking sound from the hall.

Drawing back from Richard, she turned to see that Cook was standing in the doorway, the basket of kittens in her hands. "I do be that sorry to be disturbin' ye, miss; but they be hungry again, and I'm in the midst of preparing nuncheon."

Anne moved to take up the basket which held the mewing kittens. She glanced over her shoulder. "Will you come with me, Richard, while I tend to them?"

"Of course I will," he said.

"Good, for it is the least you can do. You may count these little ones your very good friends."

"Why?" he asked, bemused.

"Because they gave me the idea of having the pair of you prove yourselves to me. I kept hoping that your previous concern for them would not fail me during the contest, and I truly wanted to give Arthur an opportunity to—" She couldn't complete the sentence.

Richard reached her side and took the basket from her. "To prove his heart was a trifle warmer than you suspected?"

She nodded. "Something like that. After our picnic, I couldn't bear the thought of seeing my children treated secondary to his notion of an *al fresco* nuncheon. Although I don't mean to criticize him overly much. He is, after all, a good man—"

"Just not the proper husband for you."

"Yes, precisely."

He kissed her swiftly upon the lips and, cradling the basket in one arm, took up her arm with his own. After a time, he glanced into the basket and said, "I will have to rename the yellow one Blink, for both his eyes are now opened."

Anne chuckled and gave his arm a squeeze. "No. He should be Wink, always, for I think he always knew there was something rather ridiculous about my betrothal to Arthur."

"I always suspected he was an unusually perceptive kitten. I daresay he will grow up to be a very wise cat."

"A very wise cat, indeed."

THE RUSSIAN BLUE

by
Martha Kirkland

ONE

"Where in heaven's name is Neville?"

Miss Margaret Denby looked around the inn yard, searching for her brother, but there was no sign of the tall, dark-haired gentleman. "This is most unlike Neville to be late."

The groom gave the young lady his hand, assisting her from the antiquated carriage. "The lieutenant will be along soon, I'm sure, miss. No need for concern."

"I am not concerned exactly. It is just that Neville said he would be at the inn before I arrived, waiting to escort me the remainder of the way home, and it is out of character for him to deviate from his plans. Now, if it were James, I should not give it a thought, for anything might detain him. A horse auction, a card game, a country fair. James always means to be punctual, but he finds life much too filled with interesting distractions. Neville, on the other hand, is never distracted from his chosen course."

Margaret looked southward down the road that led ultimately to Oxfordshire, hoping to see a post chaise approaching, but if one of the "yellow bounders" was headed in their direction, its presence was not immediately discernible. There was a rather handsome private chaise visible from the coach house beyond the stables, but she knew better than to expect one of her purse-pinched brothers to have traveled in anything half so elegant.

Of her four brothers, only Frederick kept his own coach, and she had just stepped out of that bone-rattling vehicle. Heaven be praised!

Her vertebrae still complained due to the thirty miles she had traveled from the vicarage at Compton, Warwickshire, to the market town of Spittleford, and she prayed never again to set foot in that medieval torture chamber on wheels. In fact, though some might turn up their noses at traveling by post, she was not among their number, and she quite looked forward to the final forty miles to her home.

"That is, if Neville has not found some new war to fight and forgotten all about me."

She had spoken to herself, but Frederick's groom, scandalized on her war-hero brother's behalf, said, "The lieutenant would never do that, miss."

"No, of course he would not. I spoke without thinking."

She looked down the empty road again; then with a sigh, she said, "Perhaps you should take my portmanteau into the inn, George, and see if the innkeeper can furnish me with a private room while I wait for Neville. As well, you might bespeak a meal for my brother and me, for if I know him, Neville will want to eat before we return home."

"Yes, miss. I'll tell old Terwhilliger. He'll see to your needs."

Though she would have liked to stroll about to stretch her legs, Margaret followed the groom toward the entrance to The Green Man, a half-timbered, thatch-roofed building constructed in the style of many a Warwickshire dwelling. The inn was a rambling old place at least a hundred years old, and it boasted two full stories and a gabled wing.

After stepping across the well-scrubbed fieldstone floor of the entryway and stopping before a thick oak counter, the groom explained to the innkeeper who greeted him that Miss Margaret Denby, the only sister of the Reverend Mr. Frederick Denby, of Compton, was to be met within a matter of minutes by another brother, Lieutenant Neville Denby. Once he had puffed up her consequence sufficiently to insure attentive service, the groom said, "Miss will require a private room in which to wait for her brother. And when the lieutenant arrives, they will be wishful of one of your best meals before continuing their journey."

Benjamin Terwhilliger, a middle-aged fellow with a pleasant countenance and an expanding waistline that gave evidence of his enjoyment of the bill of fare at the inn, smiled and bowed politely to Margaret before returning his attention to the groom. "Happy to oblige the vicar's family," he said. "I've a room just at the top of the stairs; I'm certain miss will find it comfortable."

To Margaret he said, "Happen your brother is delayed by the rain, Miss Denby."

"Rain? But we saw no signs of inclement weather."

"Not the first drop," the groom said.

Terwhilliger explained his surmise by rubbing his left elbow. "Rheumatism. It always warns me when we're in for a good wetting, and its telling me this one may have us looking over our shoulders for the approach of Noah's ark. Happen you'd be wise, lad, to be on your way back to Compton before the rain arrives."

Margaret searched in her reticule until she found the proper vail, then handed the two coins to the groom. "Mr. Terwhilliger may be in the right of it, George. Perhaps you should return to the vicarage while it is still possible to do so."

The servant took the shillings, but he scratched his head as if pondering a riddle. "I don't know as the vicar would want me to leave you here alone, miss. You know how he is about doing what's proper."

Don't I just!

Margaret kept her retort to herself; first because no lady should utter such slang, and secondly because she did not expect the servant to appreciate the peculiarity of her situation. It was not easy being the fifth child, especially when the first four were all males!

If the truth be known, though she held all four of her tall, handsome, well-built brothers in great affection, their overprotectiveness was the bane of her existence. They treated her as though she were a child of twelve instead of a woman of almost four and twenty, and they looked out for her as though the world was filled with ogres just waiting to take advantage of their little sister.

If, when her days on earth came to an end, Margaret departed this mortal coil as a doddering, bitter old maid, she would know whom to thank for her sorry state, the fearsome foursome. She lived in a college town filled to overflowing with young men, yet every time a likely lad looked favorably upon her, he took one glance at the glowering faces of Frederick, David, James, and Neville and took himself off with all haste.

Recalled to the present, she said, "Please, do not worry about me, George. Neville will be along any minute now, and I am convinced the vicar would not wish his coach stuck in the mud somewhere between here and Compton. Furthermore," she added, just a hint of sarcasm creeping into her voice, "for those few brief seconds I will be out of sight of one of my relatives, I believe we may trust to Mr. Terwhilliger to see that I am not abducted and dragged off like so much filched poultry."

The innkeeper hid his smile. "The lady will come to no harm," he assured the groom. "Now be off with you, there's a good lad, for did you but know it, the rain is chasing you even as we speak."

"Yes, go," Margaret concurred, "and should the vicar ask, you may tell my brother that you left me well looked after."

Obviously torn as to where his duty lay, the groom hesitated, but he finally touched his forelock in respectful salute and wished the lady a pleasant journey back to Oxford. In a matter of seconds, he had climbed aboard the box and settled himself beside the coachman. Immediately, the driver lifted the reins, and the outdated carriage lumbered its way out of the inn yard.

"And now, miss," Mr. Terwhilliger said, reaching behind him to the polished oak hutch from which hung a series of thick keys, each with a numbered tag, "let me call Polly to show you to your room. You'll find her a good girl, not afraid to turn her hand to a task, and quite willing to please."

At the innkeeper's shout, the maid came running from the kitchen area at the back of the house, her mobcap falling across her forehead as a result of her haste. She appeared pleasant enough, but any similarity between the good "girl" her employer described and the thin, fortyish individual in the starched apron was purely coincidental. After bobbing a curtsy, she took the key and Margaret's portmanteau, and while Terwhilliger turned left, returning to the tap room, the maid continued beyond to a flight of narrow wooden stairs.

At the top of the flight, they stopped at the first door to the right, and while Polly fit the key into the lock, then turned it first one way then the other, jiggling the latch without success, three gentlemen strolled down the corridor, obviously coming from the gabled wing.

Always interested in seeing new people, Margaret glanced toward the trio, who were of disparate ages. One was a portly gentleman in his middle years, another was a youth about the age of her father's first-year Latin students, and the third was a well-dressed gentleman of twenty-nine or thirty.

Tall and blond and exuding an air of outdoor good health, he might well have posed for a portrait of one of the Norse gods. Margaret gave him a second look, admiring not only the cut of his clothes, but also the easy, unaffected way he moved.

The portly gentleman seemed to be counseling the younger men upon the advisability of giving their custom to a certain wine merchant on Jermyn Street, in London. "Must allow him to stock your cellar, Jonathan, my boy. Excellent selections. Good Madeira. First rate-port. And," he added, lowering his voice, "the finest brandy to be had in all of England."

"I thank you for the advice, Uncle, but I am quite satisfied with Winton Brothers. As for Albert, I doubt he will have need of such a merchant for several years yet."

"What? Oh, yes. No cellars at Oxford," replied the youth, who was ogling Margaret unashamedly as they passed by.

Since being ogled was a daily occurrence for a female reared in a college town, she was not bothered in the least by the attention and merely turned her back. Unfortunately, she could not avoid hearing the youth's comment upon her presence.

"I say, Jonathan, a smashing female that. Quite lovely, in fact, and she appears to be traveling alone. Do you suppose she is a—"

"Keep your voice down," the blond gentleman warned. "No point in being rude."

"Not rude at all," the portly gentleman declared. "Since the chit is not drab enough to be a governess or a paid companion, that leaves only one other kind of young female who travels alone. I must say, however, that I am a bit surprised at the innkeeper allowing her to stay.

Not good for business, don't you know, taking in the *demi monde.*"

At first, Margaret gasped; then the humor of the man's assumption struck her, and she was obliged to smother a laugh. What a marvelous joke on her brothers! The fearsome foursome had shielded her all her life, and the one time they were not around, she was mistaken for a light skirt.

Still smiling, she turned to watch the trio descend the stairs, and to her surprise, the blond gentleman turned to look at her as well. He must have heard her laughter, for his eyebrow was raised in question, and as she gave him stare for stare, determined not to be the first to look away, she encountered the most captivating eyes she had ever seen in her life. They were as clear and blue as a summer sky, and for just a moment Margaret fancied they held her as if by sorcery, causing a decided acceleration in her breathing. Thankfully, the gentleman broke the spell by inclining his head as though in greeting and continuing down the stairs.

"Finally," Polly said, opening the door. " 'Tis always stubborn, this lock."

The maid's words served to remind Margaret that she stood in the corridor of an inn, and after giving herself a mental shake, she hurried into the chamber, closing the door rather quickly behind her.

"Blast!" Mr. Albert Chively said upon hearing the sudden clap of thunder. "The rains are coming again. Have we not had enough weather for one year?"

"Right you are," replied his uncle, Mr. Oscar Purley. "First we'd to endure the coldest winter I can ever recall, with the Thames freezing over and people flocking to that disreputable frost fair; then the spring brings nothing but day upon day of rain. Demme if it does not make a man wish he had stayed in his own comfortable rooms on Chesterfield Street, instead of racketing about the country for some trifling bir—"

As if realizing he was about to commit a solipsism, the gentleman stopped short and glanced at his other nephew. "Not that I would have missed your mother's birthday celebration, Jonathan. Not for the world. Always enjoy these family gatherings, don't you know. 'Twas a grand week, and nothing could have equaled the ball. Makes me quite look forward to turning sixty myself."

"Coming it just a shade too brown," observed Mr. Jonathan Holm, who was not deceived by his uncle's attempt to smooth over his error. Nor was he offended by the man's blunt remark. After all, his mother's brother was a crusty old bachelor who had lived most of his fifty-eight years pleasing himself, and his nephew found nothing so very odd in the gentleman's desire to be in town in his bachelor digs.

If the truth be told, Jonathan half agreed with his uncle. Though he was sincerely devoted to both his parents, this had not been an auspicious time for him to leave London. He was sitting in his first session as a member of parliament, and there was so much he needed to learn.

Lord Liverpool, the Tory prime minister, had been so good as to invite all the new members to his home for tea, even those like Jonathan who were among the loyal opposition. Regrettably, Jonathan had been obliged to decline the invitation in favor of traveling into Warwickshire for his mother's birthday celebration. Not that Lady Holm would have faulted her only son for being absent from the festivities; after all, she had campaigned for his election. Still, he would have faulted himself.

Like the bachelor Mr. Purley, Jonathan wished he were back in town at that very minute, and not cooling his heels in some second-rate country inn with his uncle and his Oxford-bound cousin. Furthermore, if the rain should prove heavy enough to turn the roads to liquid goo, they might find themselves obliged to remain here for several days.

As if to reinforce that daunting possibility, near-deafening thunder rolled through the sky, followed by a veritable sheet of water that seemed to come from nowhere.

"Blast," Albert said again. "Another hour of this, and we might as well settle in for the evening, for there will be no more traveling this day."

"Right," agreed the young man's uncle. "What say you then, lads, to a sampling of *mein* host's home brew?"

While the gentlemen retired to the tap room, Margaret stood at the window of her chamber and stared down the road. "Where are you, Neville?" she muttered.

Logic told her she need not be concerned for a man who had chased Bonaparte's soldiers back and forth across the Peninsula for the better part of two years, then come home without a scratch to show for his months of battle. Still, he had said he would be at Spittleford, and he was not. Furthermore, she had seen only one carriage since she arrived at the inn, and that a private one that had passed by a good hour ago headed south.

When she heard the rumble of thunder, then witnessed the deluge suddenly pour from the sky like a waterfall, she knew the innkeeper's rheumatism had proved a faithful gauge. She knew as well that such a downpour would probably turn the road into a quagmire, so if Neville did not arrive within the next few minutes, he might not arrive at all that day.

Feeling bored, and just a bit cool from the rapidly dropping temperature, Margaret decided to go below stairs. She could watch for her brother just as well from the common room, and perhaps Mr. Terwhilliger would have the fire going in the large fieldstone fireplace.

After searching through her traveling bag, she grabbed up her paisley shawl and the book her sister-in-law had given her as an early birthday present and went in search of the fire. To her delight, she discovered a nice blaze going, and except for an elderly gentleman who snored softly in a chair by the window, the common room was empty. Flanking the hearth were wing chairs covered in a pleasantly faded floral chintz, and since neither chair was occupied, Margaret chose to sit with her back to the sleeping gentleman.

She had just found her place in the book when she heard the jingle of harness and the *clop, clop* of horses entering the inn yard. Hoping it might be Neville at last, she turned toward the window. To her disappointment, it was not her brother arriving, but the return of the private coach she had spied going south over an hour ago.

A liveried groom jumped down from the box, opened the coach door, and assisted a very large, very irate middle-aged woman to alight. "This is all most inconvenient," the lady said.

"Yes, ma'am," replied the groom. "Most inconvenient."

"I do not like it, I tell you."

"No, ma'am. It is not at all likeable."

Apparently not placated by the groom's sycophantic replies, she said, "But why must it turn inclement just when I am scheduled to go up to town?"

Since there was no answering such a question, the groom merely *tsk-tsk*ed, then stood aside while the lady waddled toward the door.

"Shall I bring the basket, ma'am?"

"Yes, yes, bring it in immediately, for I do not want it out of my sight."

While the groom did the lady's bidding, Margaret's curiosity got the better of her manners, and she stared at the new arrival, whose clothing was not at all consistent with that of a person who had traveled in a private carriage, accompanied by a manservant dressed in livery.

The woman's mauve gown was made of inexpensive cambric muslin, and it was far from stylish; furthermore, her chip straw bonnet might as well have borne a sign declaring that it was trimmed by the wearer, and her pelerine, though made of good merino, was at least two decades out of fashion.

"I'll fetch Mr. Terwhilliger," the groom said, stepping across the entryway to place a large, woven basket on the oak counter.

Ignoring the offer, the woman chose a more expedient method; she yelled, "Terwhilliger! Where are you, man?"

At the sound of the shrill voice, the innkeeper ran from the tap room, hurriedly wiping his hands upon his ale-stained apron. "Lady Bardmore," he said, bowing politely, "what has happened?"

Lady Bardmore? Margaret stared in surprise, for with the addition of the basket to the woman's dowdy ensemble, she appeared quite the farmer's wife come to market.

"Why has your ladyship returned?"

"You may well ask, my good man, for we were forced to turn about. The recent rains have undermined the tree roots, and with this new downpour, a very old, very large beech tree has fallen across the road, blocking the bridge to Epping." She paused for breath.

So, the bridge is blocked. Perhaps that explains why Neville is not here.

"Naturally," her ladyship continued, "I had my coachman turn around immediately. I shall remain here at The Green Man until the obstruction is removed."

Mr. Terwhilliger had the look of a goose cornered by a fox. "I . . . I shall be honored, my lady, but what of the rains? If they should not abate, you might be obliged to remain here for days. Do you not think it wisest to return to Bardmore Hall until the weather clears? In a few days, a week, perhaps, it—"

"I cannot wait a week, man! Time is of the essence,

for I have six Russian Blues ready to sell in town." She patted the basket. "With the arrival of the tsar's sister, the Duchess of Oldenburg, not to mention the expected arrival of the tsar himself, Society has gone mad for anything Russian. You cannot imagine what a blue will bring in London."

"No, my lady, I—"

"Twenty-five pounds," she said, "at the very least. And rumor has it that Prinny himself has ordered one from Countess Lieven's cousin. Depend upon it, Terwhilliger, once that information gets about, there is no knowing how much Londoners will be willing to pay for one of my little blues."

Margaret had no idea what manner of animal, vegetable, or mineral a Russian Blue might be, nor why the Prince Regent would want one; but whatever it was, it certainly cost a lot of money. Thinking she had eavesdropped long enough on a conversation that was none of her concern, she turned back toward the fire, wondering as she did so just how long she might be required to remain at the inn. She had ten pounds in her reticule, ample pin money for a young lady whose brother would meet her halfway and take care of all the expenses, but it was not nearly enough if she should be obliged to pay her own shot for several days here at The Green Man.

She was busy calculating how much the meals would cost per day when she felt something brush her ankle. When she looked down, a small kitten was rubbing his face back and forth against her boot top. He was a pretty little thing, with a short, very thick, grayish coat and eyes as green as an emerald. "Hello," she said, swooping the tiny, delicate-boned creature up and setting him in her lap, "did you escape from the stables?"

"Mew," he said in his barely audible, baby kitten voice.

"That is just what I thought, little one. But have no fear, for I will not send you back out in the cold rain.

However," she added, looking at his sweet little wedge-shaped face, "your mother was very careless to let you stray so far from her protection."

"Mew," he said again, as if agreeing with her assessment of the situation.

Margaret stroked her finger across the incredibly soft fur between his little pointed ears, and in a matter of seconds the kitten curled up in her lap and began emitting a rhythmic purr of contentment.

He appeared barely old enough to be weaned, no more than six or seven weeks, and thinking he might be chilled, Margaret pulled her shawl from around her shoulders and used one corner of it to cover the little creature.

"You sleep," she whispered, "while I get back to my book, and when the rain lets up, I will take you back to the stables."

She had just found her place on the page when Lady Bardmore let out a scream guaranteed to rouse everyone in the house, and possibly one or two who were laid to rest in the church yard.

"Heaven help me!" the lady cried, her hand upon the basket. "The blues. One of them is missing."

Noting the group of men who had gathered in the tap room doorway to see what was amiss, Mr. Terwhilliger tried to calm her ladyship. "Are you certain they are not all there, my lady? Look again, perhaps you only miscounted."

She would not be calmed. "Do you take me for an idiot?"

"No, no. Of course not, my lady. It is just—"

"They were here in the basket, all six of them, and now there are but five."

The innkeeper looked into the basket, pointing his finger as if counting the contents. "Five," he said, looking decidedly ill at ease. "But what could have happened to the sixth one?"

"Stolen!" her ladyship wailed. "Stolen from beneath my very nose. Send for the justice of the peace, Terwhilliger."

"Your ladyship, I am certain there is a good explanation for this. Perhaps the blue has only—"

"I want the squire!" she said, her voice a screech. "At once, I say, for when I find the thief, and mark my words, I will find him, I want him arrested on the instant and put in the stocks."

At Lady Bardmore's initial scream, Margaret had spun around to see what had happened. Obviously her ladyship had misplaced one of her blues, whatever they were, and she was threatening to call in the justice of the peace to arrest someone. Several men had come to the door of the tap room, and for just a moment Margaret's gaze met that of the blond gentleman who had passed her in the corridor.

Earlier she had been mesmerized by his eyes, but now she took note of the rest of him, looking him over at her leisure, or as much of him as she could see behind the young man who accompanied him. He was a full head taller than the youth, and though he was slender, he appeared very fit, his bottle green coat showing to perfection his broad shoulders.

His face was slender as well, the shape symmetrical and the features even, but he was robbed of true male beauty by a nose with a slight irregularity in the bridge. If Margaret knew anything of males—and she did!—that nose had come into contact with a fist, perhaps more than once.

What struck her most, however, more than his blond good looks and more than those sky blue eyes, was the vitality of the man. Even standing quietly in a crowd, he was vibrantly alive, like a man who had important things to do in this world and knew he was capable of doing them.

As she continued to study him, she realized some-thing—something that sent her senses reeling. He was the waking embodiment of the man who frequented her dreams, a man the complete opposite of her four dark, brawny brothers.

"No one is to leave the inn," Lady Bardmore ordered, her tone as imperious as a queen's, "until the Russian Blue is returned to me."

Because Margaret had no knowledge of her ladyship's blue thingamabob, and because the blond man had caught her watching him, and had returned her gaze, his perusal making her feel strangely giddy, she feigned an interest in the book she held open in her hand. The fact that she had no idea what was printed on the page was immaterial; it was enough that she could withdraw and take no part in what was happening.

All too aware of the man watching her, it was no won-der that Margaret did not notice Lady Bardmore wad-dling toward her until she stopped scarce three feet away.

"There!" her ladyship declared in her eardrum-pierc-ing voice. "There is the culprit."

Surprised, Margaret stared wide-eyed at the woman who stood before her, her plump arm stretched forward rig-idly, her pudgy finger pointed accusingly. "There is my blue," she said. "The thief has it yet. Someone seize this young woman before she attempts to escape with my property."

TWO

Margaret felt every eye upon her, and though no one rushed forward to capture her, she experienced a strong urge to flee. She also experienced a stirring in her lap and heard a soft, "Mew." Recalling the kitten, she slid her hand beneath the tiny creature and lifted it, shawl and all, into her arms.

"Stop her!" Lady Bardmore said, "before she absconds with the kitten."

Abscond? With a stable kitten?

"That is my Russian Blue," her ladyship said, pointing to the tiny gray nose that had worked its way from under the shawl. "And that . . . that *person* is hiding it."

"I am doing no such thing! The kitten merely went to sleep in my lap. I . . . I thought it was cold, so I covered it with my shawl."

"Ha! A likely story."

Margaret felt the heat of mortification steal up her neck. It was unbelievable that anyone should accuse her of theft, and as she glanced around the room, each face she encountered seemed to be staring at her, each pair of eyes already indicting her for the crime. Each pair, that was, save one; the sky blue eyes of the blond gentleman appeared more amused than accusing.

"Young woman," Lady Bardmore continued, "that is a

valuable cat, and I shall see you deported for this day's work."

"Deported!"

In her entire life, Margaret had never wished more to see one of her large, capable brothers bound into the room. Unfortunately, now that she finally had need of one of them, they were conspicuously absent. If she was to be cleared of this accusation, she must depend upon her own strength, her own intelligence. Taking a deep breath, she said, "Your ladyship has misinterpreted the circumstances. The kitten came to me; I did nothing to entice it."

"You must think me a mental deficient."

"No, ma'am. I merely think you have allowed yourself to become excited, and for that reason, you are not thinking clearly."

"What impertinence!" Her ladyship's impressive bosom heaved with indignation, and the pitch of her voice seemed to go up half an octave, rendering it so shrill the kitten cried out in protest and tried to hide his head beneath Margaret's arm.

"I will have you know, young woman, that my thinking is more than clear enough to see through a fabrication of lies told by a thief. Especially if you would have me believe that the kitten climbed into your lap without any assistance, then covered himself with your shawl?"

"No. Of course he did not cover himself. The fact remains that he—"

"The fact remains that you stole an animal worth a great deal of money, and now that you have been found out, you must pay the penalty for your actions."

"Excuse me," said a deep, calm voice. "How much is the feline worth?"

Margaret looked up to see the blond gentleman strolling toward her, his manner unruffled, his hand already reaching into his coat pocket.

"This is none of your concern," Lady Bardmore informed him, her tone icy.

Margaret had not believed it possible to be any more embarrassed; she was wrong. Like her ladyship, she would have liked to tell the man to mind his own business. Unfortunately, she dared not. He had already withdrawn a leather pocketbook quite thick with pound notes, and if he was willing to expend a few of them to get her out of this mess, Margaret would let him, never mind the injury to her pride. Neville could repay him when he arrived.

The gentleman was undeterred by her ladyship's icy command to be off. "If you are wishful of selling the animal, ma'am, I shall be happy to pay the price. You have but to name it."

Her ladyship bit her lower lip, as if deep in thought; then she said, "Forty pounds."

"No," Margaret protested. "You told Mr. Terwhilliger the blues were worth twenty-five."

"Ah, ha! So you betray your own guilt."

"I do nothing of the kind. I heard you talking from where I sat here by the fire. That does not mean I left my chair and snuck over to lift the kitten from your basket."

At her words, everyone turned to look at the basket that still sat upon the oak counter, and as if on cue, a small, furry head peaked out and surveyed the area. Obviously perceiving this as an opportunity not to be missed, the animal crawled out of the woven container onto the smooth wood. A moment later he was followed by a second, then a third kitten. The fourth would have made his bid for freedom as well had he not gotten one of his back paws tangled in the handle.

"Meow!" he wailed, terror strengthening his baby cry. "Meooow!"

As if he had warned his siblings of impending doom, the other three kittens scurried down the side of the counter and fled, one dashing down the corridor and up the stairs, the remaining two scurrying past the many pairs of feet in the doorway to lose themselves inside the tap room.

"Quick!" Lady Bardmore yelled. "Catch them!"

While several men went to do her bidding, one running up the stairs, the others rushing about noisily, yelling good-natured insults at one another as if involved in some sort of game, her ladyship turned to the blond gentleman. "Twenty-five," she said quickly, as if worried he might renege on his offer to buy.

Without a word, he counted out five five-pound notes and offered them to her. She grabbed the money, stuffed it inside her glove, then waddled off toward the tap room. "Do not manhandle them," she called to no one in particular. "They are valuable animals."

Margaret still held the kitten who had hidden beneath her arm, and now she lifted it out and held it toward the blond gentleman. "Here you are," she said. "At twenty-five pounds for the purchase, I sincerely hope you like felines."

"As a matter of fact, I have little fondness for them. Horses, dogs, and pretty ladies," he said, a slight lift to his eyebrow, "those are the only creatures who interest me."

Ignoring the implication of his remark about pretty ladies, she said, "If you do not care for cats, then why did you buy this one?"

"Why? I should think that was obvious. I bought it for you."

"For me? But, I—"

Margaret could not finish the statement, for she had just remembered what the man he had called Uncle had said. The man had mistaken her for one of the *demimonde*, the kind of woman who would think nothing of accepting a gift worth twenty-five pounds from a stranger. At the time Margaret had thought the mistake quite amusing. Now, of course, it was not so funny. In fact, it was almost as mortifying as being accused of theft.

Deciding it would be far more embarrassing to try to disabuse him of his erroneous belief than to just let it be, she said, "I thank you, sir, but I already have a cat."

"In that case," he said, a smile pulling at the corners of his well-shaped mouth, "you now have two."

She would have protested, but she became ensnared once again by those blue eyes. When the man smiled, his eyes held a devilish twinkle, and the skin at the outer corners crinkled in a way that had the strangest effect upon Margaret, causing a wave of little flutters inside her midsection.

As if recalling his manners, he made her a very gallant bow. "Allow me to introduce myself. I am Jonathan Holm, at your service, ma'am."

Common courtesy obliged her to acknowledge his introduction. "Sir," she said, inclining her head politely.

When she added nothing more, he said, "And may I have the pleasure of knowing who you are?"

He was asking her name! There could be no doubt about it; he, too, believed her to be a light skirt. Under these unusual circumstances, a gentleman *might* introduce himself to a lady, but he would never be so forward as to ask her name. Still, Mr. Jonathan Holm had done her a service, and it would be churlish of her to give him a set down after he had saved her from a night in the stocks.

"I am Miss Margaret Denby," she replied.

He smiled again, and Margaret was obliged to ignore the veritable tidal wave of flutters crashing against her ribs.

"I am pleased to make your acquaintance, Miss Denby. Am I to understand that you are at the inn alone?"

"For the moment only," she said, feeling a blush travel

from the top of her head all the way to her booted feet. "I was to be met, but there was obviously some sort of trouble near Epping, for Neville has not yet arrived."

The gentleman did not even bat an eye. "Then, Mr. Neville's loss is my gain. Since it appears the rain will oblige us to remain here at The Green Man at least until tomorrow, would you be so kind, Miss Denby, as to join three rather bored bachelors for dinner?"

Margaret's initial inclination was to accept the invitation, for she was admittedly curious about Jonathan Holm, who was so like the man of her dreams. Of further inducement was the fact that an opportunity seldom came her way to be in company with a gentleman without having to tolerate the daunting chaperonage of one or the other of her brothers. And yet, there was no denying the facts: the man was a stranger, and she was alone, without even a servant to protect her reputation. With regret, she declined his offer.

"You are very kind, sir, but I think not."

Having refused him, she rose from the chair, gathered her shawl, her book, and her newly acquired kitten, and quit the common room. She knew the man watched her as she climbed the stairs, for she felt the warmth of his gaze touching her neck, her shoulders, her back. Resolved to ignore the tingling sensation that skittered up and down her spine, she forced herself to walk slowly, her head held high.

Once she reached the privacy of her bedchamber, she leaned against the door and drew in a deep, steadying breath, happy to be free of Jonathan Holm's scrutiny, though she fancied she could still feel his presence in the room below. She stayed in her bedchamber for the remainder of the day and all of that evening, getting acquainted with the Russian Blue and seeing no one except Polly, who brought the kitten a saucer of shredded chicken and Margaret a pot of tea and some sandwiches.

The rain continued throughout the night, and by morning, Neville still had not arrived.

Margaret rose early the next morning. The rain had stopped just after daybreak, but she had been awake long before the light peeped through the faded linen hangings at the window. An unaccustomed noise, a sort of purring sound, had interrupted her dreams. If dreams they were.

Still in a sort of half sleep, she had imagined she heard Jonathan Holm's deep voice bidding her share a laugh with him. His was the kind of mellow baritone that never failed to please, and she decided she could listen to him speak for hours without tiring of the sound. The thought had only just formed in her consciousness when something touched her earlobe.

"Unh unh," she muttered, reaching up to brush away whatever had disturbed her. To her surprise, her fingers encountered something soft and furry. Not immediately remembering her unplanned acquisition of the day before, she gasped and sat up quickly.

"Mew," said the kitten, who sat like a miniature sphinx on Margaret's pillow, staring at her as if pondering her peculiar nonfeline features.

"Little one," she muttered, lying back down with a sigh of relief. "You gave me a fright."

As if to demonstrate the foolishness of her fears, the kitten touched a tiny paw to her earlobe once again.

"Yes, I see what you are about, sir, but before you start deluding yourself as to the order of things, pray allow me to make one thing perfectly clear. *You* are the cat, and *I* am the cat owner. You may not wake me simply because it suits your purpose."

To illustrate his total lack of interest in discussing logic with an inferior being, the blue stretched out his right rear leg and began to pay special attention to the grooming of his short, thick fur.

"So," she said, "you mean to pretend you do not hear me, do you? You will catch cold on that, for I assure you, I am a woman not to be trifled with." Lifting the kitten from the pillow, she held him close to her face, where he rubbed his incredibly soft and silky forehead against her chin to their mutual satisfaction. "Now that we understand each other," she said, "I propose to dress and take myself outside. I feel the need of a little exercise."

Matching the deed to the words, she threw back the cover, padded barefoot across the uneven wooden floor to set the kitten in the box of dirt the maid had procured for him, then returned to the washstand where she poured water from the ewer into the shallow crockery basin.

Unfortunately, before she had finished her ablutions, the rain came again, hitting against the window with such force Margaret marveled it did not break through the glass. "Drat," she said. "Now I will be cooped up in this room for the entire day."

Appalled by the idea of even one more minute of this self-imposed incarceration, she decided to go below stairs. As a guest, she was entitled to the amenities of the establishment, if amenities there be, and she meant to avail herself of them. If nothing else, she would break her fast in the common room, where she could at least watch the comings and goings of the other guests.

The decision made, she left the kitten curled into a little blue-gray ball in the middle of the bed; then she followed her nose to the source of several tantalizing aromas, among them kippers, basted eggs, and the delightfully yeasty smell of popovers. Against the far wall of the common room stood a polished oak buffet, and upon that ancient board reposed several covered platters from which the guests were free to serve themselves. The seat-

ing arrangements were informal, and two cloth-covered
refectory tables had been drawn up quite near the fireplace for those who had not bespoken a private dining
room.

A white-haired couple was seated at the larger of the
tables, quietly sipping steaming cups of chocolate, while
at the smaller table a young man applied himself with
apparent gusto to his meal. Recognizing the youth as one
of the traveling companions of Mr. Jonathan Holm, Margaret asked Mr. Terwhilliger to seat her at the table with
the elderly couple.

As it transpired, it was a happy choice, for the elderly
couple, an attorney and his wife, were returning from a
visit with their newest grandchild, and they were more
than pleased to find themselves in possession of a pair
of willing ears. They waited only until Margaret had returned with her food to begin their description of the
new offspring, starting with the curls on his tiny head
and ending with his pink toes. While they talked, the
young gentleman at the opposite table attempted to make
eye contact with Margaret, smiling at her over the rim of
his coffee cup.

She tried to ignore his ill-bred behavior, but after a few
moments he rose from his table and approached her.
"Good morning, ma'am," he said. "May I inquire after
the health of the little kitten?"

The elderly gentleman paused in middescription of his
grandson's christening and stared at the youth who had
been so rude as to interrupt their conversation. As for
Margaret, so great was her embarrassment that she could
not think where to look.

How dare the young man approach a lady in such bra-
zen fashion, as though she were known to him! Thankfully, she was not obliged to give him the cut direct, for
Mr. Holm chose that auspicious moment to enter the
room. As if grasping the situation at a glance, he said,

"There you are, Cousin. I wondered where you had gotten to so early."

After linking his arm with the young man's, he inclined his head politely toward the three at the table. "Miss Denby," he said. Then to the older couple, "Ma'am. Sir. I bid you good morning."

"Mr. Holm," Margaret replied.

She was grateful to him for not remaining and obliging her to introduce him. Instead, he bowed again, then took himself and his young relative to the other table where they soon became engrossed in quiet conversation.

As soon as her companions declared themselves replete, Margaret excused herself and hurried back to her bedchamber, relieved to be away from the common room—the scene of yet another embarrassing episode. First she had been accused of being a thief, and now she had been accosted like some common strumpet.

She would not go below stairs again, she decided, lest something worse befall her. "Not if I expire of boredom."

"Mew," replied the kitten, who was her sole audience.

For the next several hours, she alternated between playing with the kitten and attempting to read her book. In time, however, she grew heartily bored with her situation. It was her growing ennui that sent her racing to answer the knock at her bedchamber door.

Half expecting to see the maid, Polly, Margaret was rendered speechless to discover Mr. Jonathan Holm standing in the corridor, a smile upon his handsome face.

"Good afternoon, Miss Denby. I hope I do not intrude upon your privacy."

"No, sir," she said, her voice noticeably breathless.

"I have come, ma'am, to offer you my apologies for any embarrassment my impetuous young cousin may have caused you this morning. The lad is only just turned eighteen, and he is not as savvy in company as he would like to think. As for his behavior, he has been apprised of his *faux pas* and is quite contrite. Therefore, if you should wish to venture below stairs in future, rest assured that nothing similar will happen."

"Thank you, sir. I had begun to feel as though these walls were inching ever closer."

He chuckled. "I suspected as much."

Margaret smiled, unable to resist his charm, for he had a way of looking directly at a person, as though interested in their every word.

"I beg you will let me make it up to you, Miss Denby."

"That is not necessary, sir."

"I feel it is," he said. After searching her face, he appeared to come to a decision. "Dare I risk a second rebuff? Would you hand me my head on a platter if I renewed my invitation to you to join my uncle, my cousin, and me for dinner?"

Margaret's first thought was to refuse the invitation, for no lady would dine with three strange men. After a moment's consideration, however, two things changed her mind. First, she had only ten pounds in her reticule, and with the continued rain she had not the least idea how long that money would have to last her. Secondly, now that the gentleman had assured her no further embarrassing incidents would occur, Margaret felt her old spirit return, and some imp inside her bid her do something rather daring while she was free of the oppressive protectiveness of the fearsome foursome.

"I am all out of platters, Mr. Holm. Therefore, your head is safe. Furthermore, I should be delighted to join you and your relatives for dinner."

"Excellent."

Jonathan had watched the young woman's face while she considered his invitation. She had needed to think about it, possibly because she knew the unexplainably tardy Mr. Neville would not approve. And why should he? If she were in *his* keeping, Jonathan would certainly not have wanted her dining with another man. But then, he would not have left her to travel alone, unprotected.

Whatever this Neville fellow might have to say to the matter at some later time, Miss Denby had decided to do as she pleased for the evening. A rather impish light had shown in those soft green eyes, and Jonathan had known the moment she made the decision to suit herself regarding his invitation.

He was delighted, of course, for what man would not enjoy an evening spent in the company of a pretty woman? And she was pretty. No longer in her first blush of youth, she was already showing signs of the real beauty to come. A velvet band held the gathered muslin of her dress beneath her rounded bosom, revealing curves enough to catch the eye of any male, while medium brown tendrils that had worked loose from her coiffeur kissed her temples, brushing against slightly darker eyebrows that were a perfect frame to her green eyes.

She was one of the few females he had met who actually possessed that complexion touted as English Rose, and Jonathan could imagine the pleasure it would give a man to rub his hand against her satiny skin.

Furthermore, she showed none of the hardness so often discernible in females who eschewed the role of wife and mother in favor of a less permanent arrangement. In fact, from her speech Jonathan had the notion she was well-educated. Unusual, of course, for one of the *demimonde*, but for his part he liked intelligent women. If the truth be known, it was the lack of depth in the young ladies presented to his notice this Season that had kept him from paying special attention to any one of them.

The leader of his party had already hinted to him that if he wished to advance in parliament, he would need a clever wife. "And if possible," his mentor had said, "choose one with exemplary family connections and a handsome dowry."

Jonathan had taken the advice to heart, especially the part about brains and connections. As for the handsome dowry, he did not need to hang out for a rich wife. He had three thousand a year left him by his maternal grandfather, and if that was not a fortune, it was certainly a comfortable living. Also, though his father was only sixty-two, and robust enough to live another quarter century—praise heaven!—upon the gentleman's demise, Jonathan would inherit the baronetcy and a very profitable estate.

"What time?" Miss Denby asked, bringing his thoughts back to the present. "I imagine they keep country hours here."

"I have no doubt of it, ma'am. Shall I call for you at half past five?"

THREE

"Mark my words, miss," Polly said, holding out the jonquil lustring dinner dress she had just ironed, "naught but ill will come of it. Why, everyone knows the only good cat is a stolen cat. 'Tis bad luck to buy one."

"Everyone may be in the right of it," Margaret said, stepping into the dress, then turning so the servant could do up the tapes and hooks, "but I did not buy this particular feline. Mr. Holm purchased him. And though I have no doubt my brother will repay the gentleman once he arrives, surely any bad luck will have worn itself out by that time."

The maid *tsk tsk*ed, apparently unconvinced.

"Besides," Margaret added, "how much harm could such a tiny creature do?" She glanced toward the bed where the blue-gray kitten lay in the center of the counterpane. Only moments ago he had been watching them as if following every word of their conversation; but now his tiny eyelids had fallen shut, and he slept.

The maid put her finger across her thin lips. "Shh," she warned, "mind what you say, for 'tis unwise to speak before a sleeping cat. Them as do so soon find their secrets revealed and their plans exposed to them as would do them mischief."

"But who would wish to do me mischief?"

"Who can say, miss? All I know is, them as speak before a sleeping cat will live to rue the day."

Familiar with most of the popular superstitions, Margaret supposed next she would hear that the bread dough in the kitchen would not rise, or that the loaves had burned to cinders, all because of the presence of one little kitten. Thankfully, she was spared further dire prophesies by the sound of a knock at the door.

After stepping into her yellow kid slippers, she nodded for the maid to answer the knock. It was Jonathan Holm, looking tall, lean, and heart-stoppingly handsome in an evening coat of dusty black worn over a silver waistcoat and slate gray pantaloons.

"Good evening," he said. "Dare I hope, ma'am, that you are one of that rare breed, a punctual female?"

"Since there is no way to answer that remark without condemning my entire sex, I shall ignore all but your greeting, sir, and wish you a good evening as well."

After a moment's hesitation, he smiled, inclining his head in a brief bow. "I see I shall need to watch what I say with you, ma'am."

"Oh, no. You may say whatever you like. However, if you choose to give voice to blanket statements, I make no promise to let them go unchallenged."

Surprise was writ plainly upon his face, but after a moment he chuckled. "Good heavens," he said, "come along, do, for time is wasting. I want you to meet my uncle while the vinegar is still flowing in your veins. I am persuaded this will prove to be a most interesting dinner."

As it turned out, Margaret had a delightful time. They had the common room to themselves, for the other guests at the inn, Lady Bardmore included, had obviously chosen to dine in private rooms. Since there were just the four of them, only the smaller of the two oak tables was set, and for all practical purposes, theirs was a private parlor.

Though she doubted a more disparate quartet had ever broken bread at that table, Margaret thoroughly enjoyed the evening, for it was unlike anything in her previous experience.

Mr. Albert Chively, after stumbling through an apology for his behavior that morning, assumed an air better suited to a man of thirty, and during the entire meal he tried all within his power to strike up a flirtation with her. As for Mr. Oscar Purley, the uncle of both the gentlemen, his conversation seemed limited to hunting, horses, cards, and potable spirits, and once he discovered that Margaret was without opinion on any of those subjects, he applied himself to his dinner without further interruption.

"So. Er, um, *so,*" Mr. Chively said, lowering his voice for the second utterance, "how does the kitten fare, Miss Denby?"

Margaret pretended not to notice his vocal shift; instead she smiled pleasantly at him. "The kitten appears content, Mr. Chively. I had thought he might feel the loss of his littermates, but he seems to be adjusting quite well to his new, solo existence."

"Please, ma'am. Call me Albert."

Since he was still a youth, Margaret complied with his request. "Why, thank you, Albert."

"And what shall I call you?" he asked, leaning his elbows on the table and gazing at her in a manner he must have thought debonair.

Margaret found his attempts to charm her amusing in the extreme; after all, she had watched four brothers go through this stage of adolescence. On the other hand, she was unsure if he would know when to draw the line if she did not draw it for him, so she replied, "You may call me Miss Denby."

Jonathan Holm was seized by a fit of coughing, but Margaret had the suspicion that the paroxysm was feigned to cover a laugh.

"Speaking of names," the afflicted gentleman said, "have you chosen one for the Russian Blue?"

"Tyger, Tyger," she replied.

"Tiger?" Albert said. "Is that not a rather ferocious name for such a small animal? Furthermore," he continued in his pseudo-jaded voice, "if I am not mistaken, tigers come from India, not Russia."

"I believe, Albert, that Miss Denby is making a literary allusion."

When the young gentleman stared blankly, his cousin continued. "The name comes from Mr. William Blake's *Songs of Innocence/Songs of Experience.* 'Tyger, Tyger, burning bright; in the forests of the night.' "

"Oh, yes, of course. I see," Albert replied, the confused look on his face giving the lie to his declaration of understanding. "It is a sort of pun. Very clever, Miss Denby."

"Very," Jonathan said, lifting his glass in salute.

While he sipped the white wine, he studied the dark-haired beauty over the edge of his goblet. She would bear watching, for she was, indeed, clever. Beauty *and* brains. A dangerous combination.

Was hers, he wondered, a song of innocence or one of experience? If the truth be told, he was having difficulty with the answer to that question. So far she had handled Albert's puppyish attempts at flirtation with adroitness, parrying them without giving offense, but would she continue to dismiss the lad if she should discover that his father was one of the wealthiest men in England?

"Demme fine wine," his uncle said, adding his mite to the conversation. "Think I'll ask the innkeeper if I may purchase a few bottles. Take a pipe if he's got it." He emptied his goblet, then smacked his lips in satisfaction. "Yes, demme fine wine. I'll vow Winton Brothers has nothing to match it. If we remain at the inn through tomorrow, think I'll just take a look in Terwhilliger's cellar. Beginning to think it's true what they say about an ill wind blowing good."

Jonathan glanced at Miss Denby to see if she would correct his uncle's misquoted adage. Though she returned his gaze for several moments, obviously enjoying their mutual amusement, she made no comment, merely smiled and lowered her lashes.

"Come, come, Miss Denby," Jonathan said, lifting the wine carafe, "allow me to replenish your goblet. I believe you have run out of vinegar."

The kitten woke her again the next morning, but this time Margaret offered no objections, for if her ears were not playing her false, the rain had stopped.

"Hallelujah!" she said. "Please let it be gone for good."

"Meow!" her companion said, not at all pleased by her noisy outburst.

As if in apology, she stroked his head until he settled back down on the pillow. "I see it is quite all right for *you* to disturb *me*, but the same standard does not apply to my behavior."

"Prrrr," he replied softly, nuzzling his head into her palm in hopes of encouraging her to further displays of affection.

Longing to be out-of-doors, if only for a short time, Margaret told him he was fast becoming spoiled; then she threw back the covers and went straight to the washstand. Once her face and teeth were clean, she combed and pinned up her long hair; then she pulled on her sturdy walking boots, donned a sprigged muslin that was far from new, and topped it with a jasper green kerseymere cloak. After bringing the hood up over her head, she quit the room and descended the stairs.

From the kitchen region at the back of the ground-floor corridor, the homey sound of spoons clanging against pots greeted her ears, and the sweet smell of porridge teased her nostrils. At that moment, however, Margaret was more interested in fresh air than in breaking her fast, so she hurried toward the front entrance and out the heavy wooden door.

Not unexpectedly, the morning was cool, the air was thick with moisture, and the inn yard and the road were stretches of near viscous goo just waiting to suck up the boots of the unwary. Fortunately, there was no fog, so Margaret felt reasonably safe in exploring a bit of the village. After determining that the grassy verge on the side of the lane offered secure footing, she turned right, passed beneath the rectangular swinging sign depicting The Green Man, and strolled toward the two dozen or so shops that lined the high street of Spittleford.

It was a small village, with only the stone-based market cross, which reached eight feet into the air, to indicate that it was a market town. Familiar with such towns, she knew that four days out of every week farmers and craftsmen set up stalls from which they exhibited and sold their crops and wares. With the recent heavy rains making travel difficult, it was no surprise that no one had come that day to trade. In fact, the high street was empty save for Margaret and a tall gentleman who had only that moment stepped from a saddler's shop.

Even from a distance, she recognized the broad shoulders and the assured posture of Mr. Jonathan Holm. As if feeling her presence, he looked in her direction, and after a momentary pause, he lifted his tan beaver hat in salute and walked toward her. He moved with purpose, and even at a distance Margaret fancied she could feel the force of his energy.

The fancy did not diminish as he drew near. There was something about him, a vibrancy of personality; it was in his warm smile, in those summer blue eyes, even in his blond hair, which seemed almost a substitute for the absent sun.

Beware, wisdom told her. *Those who would get too close to the sun do so at their own peril.*

"Well met, Miss Denby."

"Sir," she replied, curtsying. "I did not expect to come upon an acquaintance at such an early hour."

"Nor I," he said. "I bethought an errand, and the execution of it gave me a good excuse to be out and about."

"Was an excuse necessary?"

"Of a certainty. In such weather as this, one risks being labeled a lunatic for quitting a comfortable chair by the fire."

"Rest assured, sir, that I will utter no such animadversions, since I, too, felt the lure of wider spaces. There, unfortunately, our similarities end."

"Oh? And in what ways are we dissimilar?"

"Apparently I lack your imagination, for it never occurred to me to invent an errand to protect me from being thought a bedlamite."

"Very short-sighted of you," he said. Then, without asking or receiving consent, he lifted her hand and tucked it in the crook of his arm. "Shall we?" he asked, indicating the far end of the village.

This close to the man, Margaret felt a hum of awareness resonate throughout her person. A faint whiff of sandalwood shaving soap emanated from his skin, enticing her to breathe deeply of the masculine, cedar scent; while at the same time, the feel of his rock-hard arm beneath her hand caused a noticeable slowing down in the action of her lungs.

At one point, she turned her head to look up at him, and though he seemed conscious of her appraisal, he remained silent. After allowing her a few moments quiet examination, he said, "Well, Miss Denby, what is your verdict? Have you drawn a conclusion regarding my profile?

Should I don a mask to keep from frightening the local children?"

Though Margaret's thoughts had run more in the direction of the possible number of female hearts broken by that particular profile, she responded to his foolishness by stating that she believed a mask unnecessary. "On such a day as this, the children are not likely to leave their homes."

He looked down at her, a smile pulling at the corners of his mouth. "I see the vinegar is flowing once again in your veins."

Though she knew he was teasing her, she pretended to be taken aback by his statement. "Oh, sir. Did I give offense? Ought I to have praised your manly charms?"

He gave her a sidelong look that was half astonishment, half amusement.

Unrepentant, she continued, "If I had realized you were on a fishing expedition, I am persuaded I could have thought of some suitable compliment. You must forgive my lack of finesse, sir, for I am but a country girl, unversed in the ways of you town beaus and dandies."

"Dandies! Now you have gone too far. It may interest you to know, madam, that I am not a member of the dandy set."

She sighed dramatically. "There, did I not say I lacked finesse? Should I have ranked you with the Macaronis?"

With this he laughed aloud. "Fine words from a damsel who only moments ago promised to utter no animadversions. Persist in this name calling, Miss Country Girl, and I shall not be responsible for the consequences."

"Do I detect a threat?"

"Without question."

She looked up at him again, her green eyes wide with affected innocence. "Never say you would toss me into the mud."

"No," he replied, dragging out the vowel, "I had a slightly more enjoyable form of retribution in mind."

"Enjoyable for whom?" she asked, her eyes now alight with laughter.

"Who can say, madam? Who can say?"

Earlier Jonathan had been just a bit taken aback by her examination of his face, for she had looked at him as if trying to determine what manner of man lay behind the facade of his features. During her scrutiny, she had exhibited none of the coquetry one might expect from a female of her chosen life-style; in fact, her look had almost a guileless quality to it, an honesty that cut right to the heart of the matter.

Then she had answered his teasing about the need for a mask with a teasing of her own, and to his surprise, he had found her as refreshing as the morning air. He was less surprised a few minutes later to discover within himself a desire to take her in his arms and kiss her full, satiny lips. Unfortunately—or, perhaps, fortunately—such activity was prohibited, for they stood in the middle of a public street; otherwise, Jonathan might have been tempted to show her just what sort of retribution a saucy minx could expect.

They continued their stroll, staying on the right side of the high street where they passed several half-timbered shops: the saddler's, a combination seamstress and millinery store, a cobbler's, and as they neared the end of the businesses, a blacksmith's and lastly a horse-trading corral. It was doubtful if they could cross to the other side of the village without becoming one with the mud, and since the shops that awaited them on that side included the butcher's and the pig killer's, the outdoor enthusiasts decided to continue down the sloping street to where it ended at a centuries-old stone packhorse bridge.

They stopped midway on the bridge, which was erected over what was probably, under normal circumstances, a shallow, peaceful brook, and as people will do the world over, they rested their hands on the rough parapet and leaned over to view the water. Up and down the length of the brook, pale green willow trees grew almost to the water's edge, while in the distance, past a small gray stone church and an ancient churchyard, lay a wide sweep of prosperous-looking pastureland dotted here and there with clusters of white sheep. The green pastures seemed to go on forever, traveling up the shoulder of the far hills and not stopping until they reached the clouds hanging low in the sky.

Jonathan could imagine that at most times this spot would be enchantingly tranquil, inviting a person to stop and enjoy the gentle lapping of the clear water over the occasional boulder. After the heavy rains, however, the water was muddy, and several feet deep, and it raced southward with a surprising current that made his companion shiver.

"Are you cold, Miss Denby? Shall we turn back?"

"Yes," she replied, her tone devoid now of all playfulness, "I believe I have had enough of nature for one day."

They turned and retraced their steps, and for the next quarter hour, as they walked through the town, his companion was quiet, apparently lost in private thoughts. Just before they reached the market cross, she looked up at him, gave him a half-hearted smile, and begged his pardon for being such poor company. "I fear I am become as dismal as the day."

"I cannot agree, Miss Denby. Any man must consider himself fortunate to have such a pretty woman on his arm."

Noting the sudden coolness in her expression at his automatic compliment, he added rather hastily, "And I feel especially blessed to have spent a goodly number of minutes in your company without being subjected to another rude reading of my character."

At this she chuckled. "I thought you had forgiven me my lack of tact, sir, on the understanding that I am but a—"

"Yes, I know. You are a simple country girl."

"Not at all," she corrected, her eyes filled with mischief, "I never used the word 'simple.'"

Nor was she, Jonathan thought. Not by a country mile. Miss Margaret Denby was as sharp as a freshly honed razor, and he suspected she could be just as cutting if required to suffer fools overlong.

They had reached the sign of The Green Man when Jonathan gave in to an impulse and asked what had upset her at the bridge.

Far from snubbing him as his impertinent question deserved, she answered frankly. "I was thinking of Neville. After seeing for myself how treacherous a gentle brook can become when swollen, I bethought the possible condition of the Thames. In order to meet me, Neville was obliged to cross the river twice. I pray no accident has befallen him. He can be quite overbearingly stodgy at times, but I should be heartbroken if anything happened to him."

"Yes. Of course. I had quite forgotten about Mr. Neville."

Jonathan had purposefully put the young lady's protector from his thoughts. Upon being reminded of the fellow—"overbearingly stodgy," she had called him—he had felt an unexpected surge of anger travel through his entire body, anger that would, in another man, have passed for jealousy. Not that *he* was jealous. Far from it. It was just that he liked Margaret Denby, who was no ordinary light skirt.

A country girl, she had called herself, and Jonathan was beginning to think she was just that. Though she was possessed of a fine brain and a quick wit, and apparently a better education than the average female of his acquaintance, there was an unspoiled quality about her, an aura of innocence that had not yet been eroded by her chosen life-style.

He hated to think of that innocence becoming tarnished, and as they bore left and passed through the entrance to the inn, Jonathan found his hands balling into fists. To his surprise, he knew a strong desire to rearrange the face of the mysterious Mr. Neville.

"I say, Miss Denby," Albert Chively called from the refectory table nearest the fireplace, "hello."

Jonathan's young cousin lifted a fork stacked high with basted eggs and shaved ham. "Have you broken your fast, ma'am? I recommend the eggs. First-rate ham, too. Won't you join me?"

"Meow!"

The reply came not from the young lady, but from a blue-gray kitten who jumped up on the table as if in answer to Albert's invitation. After settling himself comfortably on the end of the table, the feline fixed his attention upon the diner's plate. "Mew," he uttered pitifully, as if only moments away from starvation.

"Mrrow," added a second voice.

The newcomer followed her sibling onto the table, but apparently lacking the decorum of her brother, she sauntered right up to Albert, her tiny gray nose twitching with interest. She must have found nothing to dislike in the aroma of the chosen breakfast, for without so much as a by-your-leave, she made a swift swipe with her little paw, commandeering the ham from the gentleman's fork. Then, as though such rag manners were quite good enough for a second-rate inn, she sat back on her haunches, totally disregarding the outraged look on the young man's face, and began to devour the stolen morsel.

"Here now," Albert protested, "none of that." Only when the third kitten joined his fellows did Mr. Chively swing his arms about to shoo them away.

"No, no, my dears," Lady Bardmore called from the bottom of the stairs. "Come away at once! Here kitty, kitty, kitty. Do not eat the young man's food, for we know nothing of him, and he may be sickening from some ailment you could contract."

The face of the supposed disease carrier grew red with outrage, but before he could protest her ladyship's maligning of his health, Margaret hurried over to the table, swooped all three kittens into her arms, and conveyed them to their owner, who wore her bonnet and pelisse, as though intending to go outside.

"Oh, thank you," Lady Bardmore said, holding open the woven basket so Margaret could deposit the furry threesome into its depths. Obviously forgetting her accusation of two days ago, her ladyship said, "How kind of you, my dear. I mean to take the blues up to the vicarage. They can run around safely there, and I am persuaded the vicar will not object in the least to taking them in for a day or two until I can continue on to London."

"An excellent idea, ma'am. Can you manage alone, or do you need assistance? I should be happy to—"

"No!" her ladyship interrupted, clutching the basket to her plump bosom as if suddenly recalling that the young woman before her had purloined one of the original six kittens. "That young man can assist me."

The young man in question, being the same disease-ridden person whose ham the kitten had snatched, protested this cavalier assumption that he was her ladyship's to command. "As you can see, ma'am, I am at table. Surely the stables of this establishment must be filled with grooms and postboys who would be only too happy to carry the animals for you."

Lady Bardmore dismissed his protest with a wave of her plump hand. "Do not be tiresome, sir. You must have eaten your fill by now, else you would not have been trying to entice my Russian Blues with the scraps. Come along, do, there's a good fellow, and take these kittens. Young bones make quick work of errands, and you should be back here in no time."

Though Albert looked to his cousin for help, none was forthcoming, and while he muttered beneath his breath about persons who used their age and social position to impose their will upon others, he took the basket from her ladyship and hastened toward the door. "I shall return," he called over his shoulder. "Do not let anyone remove my plate."

"Poor Albert," Margaret murmured.

"Not at all," Jonathan replied, not bothering to hide his laughter "It will do him no harm to make himself useful. Because of his father's wealth, Albert has been a bit cosseted. He—" Jonathan stopped short, remembering too late that he had hoped to keep it from her that Albert's father was one of the richest men in England.

"Oh?" she said. "Is Albert's father all that wealthy?"

Damnation! She was too quick by half. Thankfully, Jonathan was not obliged to answer her question, for at that moment Albert came rushing back into the inn, his breathing labored. "Jonathan! Miss Denby! Help! One of the kittens reached out and scratched me on the hand, and I dropped the basket. Now all five of the cursed varmints have escaped, each running in a different direction, and Lady Bardmore is threatening to make me pay for the lot. At fifty pounds per kitten!"

FOUR

"Catch them! Catch them!" Lady Bardmore screamed, succeeding in nothing so much as adding further chaos to the situation.

"There is one!" Albert cried. Since Mr. Chively held a squirming ball of blue-gray fur in each hand, he inclined his head toward a kitten who was trying valiantly to scale the half-timbered front wall of the inn. "Grab him!"

"Right you are," muttered Lady Bardmore's groom, who had come from the stables at the sound of his employer's screams. While he fetched the climbing kitten, one of the inn's young ostlers cornered another of the escapees behind a rain barrel.

"Come 'ere, you little varmint," the ostler ordered. As he reached around the overflowing keg, he bumped it with his shoulder, causing it to tip slightly and spill a few drops of water on the hiding kitten.

"Hssst! Hssst!" protested the trapped feline, indignant at the sudden dousing. "Hssstt," the animal repeated when the ostler grabbed him by the scruff of the neck and lifted him out.

Margaret, perceiving the last of the five, who thought himself hidden because his small head was tucked behind an oaken bucket, crept slowly forward. When she was but inches away, she bent and slipped her left hand beneath the kitten's chest, scooping him up.

"Meoow!" he howled, squirming about in an attempt to escape her hold on him.

"No, no, little one," she said, catching his back paws in her right hand and immobilizing those needle-sharp claws before they could scratch her arm. "You must not repay me with violence, for I promise you, I mean you no harm."

"Meooow," replied the captive.

"Poor baby," she cooed. When the frightened creature grew quiet, she cradled him gently in her arms, using one finger to stroke that sensitive spot beneath his chin. Within seconds he was purring.

The ostler, a resourceful youth, had retrieved the basket, taking it around to collect the small miscreants, and now he brought it to Margaret. Once she had deposited the final kitten, the lad yanked the spotted kerchief from around his neck and used it to tie the basket handles shut. "Whew," he said when all was secure. "If it was me as owned these valuable kittens, think I'd get them to town as fast as ever I could, 'fore they take off for parts unknown, never to be found again."

Lady Bardmore placed her mittened hand over her heart, apparently frightened by the thought of losing the quintet. "Hand them to me," she instructed, "before they escape again, for the blues are worth a hundred pounds each."

"Cooee!" said the ostler, his eyes wide with astonishment, "as much as all that for a cat? Always knew them Lunnon folk was daft."

Because the groom came forth and took possession of the basket, Lady Bardmore allowed him to accompany her to the vicarage in Albert's stead. While the pair passed beneath the inn sign and turned right, Mr. Chively tossed a coin to the ostler, who touched his forelock respectfully and returned to the stable.

The gentleman, a bit disheveled from having chased

kittens about the inn yard, straightened his cravat and ran his fingers through his dark hair in an attempt to right himself. "I must thank you," he said, bowing to Margaret, "for your assistance. I doubt we could have rounded them up without your help."

"I did very little, Albert. If anyone is to be praised, it is you, for you were wonderful, organizing the operation in a most timely manner."

The young man turned a rosy shade, but if his smile was anything to go by, he was not displeased with the picture of himself as hero of the moment.

"Furthermore," Margaret continued, "I am persuaded that when her ladyship is less agitated, she will express her appreciation to you for not deserting her in her hour of need."

"Quite unnecessary, ma'am, I assure you. Anyone would have done as much."

"I beg to differ," Margaret said, "for there are those who did not so much as lift a finger to assist in the rescue." She glanced meaningfully toward the doorway, where Mr. Jonathan Holm had leaned negligently against the jamb, watching their frenzied attempts to catch the kittens. If he found her stare at all disconcerting, however, he gave no indication of it.

"Blast it all, Jonathan," his cousin protested, "you might have lent us a hand. While the rest of us raced around like . . . like . . ."

"Bedlamites?" he offered.

Margaret was forced to repress a chuckle. "I should prefer to think of us as concerned citizens assisting a fellow traveler."

"Quite right," Albert said, apparently liking the phrase. "We were concerned citizens. And I should think a member of parliament would take note of his constituents' needs and offer them his aid, instead of standing about watching them as though they were some sort of raree-show."

Jonathan merely smiled. "Someone was needed to admire the performance, cousin. I filled that need."

Thinking it prudent to interrupt the conversation before Albert became angry, Margaret said, "I did not realize, Mr. Holm, that you were in politics. Are you a Whig or a Tory?"

He made her a sweeping bow, as if only just then introducing himself. "I am a member of the loyal opposition, madam, at your service."

"Ah, yes," she said. "A Whig."

Jonathan looked up quickly, surprised at her knowing which party was in power. In his experience, most young women had little interest in politics and even less knowledge of the subject. "Is Mr. Neville politically minded?"

She returned his look, her own gaze questioning, seemingly unable to make the connection between her last statement and his. "Neville? Political? Why, no. He is army mad. Always has been. Nothing interests him but his regiment. In fact, I doubt he knows that Lord Liverpool is prime minister, or that the Tories—"

She paused, apparently just realizing the significance of Jonathan's question. "I see what you were thinking," she said, her voice noticeably cool. "You assumed that because I am a female, I have no thoughts or opinions save those put into my head by some male."

Jonathan had the grace not to attempt to extricate himself; he had been intolerably judgmental, and he knew it. Instead, he said, "Once again you find me guilty of making blanket assumptions about the members of your sex. I ask your pardon, Miss Denby."

"As well you might, sir. Politics affects the lives of us all, and though I may not be allowed to vote, that is insufficient excuse for my not being informed about matters of paramount interest to my country and to the world."

"Madam, I could not agree more."

Jonathan had intended to tell her that he admired her philosophy, and wished more citizens shared her view, but before he could do so, Mr. Oscar Purley chose to put in an appearance. Pausing at the door just behind his nephew, he added his tuppence to the conversation. "A waste of time, my boy, talking politics with a female, for their brains are not equipped for reasoning."

"Uncle!" Albert said, his face beet red. "Miss Denby is—"

"A female," interrupted Mr. Purley. "A handsome one, I'll grant you that, but the ladies, bless 'em, lack the necessary number of what-d'ye-call-'ems in their brains. I forget the scientific name for it, but it is a proven fact they do not have them."

He returned his attention to Jonathan. "Steer clear of certain topics with those of the gentler sex, nephew, for you will only confuse them. Take my word for it, they are happiest when they concentrate upon fashion and family and leave such things as politics to the men in their lives."

No less appalled than his young cousin at their uncle's prejudice, Jonathan said, "You forget, Uncle, that my mother campaigned for me, giving speeches from one end of Warwickshire to the other, and quite often explaining to those who did not understand them the major issues facing parliament. Her help was of inestimable value, and I do not believe I would have won the seat without her."

The older gentleman's eyes fairly bulged with surprise. "My sister, speechifying? By Jove! Quite fond of the old girl, and all that, but she had much better have stayed at home. But then, she was ever an outspoken female. And far too opinionated for my taste! A most unsettling creature, even when she was still a girl. I daresay that is what turned me off marriage, and why I am a crusty old bachelor to this day."

At that moment, the bachelor, blissfully unaware that he had insulted Miss Denby and angered both his nephews, spied the innkeeper coming from the back of the house. "I say there, Terwhilliger. A moment of your time, my good fellow, for I would speak with you about that Madeira you served last evening. Demme fine wine. I'll take a pipe of it if you have any to spare."

Waiting only long enough to motion to Albert, Mr. Purley said, "Come along, my boy, while I inspect Terwhilliger's cellar. You'll learn something of value there."

Albert, though reluctant, allowed his uncle to drag him off toward the waiting innkeeper. Meanwhile, Jonathan returned his attention to Miss Denby. He would not have been surprised to receive a tongue-lashing, for he knew the country girl would not suffer fools gladly. In this, she amazed him once again, for though she gave him look for look, sparks flying from her eyes, she remained in control of her emotions.

Jonathan could not take his eyes off her, for she held her head high and proud, and she looked positively regal. When she finally spoke, her tone was evenly modulated, demonstrating to any who cared to notice just who among them was in possession of the requisite *what-d'ye-call-'ems*.

"I shall ask but one question of you," she said. "If it were possible for your mother to vote, who would be more likely to make an informed choice, she or your uncle?"

"I think you know the answer to that, Miss Denby, and I beg you will forgive my uncle's display of unmitigated stupidity. He was ever a pompous windbag, but until today I had not known he was an imbecile as well."

To Jonathan's relief, a smile teased the corners of her mouth. "An imbecile you say. Is it a family trait, sir?"

"Only in the males, Miss Vinegar. Only in the males."

* * *

Margaret returned to her room to leave her cloak and boots, and when she arrived she discovered that Polly had brought her a breakfast tray and left it on the little table by the window. Deciding she would do well to remain above stairs, rather than risk seeing Mr. Oscar Purley and perhaps giving that misguided gentleman a piece of her mind, Margaret sat down at the table and poured out the now lukewarm tea. She ate the meal, drank the tea, and had just reached down to offer the last bite of her shaved ham to Tyger when she heard a knock at the door.

"Miss Denby." It was Jonathan Holm's voice. "May I speak with you for one moment?"

Somehow, she was not surprised at his visit, and as she opened the door and saw him standing there, so vibrantly male, with his hair still a bit windblown from their walk, she experienced a distinct acceleration of her heartbeat. These reactions to the man were becoming more common with each encounter, and she prayed that only she was aware of them.

Feigning a calmness she was far from feeling, she stepped into the corridor and closed the door behind her. "So the kitten will not be tempted to come out," she explained. He is, after all, from the same litter as that group of scamps who escaped earlier."

"Of course. Actually, it is on the feline's behalf that I am here." Having said this, he reached inside his coat and produced a small parcel wrapped in plain brown paper. "It is a gift," he said.

Margaret drew breath to tell him that she could not possibly accept a gift from him, but he forestalled her refusal by informing her the parcel was meant for Tyger.

"Oh," she said, unaccountably deflated.

"It was my reason for being at the saddler's this morning."

She took the parcel and removed the paper. Inside was a small, delicately wrought collar, and tooled into the soft Moroccan leather was the kitten's name. "Oh, Mr. Holm, this was kind of you. Now I can let Tyger out of the room without fearing he will become one of Lady Bardmore's menagerie once again. I do not know how I am to thank you for such thoughtfulness."

"I do," he said, his voice unusually soft. "You might try calling me by my name."

Only moments ago, Margaret's heart had been rapid; now it pounded frantically inside her chest. Though she knew she should not accede to his request, she said, "Thank you, Jonathan."

Some time around midmorning, Margaret took Tyger out to the inn yard to let him play. She had fastened the small collar around his even smaller neck, then tied to the collar a string the maid had brought her from the kitchen. Lastly, she tied the other end of the string around her own wrist, to keep the kitten from running away.

"You'll not need the string," Polly informed her, "if you first take the animal to the fireplace, where you dab warm milk on his nose, then circle the room three times. After that," she said, "he'll never stray from home."

Promising to try that method when she reached her own home, Margaret scooped the kitten up and hurried down the stairs, not stopping until she was outside in the fresh air. To her surprise, she found Jonathan waiting for her beneath the inn sign.

"I thought you might come out," he said, coming to meet her. "The sun made an appearance for about three or four minutes, but I am afraid you missed it."

"Perhaps it will return. In the meantime, I am grateful the rain appears to have gone elsewhere."

She set the kitten down upon the still damp ground, then laughed when he looked up at her as though she had played him a mean trick. Not liking the dampness, he lifted first one paw then the other, trying to shake off the moisture that clung to his soft pads. In time, however, he grew accustomed to the new surface and, upon discovering the empty shell of a garden snail, began to bat the relic back and forth, hopping about and chasing it with all the ferocity of a born hunter.

Jonathan was watching Margaret encourage the kitten, enjoying the sound of her laughter, when their idyll was interrupted by a man who approached them from the lane. The fellow wore the rough trousers and smock of an itinerant workman, and across his bony shoulders was slung an old infantry haversack. His boots, also army issue, were caked with mud, as though he had walked a long way.

"Beggin' your pardon, sir," he said, doffing his wide-brimmed felt hat, "but I've a message to deliver from a gentleman what's injured and unable to travel. When I passed through Epping yesterday afternoon, I chanced to meet a young lieutenant at The Pig and Whistle. Me once being an army man and all, he treated me to a pint, and when he heard that my journey would take me past The Green Man in Spittleford, he give me a message for a Miss Denby, as is thought to be stopping at the inn."

She had bent to push the shell for the kitten, but at the traveler's words, she looked up. "Neville," she said, the name little more than a strangled whisper.

Her eyes grew wide with fear, and upon witnessing her anxiety, Jonathan felt an unexpected knot form in his solar plexus. It was all he could do not to go to her, to put his arms around her and offer what comfort he might. Controlling that impulse, he chose instead to step toward the traveler, a coin in his outstretched hand. "Let us have the message, for that is Miss Denby."

The man took the proffered shilling, then reached inside his smock, withdrawing a single sheet of cheap paper, haphazardly folded and sealed with a crude blotch of wax.

Concerned only with the contents of the missive, Margaret took the crumpled paper, broke the seal, then hurriedly perused the half dozen lines. "It is from Neville," she said. "He was thrown from his horse and has sustained a sprained ankle. The poor dear must keep it elevated for several days, so he bids me come to him as soon as possible."

Turning to the messenger, she asked, "How did he appear? Was he in pain?"

From the sheepish look on the laborer's face, and the fact that he had mentioned the lieutenant's having treated him to a pint, Jonathan was of the opinion that the *poor dear* was alleviating any possible pain by availing himself of the tap room.

"A sprain is not so very bad," Jonathan assured her. "I mangled my own ankle when I was a lad, with no permanent ill effects." To the messenger he said, "I assume a physician was called to see to the injury."

"Yes, sir, but that was before I happened by. By the time I come along, the lieutenant's ankle was wrapped snug as a bug, as the saying is, and he was making a funny story of his fall, saying how he had chased Boney's men from Portugal to Belgium, without a scratch, only to be tossed like the veriest greenhorn on an English country lane." He smiled at the memory. "A most affable gentleman, the lieutenant, if I may make so bold as to say so."

Affable, perhaps, but Jonathan took leave to doubt the lieutenant knew the meaning of the word "gentleman." Surely no gentleman—even one with a sprained ankle— would sit in an ale house buying rounds and entertaining the locals with his war stories while an innocent young woman was left to fend for herself upon the road. Such thoughtlessness was inexcusable.

The way Jonathan viewed the situation, the fellow should have been escorting Miss Denby the entire way. He should have been looking out for her. Why, who could say what might have happened to her if circumstances had marooned her at some other inn. Instead of encountering men like his cousin and himself, she might have been thrown into the company of rakes and roues, men without scruples, men who would have done all within their power to seduce her.

No, he thought, Neville might be an officer, but he was no gentleman.

She is too good for such a thoughtless lout. She has charm, beauty, and intelligence, and if I had the keeping of such a superb creature, I would—

Jonathan called himself to order, not a little surprised at the direction of his thoughts. He was not looking for a mistress. Far from it!

After a moment's thought, however, he realized he had been lusting after Margaret Denby from the moment he first clapped eyes upon her. He would not dignify his original feelings by calling them anything more exalted than lust, even though after getting to know her—after discovering her sense of humor and her intelligence—his feelings had undergone a change. He still found her a beautiful and desirable woman—what man would not—but his desire for her was now coupled with an admiration for her spirit, for the woman within.

No matter her chosen lifestyle, she had proven herself worthy of admiration, a lady in the best sense of the word. Only that morning she had comported herself with dignified restraint when faced with his uncle's display of idiotic male superiority. As for her encounters with Lady Bardmore, who exhibited the breeding of a fishwife, on those occasions Miss Denby never failed to deal with the old harridan in a kindly and respectful manner.

As well, the young lady had chosen to ignore his cousin

Albert's youthful attempts at flirtation, treating the lad with a delicate blend of friendliness and reserve. Even with Jonathan, she had always behaved in a circumspect manner, never once showing a lack of refinement, never once attempting to gain his admiration.

And yet, she had it. Admiration and more.

No, *he* would not have left such a woman alone and unprotected.

Damn Lieutenant Neville and his careless disregard for her welfare! If Jonathan had the keeping of her, he would make certain she was treated with every consideration. He would see to it that she traveled in the first style of elegance, dressed in a fashionable wardrobe to complement her beauty, with a maid to see to her comfort, and—

Now he thought of it, what kind of protector was this Lieutenant Neville that he failed to supply her with a servant of any kind? Furthermore, if the lady's rather provincial wardrobe was anything to go by, the lieutenant was downright niggardly with his pocketbook. If that was the situation, then what kept her with him? Was she—could she possibly be in love with the scoundrel?

For some reason, Jonathan found this possibility more irritating than all Neville's shortcomings. In fact, he was seized with an almost uncontrollable desire to have Neville at his mercy that very moment. Never mind the man's injured ankle, Jonathan wanted nothing so much as to give the fellow a sound thrashing.

The feel of Margaret Denby's fingertips upon his arm recalled him from the happy vision of himself knocking the lieutenant to the ground. The traveler had taken himself off to the tap room, and the lady had obviously been speaking to Jonathan while he wool-gathered, though he had no idea what she had said.

"Will you do it?" she asked softly.

Jonathan looked into her upturned face; it was pink with embarrassment. "Why, what is it, my dear?"

The familiarity had slipped out, unchecked, but if she heard it, she gave no indication of the fact.

"Will you see to the hiring of a mount for me? I know little of horseflesh, and I am persuaded I will need a strong yet tractable animal if I am to travel in this mud."

What is she talking about? "You cannot mean to leave Spittleford!"

"Why, yes. That is exactly what I mean to do. I must go to Epping."

"But must it be today?"

"Within the hour. And, sir," she continued, her face growing pinker by the minute, "if you would be so kind, please explain to whoever runs the stable that Neville will pay for the rental of the horse when I arrive at The Pig and Whistle."

Indignation robbed Jonathan of whatever manners he possessed. "Never tell me you are on the road, alone, without sufficient money for your needs?"

"No, no. I have ten pounds."

He refrained from commenting upon such a paltry sum, merely adding tight purse strings to his growing list of the lieutenant's shortcomings.

"I could, perhaps, pay for the horse myself," she said. "It is just that I have no idea how much my bill will be here at the inn. Mr. Terwhilliger has been most hospitable, and I should not like to ask him to extend me credit. Nor would I wish to leave without a vail for Polly, the chambermaid. She has been so kind to me, taking care of my needs, as well as those of the kitten, and—"

"Oh, my heavens," she said, tugging at the string as though to reel in the kitten, "I almost forgot about my little Russian Blue. I will need a suitable basket in which to carry Tyger."

"A basket? You cannot mean to take the animal with you, on horseback?"

"Of course I do."

"But transporting a kitten will only add to the difficulty of the trip."

"Be that as it may, I will not leave him behind."

When she looked up at Jonathan, her eyes put him in mind of the kitten's, for they were wide and green and altogether too trusting. "I know you will think me foolish, sir—after all, I got Tyger but three days ago—but somehow, in that short time, he has managed to steal a substantial piece of my heart."

Jonathan understood perfectly, for the young lady before him had made an unexpected impact upon his own senses, so much so that he found the idea of her leaving quite disconcerting. "Time is never a reliable measure," he said. "Not when one's heart is involved."

"You do understand." Her smile was like the appearing of the sun after days of rain, and it was all Jonathan could do not to take her face between his hands and claim that smile with his lips.

"It is the sweetness of his temperament that captivated me," she said, still talking about the kitten. "He is a beautiful animal, that goes without saying, but he is bright as well and has a deliciously playful nature. And to hear him purr is to fall in love. Oh, I cannot explain it."

"No need to explain, ma'am. I know exactly what you mean. I, too, have been captivated."

"You have? But I thought you did not care for cats."

"Nor do I. The creature who charmed me is not a feline. Though I confess," he said, his voice low, "that I should dearly love to hear her purr."

She looked at him then—really looked at him—and as their gazes met and held, a question seemed to hang suspended between them. Though neither of them spoke, Jonathan felt as if volumes had been said. He wanted Margaret Denby, and she knew it. Women always knew.

After several moments, he caught her hand and lifted it to his lips, turning it at the last moment so that it was her palm he kissed. When she did not pull away, but closed her eyes, as if savoring the feel of his lips upon her skin, he was obliged to use all his willpower to stop himself from taking her in his arms and covering her mouth with his own.

In his entire life he had never wanted anything as much as he wanted to kiss her. He ached to hold her close, to feel her soft body conform to his while he kissed her as she deserved . . . slowly, gently, until the honey-sweet warmth of passion made her purr with excitement.

Aware of their surroundings, and the inadvisability of acting upon his thoughts, he released her hand and stepped back. "Return to your room," he said, "and pack a small bag with your overnight necessities. Your portmanteau can be delivered to The Pig and Whistle later. Meanwhile, I will search out a basket and arrange for the horses."

"Horses? In the plural?"

"Horses, plural," he replied. "I will escort you to Epping."

"You will?" Her voice was uncertain, almost shy. "Why would you do that?"

"Why?"

Unable to resist the desire to touch her, he reached out and slowly traced the tip of his forefinger along the curve of her jaw, enjoying the incredible smoothness of her satiny skin. "You are an intelligent woman," he said, his voice noticeably hoarse. "Give it a little thought, I am persuaded you will discern my reasons."

FIVE

Margaret stood as though rooted to the spot, watching Jonathan cross the inn yard to the stable. Only after he disappeared into the dimness of the building was she freed of the spell he had cast upon her by the merest touch of his finger.

She had felt drawn to him from the first moment she looked into those sky blue eyes. Then, as she came to know him—to witness his assurance, his kindness, his intelligence—she soon came to believe that Jonathan Holm was the one man in the world she could love.

Now he had committed himself to escorting her a full fifteen miles, in the mud, so she might join her injured brother. Surely such attention spoke of a certain sort of particularity, of a shared feeling between a man and a woman.

"I am persuaded you will discern my reasons," he had said. Was it possible? Could Jonathan love her as well? With a sigh of contentment, she decided there could be but one answer.

Excited, and happier than she had thought possible, Margaret gathered the kitten close and fairly flew up the stairs to her bedchamber.

Within less than half an hour, she was once again in the inn yard, a small bag on the ground beside her, the kitten in her arms, and a copy of her inn bill in her reticule. When she had asked Mr. Terwhilliger for the reckoning, the innkeeper informed her in a slightly frosty voice that it had been taken care of. "Mr. Holm saw to it, miss."

Surprised and more than a little embarrassed, she mumbled something about having forgotten. "Make me a copy, if you please," she said, "for when we get to Epping, my brother will wish to repay Mr. Holm."

"As you wish, miss."

She had meant to speak with Jonathan about the matter immediately, but the moment she saw him, looking positively magnificent astride a spirited bay gelding, all thoughts of bills and innkeepers left her mind. The sun had come out, and its appearance seemed an omen of happy things to come. Life was perfect. The sky was blue, Margaret was in love, and she was to spend the next two hours or so with this remarkable man, a man who loved her in return. She could ask for nothing more.

The trip was not as difficult as they had expected, even though there were a few patches of road that were more like bogs than coach routes. Before they had traveled very far, the hem of Margaret's dark green habit was liberally splattered with mud, as were Jonathan's top boots and his Devonshire brown breeches, but compared to the joy of riding together, talking and laughing like old friends, a bit of mud seemed insignificant.

Margaret listened with unallayed interest while he discussed his life and his dreams for the future—a future she was excited about sharing.

"And should you like to be prime minister one day?" she asked.

"Whoa," he said, laughter making him appear carefree and more relaxed than she had ever seen him, "I only just took my seat in parliament. Allow me at least this first year to learn my way about."

"Very well," she said, "but I give you fair warning, if

you are not prime minister by the following year, I shall be obliged to write a letter to the editor of *The Times* complaining of the lack of vision among the members of the Whig party."

He smiled at her foolishness, but after a moment his face grew serious. "Why," he asked, "could I not have found you sooner?"

"Sooner than what?"

He hesitated only a moment. "Sooner than Neville."

She was about to ask him to explain what her brother had to do with anything; but at that moment Jonathan reached across and took her hand, and all else was forgotten. They rode thus for several minutes, their fingers entwined, until her mount took exception to a beech bough in the lane and began to sidestep, requiring them to break their connection.

"Meoow!" Tyger protested from inside the disreputable old saddlebags thrown across the gelding. Holes had been punched in the worn leather, and through one of those holes Margaret spied one bright green eye peeking at her.

"Poor baby," she cooed. "I know you dislike your journey, but for myself, I should not mind if we never arrived."

At her disclosure, Jonathan gave her a look that stole her breath away. "You are quite beautiful," he said. "The most beautiful girl I have ever known."

Until that moment, no one had ever said those words to her, and while Margaret basked in the glow of her beloved's admiration, they arrived at the Epping bridge, a gray stone structure that stretched across a small tributary of the Thames. Gone was the tree that had blocked the bridge when Lady Bardmore tried to cross several days ago. There were no remaining traces of the obstruction, and just across the stream, a mere stone's throw away, stood The Pig and Whistle.

The two-story inn was much older than The Green Man, and not nearly as well kept. The roof was in need of the services of a good thatcher, and the leaded panes of the windows would have been greatly improved by the judicious application of soap and water.

The inn yard was neat, however, and to the left of the small building grew a pretty hawthorn, the type country people called the May tree. The limbs of the tree were filled with white, pink-tinged blossoms—blossoms that scented the air with their delicate aroma—and circling the base of the tree was a wooden bench. A young ostler sat upon the rustic bench, but the instant he saw the riders, he came immediately to take their horses.

Jonathan dismounted first, then came around to assist Margaret from the saddle, lifting her down as though she weighed no more than Tyger. Even after her feet were firmly on the ground, he kept his hands upon her waist for several seconds, all the while looking into her eyes, his expression telling her plainly that he wanted to kiss her.

Margaret would have liked nothing better. She longed to have Jonathan enfold her in his strong arms, to feel her heart pressed against his; but the ostler stood at the horses' heads, and Tyger was wailing as though consigned forever to feline perdition.

"Meooow!"

Jonathan released Margaret, albeit reluctantly, and stepped back. After returning to the gelding, he freed the indignant kitten from his less than elegant enclosure, lifting him out of the saddlebag by the nape of his neck.

"Hsst!" Tyger said, informing one and all of his displeasure at such ignoble treatment. "Hsst. Hsst." Only when the kitten was once again in Margaret's arms did he settle down.

"Come," she said, fondling the soft, silky head, "let us

go inside so that I may introduce you to Neville. I am persuaded you will like him prodigiously."

"And what of me?" Jonathan asked.

Something in his tone made her look up quickly. "Everyone likes Neville, ladies and gentlemen alike. You two should get along famously."

"I doubt it. I have a question to ask you, and if your answer is the one I wish to hear, the lieutenant will most definitely not care for me."

A question? Excitement made Margaret's heart feel so light it threatened to float right out of her body. This was the moment she had waited for. The man she loved was about to make her an offer of marriage. That being true, she would probably need to revise her opinion about Jonathan and Neville getting along, at least for the time being.

Chances were the fearsome foursome would not like any man who proposed to her. Not at first. To them she would always be their baby sister, someone in need of their protection, but she felt confident that all her brothers would come to admire Jonathan in time. How could they not?

"You have something to ask me?"

"Yes," he said. "But the answer is of prime importance to me, and for some reason I feel nervous about putting my luck to the test."

She felt tears of happiness fill her eyes. "I believe we make our own luck, Jonathan, but if it makes it any easier for you, I give you permission to ask me anything you like."

He caught her hand and brought it to his lips. "Margaret, my beautiful girl," he said softly, "you are so wonderful."

Finding nothing to dislike in this discussion, she said, "You make me feel wonderful."

"I know you and I will be happy," he said. "You will

like living in London, I am certain of it, and I look forward to showing you all the famous landmarks. I want to buy you pretty clothes and take you riding in the park and to the theater, and when the day is finished, I want to be with you, to share with you my successes and my disappointments."

"It sounds wonderful."

"And when the night comes," he said softly, his words sending delicious chills up Margaret's spine, "I want to hold you in my arms and love you. Would you like that, my sweet?"

Margaret was obliged to swallow before she could speak. "Oh, yes," she said, "I would like it of all things. But, Jonathan," she said, wanting to tease him just a little, "you still have not asked me the most important question."

He chuckled. "I told you I was afraid to put it to the test."

"Nevertheless, you must not expect me to forfeit the words I long to hear."

"Very well, sweeting, it shall be as you wish." Still holding her hand in his, he said, "Margaret, my lovely girl, will you come to town with me and be my mistress?"

SIX

Margaret could not believe her ears. "What did you say?"

Noting the look of surprise in her eyes, Jonathan said, "Forgive me, my love, if my question lacked finesse. I should have told you first how much I admire and esteem you, and how from the first moment we met I felt as though fate had brought us together. You are everything I have ever wanted in a woman—everything I always dreamed of, but never thought to find."

"You want me to be your mistress," she repeated, her voice flat.

"Why, yes, I—" Something was wrong. Jonathan had never seen her face so pale. "Are you ill?" he asked. "Was the ride too much for you? Come, take my arm. You can sit beneath that tree; then once you are settled, I will procure something for you to drink. A glass of wine, perhaps?"

"No," she said, ignoring his proffered arm. "I need nothing."

Her voice was definitely strained, and while he watched, her face regained its color, more color even than was usual. As well, her green eyes—eyes that only moments ago had looked at him with love—seemed to fill with fire, and Jonathan would not have been surprised to hear her hiss at him as the kitten had done a few minutes earlier.

"Please," he said, "tell me what has distressed you so. Was it something I said? Something I did? Was I too precipitous? I had thought we understood one another. I thought you knew how much I wanted you."

"You want me?"

"Of course I do, and during the ride, I thought surely you returned my feelings. Was I mistaken? Should I have waited to ask you? Should I have given you more time?"

"No," she said, the word devoid of all expression, "time would have made no difference."

The fire that had flashed in her eyes was now banked like embers, no longer aflame, but smoldering still. "I gave you leave to ask me anything, and you have asked your question. To say it takes me by surprise is to understate the circumstances; yet I believe you deserve an answer. Unfortunately, I . . . I cannot make such an important decision alone, for my going with you would affect more than just me."

"Neville," Jonathan said.

"Most especially Neville, since it was he who was to have met me at The Green Man. For that reason, I am persuaded the decision should be left to him. If Neville gives his blessing to the scheme—if he says I may go to London with you to become your mistress—then I shall be happy to accept your offer."

This was not exactly the way Jonathan had pictured this scene. He had meant to speak to Neville right enough, but merely to give the man a piece of his mind and perhaps draw his cork for good measure. He had never figured on asking the man's permission to steal his mistress away from him.

"Come along," she said, taking the matter into her own hands, "let us find Neville. No need to delay."

She turned and strode toward the entrance, her back ramrod straight, almost as though she were using the rigidity of her body to hold her emotions in check. Upon entering the inn, she spoke directly to the innkeeper, who smiled a welcome.

"You are expecting me, I believe. I am Miss Denby."

At the coolness of her voice, the smile of welcome slipped from the man's face. "Your room is ready for you, miss. Up the stairs and to the left, next door to the lieutenant's room, just like he requested. If you will be so good as to follow me, I will take you there immediately."

"And the lieutenant," she said, "is he above stairs?"

"No, miss. The lieutenant is in the tap room having a bit of a visit with some of the local lads who served in the Peninsula. You want I should get him for you before you go up?"

"That will not be necessary. It is this gentleman who has business with him."

Turning to Jonathan, she said, "You heard the innkeeper. Neville is in the tap room. Since his ankle is bound, I daresay you will have no difficulty in recognizing him."

With that, she walked purposefully toward the stairs. She had only just placed her hand upon the newel post when she turned and looked at Jonathan. He remained near the door, uncertain what had happened in the last minute and a half to turn his warm, sweet Margaret into this dispassionate, distant creature.

"Tyger and I eagerly await the outcome of your meeting with Neville. If he gives his approval to our . . . our liaison, you need only knock at my door."

Within a matter of moments she had disappeared down the upper-floor corridor, leaving Jonathan staring after her, wondering what had become of the happy, smiling woman who had ridden with him from Spittleford. Where was she; and who was the angry young woman who had just said she would be waiting for him?

* * *

The tap room was smaller than its counterpart at The Green Man, and when Jonathan pushed open the door, he scanned the room and the entire assemblage of men at a glance. Two elderly men, wearing the rough breeches and smock of the laborer, occupied a wooden settle near the fireplace, while three others, their bodies young but their faces old before their time, were gathered around one of the four tables, listening to a tall, dark-haired gentleman whose bound foot rested on a chair.

At Jonathan's entrance, all eyes turned his way. The two men by the fire paused midgulp, then lowered their tankards from their mouths. As for the young men at the table, they merely stared, their conversation momentarily suspended.

"Come in, sir," the lieutenant called in a friendly voice that was just the least bit slurred. If the number of empty tankards upon the table was anything to judge by, the men had been sampling the innkeeper's home brew for some time. "You find an impromptu reunion of old soldiers, sir. But rest assured, we will not interfere with your privacy, if privacy is your wish. If we grow too loud, you have but to give us a wave, and we will try to contain the volume of our reminiscences."

Jonathan stared at the speaker, who was not at all what he had expected. The lieutenant was a fine figure of a man; broad-shouldered, powerfully built, and strangely familiar looking, though Jonathan was certain they had never met before.

Possessed of a ready smile, he had a direct way of looking at a person that would, under any other circumstances, have made Jonathan disposed to like him. Of course, Margaret had told him that everyone liked Neville; she had even predicted that the two of them would get along famously. In that she was wrong, of course, for Jonathan could never like any man who had had her in his keeping.

Trying to rekindle his desire to land Neville a facer, he recalled all the reasons he had to abhor the man, not the least of which was his lackadaisical attention to Margaret's comfort.

"I escorted a young lady to the inn," he said, his tone sounding belligerent even to his own ears. "I do not wish to mention her name in a tap room, but I am certain you will know to whom I refer."

The smile on Neville's lips was replaced by a questioning lift of his brow. "I do know, sir, and I thank you very much; but why the deuce did George not escort her?"

"George? I met no such person."

"Frederick's groom," the lieutenant said. "Never tell me he left her at The Green Man alone?"

"When I met the lady, she was quite alone. And who, if I may ask, is Frederick?"

"My brother, the vicar of Saint Anne's Church, Compton. The lady you escorted spent the past month with him and his wife."

"The devil, you say!"

Jonathan had never asked Margaret where she had been prior to arriving at Spittleford, but not in a million years would he have guessed that she was in company with the wife of her lover's brother, the vicar.

Had the world gone mad, or had he?

"She never mentioned the vicar or his wife. Yours was the only name I heard, for she was concerned for your welfare."

The lieutenant smiled. "She is forever worrying about me and my brothers. Though, I assure you, we are all fully grown and quite able to take care of ourselves. Women," he said good-naturedly, as if that one word explained it all.

Though Neville's manner was teasing, Jonathan was consumed with anger at the man's cavalier disregard for Margaret's concern. Furthermore, if he did not remove that ale-induced smile within the instant, Jonathan would be obliged to remove it for him!

"Whatever your feelings upon the matter," Jonathan said, "the lady was concerned for you, and that is why I escorted her here. That and one other reason. I . . . I asked her a question, but she refused to give me an answer, insisting that I must ask the question of you."

Jonathan looked around the room, searching out a private corner. "If I might have a moment of your time, Lieutenant. Alone."

Neville's face was suddenly serious, almost pugnacious. "If the question is what I think it is, you've no need to speak privately with me. And for that you should be grateful, for I've drawn the cork of more than one fellow whose gaze lingered overlong on the lady."

"But she said—"

"No," he interrupted, "you had best ask your question of my father."

"Your father! What the deuce does he—"

"*Our* father, I should say."

Jonathan stood as if turned to stone, staring at the lieutenant, unable to credit what the man had said. *Our father.*

The innkeeper chose that moment to brush past Jonathan, his purpose to gather up some of the empty tankards from the table. "Your pardon," he said, his voice sounding to Jonathan as if it came from a great distance, "I'll just get these out of the way. Would you care for some ale, sir? What of you, Lieutenant Denby, would you like aught else?"

Denby! Jonathan felt as if he had been kicked in the head by a horse, for his senses reeled, and he had trouble assimilating the facts before him. "But . . . but your name is Neville."

"Right you are," he said. Rising to his feet with some difficulty, the tall, dark-haired man attempted a bow.

"Lieutenant Neville Denby, of His Majesty's fifty-second, at your service."

Margaret paced the small bedchamber, ignoring the small blue-gray kitten who had sensed her anger and hopped up on the windowsill on the far side of the room. "I hope Neville murders him!" she said. "I hope he tears the blackguard limb from limb, then tosses his lifeless body into the inn yard."

She crossed the room once more; then, her anger suddenly spent, she sank down upon the edge of the bed. "Oh, Jonathan, how could you have thought I would . . . that I was a . . . ." Her voice broke. In her entire life, Margaret had never been so hurt, or so humiliated.

"Will you come to town with me," he had said, *"and be my mistress?"*

The memory of his words, the mortification of their implication, made her want to scream her frustration. She loved Jonathan Holm, and she had thought he wanted to marry her. What a fool she had been, for marriage had obviously never entered his mind. And why should it? Gentlemen did not give their hand in marriage to women of questionable reputation, and he believed her a light skirt, had believed it from the first moment he saw her.

Of course, when the mistake was first made, Margaret had thought it amusing. Later, when she might have corrected the erroneous impression, she was too embarrassed to broach the subject. As the days went by, and she and Jonathan seemed so attuned to one another's thinking, she just naturally assumed that he had realized she was a lady.

No one had asked about her family, and she had never offered the information that she was the daughter of an Oxford don. And never in her wildest dreams had it occurred to her that anyone would think Neville was her inamorato. He was just Neville—one of the fearsome foursome—one of the quartet of overprotective brothers who had frightened away every male who had ever shown the least interest in her.

A picture came to mind of the last young man who had paid her court, a picture of him creeping away, fear in his every aspect after being stared down by one or the other of her brawny brothers. Fast on that recollection came a new image, one of Jonathan lying unconscious on the floor of the tap room, Neville standing over him ready to thrash him within an inch of his life.

"No!" she said.

Jumping up from the bed, she sped across the room and threw open the door, which slammed against the wall with a loud bang. At the sudden noise, Tyger let out a howl and jumped from the windowsill, scurrying beneath the bed with all due speed. Margaret did not pause long enough to comfort the kitten; all she could think of was stopping Jonathan before he asked Neville the question he had asked her. Once the words were out, who could say what Neville might do.

Afraid for the safety of the man she loved, Margaret sped down the stairs, her feet barely touching the risers, and pushed open the door to the tap room. She spied Jonathan right away. He stood before a table where Neville and three strangers sat, and upon his face was a look of incredulity.

As she watched, her brother slipped his injured foot from the chair, struggled to his feet, and bowed awkwardly. "Lieutenant Neville Denby, of His Majesty's fifty-second," he said, "at your service."

Feeling frightened, and more than a little guilty for having sent Jonathan to face her brother's wrath, she came to the totally unfounded conclusion that Neville had just challenged her beloved to a duel.

"Neville!" she screamed. "Do not kill him!"

"Meggie?" Her brother blinked uncertainly. "What the deuce are you doing in here?"

Uncaring that he would think himself justified in ringing a peal over her for entering this male bastion, Margaret covered the short space that separated them and grabbed at her brother's sleeve. "Do not hurt him, Neville. Please. It is all my fault. I sent Jonathan in here because I was angry that he had asked me to be his mistress, but in all truth he did not know I was not a light skirt. I never told him, and—"

"Mistress!" her brother bellowed, putting her in mind of a bull spying a red flag. "Light skirt!"

Without another word, Neville took her by the shoulders and put her firmly aside, out of harm's way; then, in one fluid motion, he turned and drove his large fist into Jonathan Holm's face.

SEVEN

Margaret lay upon the counterpane, looking up at the cracked ceiling, wishing she had never come to this inn. Her tears had finally ceased flowing, yet there seemed little else she could do but relive the last hour, surely the most wretched of her entire life.

After Neville socked Jonathan, knocking him to the floor, she had run to him, afraid he might be seriously injured. He was not injured, but the skin covering his left cheekbone was turning pinker by the second . . . and he was furious. At her!

When she tried to help him up, he pushed her hands away. Once he was on his feet again, he stared at her, the look in his eyes murderous, as though he seriously contemplated wringing her neck.

"Jonathan," she said, "let me explain. I—"

"Madam," he replied, "explanations are unnecessary, for it is clear you have been making sport of me for days. I understand how it was, for you were marooned at a country inn with nothing to occupy your time, so you amused yourself with a bit of a charade."

"That is not the way it happened, not at all. I—"

"I trust you found the game enjoyable, Miss Denby. I assure you, I did not."

"But I was not playing any games. Please believe me."

"Unfortunately, I do not. Now, if you will excuse me,

I wish to return to Spittleford while there is still sufficient daylight to see the road."

He turned and walked to the door, and though she called after him, he did not stop, nor did he once look back.

There had been nothing she could do or say to convince him to stay, and in time she returned to her room, where she threw herself upon the bed and gave vent to a flood of tears. Unfortunately, the tears did not possess the power to wash away the pain that had settled in her chest like some living, growing entity, and once the salty flow was depleted, she knew she must face the remainder of her life knowing she had driven away the one man whose heart beat in rhythm with hers.

They were perfectly suited for each other, and they could have had such a wonderful life together . . . if only she had not given him a distaste for her. They could have worked through their misunderstanding, if only he had given her the opportunity. But what was the use of tormenting herself with "if only"? What was done was done, and Jonathan had made it perfectly clear that he never wanted to see her again.

Fearing she would become ill if she did not find some occupation to take her mind off her misery, Margaret recalled the kitten and the feline need for a sand box. Poor Tyger, he must have been distressed by all that had happened today.

"I will find you a box," she said, sitting up and swinging her legs off the side of the bed. "Here, Tyger. Here, kitty, kitty. You must be hungry by now, sweet boy, though you have been remarkably patient about the delay."

When her calls were greeted with nothing but silence, Margaret began to search the room for the little Russian Blue. He was nowhere to be found. It was while she got up off her knees, after having looked beneath the bed, that she remembered the sound of the door banging st the wall. She had run from the room earlier, d Neville would hurt Jonathan, and she had left the door open.

"Tyger," she said, a sob tightening her throat, "please do not be lost. I have had all the heartbreak I can endure for one day, so please be hiding somewhere in the inn."

Deciding to begin her search on the ground floor, she hurried down the stairs. She had not been there above a minute when she heard a familiar voice coming from somewhere outside. It was Jonathan! Thrilled to discover that he had not ridden away as he had threatened, she rushed to the entrance where she flattened her back against the open door, her purpose to remain unseen while she eavesdropped upon his conversation.

"What am I going to do?" he said.

"Mew," came the answer.

"I know what you are thinking, Tyger, my boy. You are saying to yourself that I am a fool. And if you should call me a complete imbecile, I should be obliged to berate you for stating the obvious."

Moving cautiously, Margaret peeped around the door-jamb. To her right was the May tree, and beneath the fragrant, pink-tinged white blossoms sat Jonathan Holm, his back against the smooth bark.He used one hand to hold a damp cloth over his left cheek, but with the other hand he stroked between the ears of a green-eyed mound of blue-gray fur that was curled contentedly upon his lap.

Margaret could only stare, for the man who had professed to have little fondness for felines—the man who liked only horses, dogs, and pretty ladies—had caressed the kitten into a near hypnotic state. Even from a distance of several feet, she could hear the kitten's soft purrs. Not that she blamed Tyger in the least. If Jonathan were holding her, speaking softly to her, and mesmerizing her with tender caresses, she would be purring, too.

"Yes," he said, "there was I, embarrassed at my uncle's

bigotry for judging her by his own limited view of fer
when I was no better. A light skirt! What arrogant bl
ness! Who but a cretin could be in Margaret Denby's company above a minute and not perceive her true nature?"

"Mew," replied the blue, nuzzling his head into
Jonathan's hand to encourage him to continue his min-
istrations.

"I love her, Tyger. It is that simple."

Margaret's breath seemed to catch in her throat, and
her heart began to beat in cadence with the kitten's renewed purrs. *He loves me! Jonathan loves me.*

Who said eavesdroppers never heard any good of themselves?

Margaret could scarcely contain her joy, for she had
never expected to hear such wonderful words upon
Jonathan's lips. *If* she had truly heard them. Afraid to
move, lest she discover she was actually above stairs lying
upon her bed and that this was all a dream, she remained
hidden, shamelessly listening for further proof that the
man she loved with all her heart did, indeed, love her.

"I had not known her above a day," Jonathan continued, "when I was convinced she was the perfect girl for
me. She is beautiful, intelligent, and adorably caustic at
times, yet she possesses a genuine kindness. Though not
enough kindness, I fear, to forgive me."

Unable to remain still another minute, Margaret
stepped out into the open. "There you go again, Jonathan Holm, making more blanket assumptions."

"Margaret!"

Surprised at her sudden appearance, Jonathan jumped
to his feet, dropping the damp cloth from his cheekbone
and revealing a decided swelling. Thankfully, he managed
to grab the sleeping kitten, saving the little blue from a
rude awakening. "How long have you been there?"

"Why?" she asked, taking several steps toward him.
"Did you say something I ought not hear?"

"I cannot be certain," he said, watching her as she
ed even closer.

hen she stopped mere inches from him, he studied
her face, a question in his eyes. It was a question Margaret
suddenly felt too shy to answer, so she nodded toward
the kitten he held against his chest. The blue was fast
asleep. "Not being fond of felines," she said, "you will
not know that it is unwise to speak before a sleeping cat.
Those foolish enough to do so soon find their secrets
revealed and their plans exposed."

"I did not know that," he said softly, his gaze holding
hers. "Is Tyger likely to betray me, do you think?"

"I am afraid he would."

"To whom?"

Earlier, when Margaret feared she had given Jonathan
a disgust of her, she had longed for the opportunity to
work through their misunderstanding. This was that opportunity, and she dared not let it slip by. "Tyger would
reveal your secrets to me."

"The little scamp. And what exactly would he say?"

Margaret licked her suddenly dry lips. "He would tell
me that you love me."

Jonathan's gaze did not waiver. "And what, if anything,
would you say to the little talebearer?"

"There would be no need to tell him anything, for he
already knows that I love you with all my heart. He has
known it for some time."

"Has he, indeed? I could wish he had shared the information with me, so that I might have done something
about it."

As if to demonstrate what he might have done,
Jonathan slipped his hand around the side of her neck,
letting his warm fingers fan out across the sensitive skin
of her nape, while his thumb caressed her throat until
she sighed. Shameless as a kitten, Margaret nuzzled her
face against his hand; then she placed a kiss in his palm.

"My sweet girl," he whispered; then he tugged her ev
so gently toward his waiting mouth. Their lips touch
the kiss soft and incredibly sweet, and Margaret wonde
if it was possible to be any happier than she was at that
moment.

Her answer came when Jonathan slipped his hand from
her nape down to her waist, drawing her close. When he
claimed her lips the second time, he kissed her until she
was breathless, the passion in him igniting a fire inside
her that sent heat all the way to her toes. It was only
when they heard a cry of protest that they drew apart.

"Mrrrr!" Tyger complained, not a little dismayed to
have found himself squashed between two humans who
seemed to have forgotten his very existence.

"Poor baby," Margaret cooed.

"Poor *me*," Jonathan said. He released her long enough
to bend down and set the kitten on the ground; then he
straightened and drew her firmly into his embrace. "After
what happened earlier, I am almost afraid to try my luck
again. Nevertheless, there is a question I really must ask."

Margaret knew a moment of trepidation, but when she
looked deep within those sky blue eyes, the emotion she
saw there was warm as sunshine and sweet as honey.
"What would you ask me?"

"Just this, my love. Will you marry me? Will you be my
wife?"

"Under one condition," she said.

"And what is that?"

"That you agree to be my husband."

"Darling girl," he said, molding her soft body against
him, "I will most definitely be your husband."

The matter settled to their mutual satisfaction, Margaret wrapped her arms around her future husband's
neck and turned her face up for his kiss. "I love you,"
she said.

"And I adore you."

"Mrrr," Tyger added.

When it became apparent that the humans were going to be busy for some time, the little Russian Blue leapt up onto the wooden bench, made several turns until he found just the right position, then settled down for a nap. It had, after all, been a very busy day, and a kitten needed his sleep.

LOOK FOR THESE REGENCY ROMANCES